The Restarting Point

Cover design by Okay Creations
Book layout by Lori Colbeck

ISBN: 978-1-950348-57-2

The Restarting Point

MARCI BOLDEN

PINK SAND
PRESS

For Laura Lou

ONE

AS JADE KELLY slid from her silver sedan, the high-pitched melody of windchimes rang with an early morning breeze. The wind that lifted strands of hair from her forehead lacked the scents she was so accustomed to. Rather than smelling of exhaust fumes, the air was fresh. Clean. There were no sounds of the city, only the song of the chimes and chirping of birds.

The scene should have been serene, however, as Jade compared the address on her rental agreement to the cabin in front of her, the fresh air and sounds of nature were dulled by her growing sense of frustration.

The cabin was *not* what she was expecting.

While she had noticed the ratings were closer to mediocre than that of the higher end places she would usually reserve, she'd been taken by the views in the photographs. Standing outside the cabin was a powerful reminder of why she'd always been more thoughtful than spontaneous. Despite knowing to do thorough research before clicking the "Reserve Now" button, she'd been so excited to take the trip, she'd jumped in without proper research. That wasn't like her. Now, she was mentally kicking herself for not digging deeper into the reviews. Others likely knew and tried to warn unsuspecting vacationers that Tranquility Cabin did not match its description.

The images she'd seen online were similar to the wood-planked shack, but she'd been expecting something larger, something *significantly* larger than this shoebox. However, the turquoise shutters and door matched the image on Jade's printout. She looked from the structure in front of her to the paper again. The owner had described the cabin as "cozy with an enchanting view," but the building she was staring at was more like "minuscule and within walking distance of a view."

Jade headed down the sloped gravel path toward the water, hoping to find the images that had won her over. The path ended at a sandy stretch of beach that led into a small tree-shrouded cove, and she groaned with disappointment. Though the inlet was calm and quiet, this was not what had been shared on the website. About fifty yards to her right, the mouth widened to show the more expansive body of Chammont Lake that had been shared on the website.

As someone who had spent her entire career in marketing, Jade was tempted to call the owner of the rental —Darby Zamora, according to the agreement—and congratulate him on a successful, though somewhat shady, description. Had the listing for this "cabin" been honest, Jade never would have locked herself in for a week-long rental.

For the first time since waving goodbye to her husband, Jade was glad Nick hadn't been able to join her on this trip to Chammont Point. When he'd sat her down to explain that he couldn't take their vacation because of a work conflict, Jade had intended to reschedule. Their two grown sons had already backed out of what was supposed to be a family vacation.

However, Nick had insisted she go without him. He'd told her repeatedly how much she needed to rest, recalibrate, and refocus. Those had been the keywords for his sales pitch when he'd sent her to the small lake town on her own.

One of the first vacations they'd taken when the kids were young was to this little-known vacation spot in eastern Virginia. Though Chammont Point was just an hour away from their home in Fairfax, they'd only visited the area once. Funny how Jade had mostly remembered the mosquito bites and sunburns. It was only in the last year or so when talking about memories and looking at old photos had become a regular part of their lives that she'd learned to cherish their time in Chammont Point. She'd recently developed the habit of clinging to the precious few times they'd spent focused on being a family rather than bills, careers, and planning for the distant future. This vacation was her attempt at making new memories, at restarting their lives as a family instead of as four people hovering in the same orbit. She'd learned the hard way just how important family was to her.

One bright and sunny afternoon a little over a year ago, Jade had sat next to her husband while a doctor said one sentence that had changed her life forever. A few words had given Jade an unexpected wakeup call that the future she'd always seemed to be working for wasn't guaranteed. She'd had to learn to focus on the now, the moment, the things she *had* rather than the things that might come to be. Staring down death had changed everything. Her focus had shifted, and she'd become almost desperate to reconnect with her husband of over two decades and form deeper bonds with her sons.

When Nick had suggested they take a vacation to celebrate Jade's recovery from colorectal cancer, he said they could go anywhere she wanted. He was probably expecting her to plan a trip to London or New York City, since Jade had always preferred fast-paced destinations over places like this. But she'd chosen to return to Chammont Point and the lake that had been so prominent in the photos of that first vacation many years ago.

He'd been confused over her choice until she'd explained how much she'd come to cherish the memories they'd made there. Xander and Owen had learned to water ski on Chammont Lake. They'd all sat by a fire and roasted marshmallows while they shared stories and jokes. Jade couldn't remember a time when they'd felt more like a family than their time exploring the small town and playing in the water. She wanted more of that.

After her recent health scare, the bright lights of Broadway and a city filled with endless dining options no longer had the same appeal to her. She'd fought hard for this second chance. Spending it in crowded theaters and noisy restaurants seemed like a waste of time when she could enjoy the quiet lake with her husband. Of course, now she just had the quiet lake, but maybe that was better.

Having a week on the lake should help her figure out what she needed to do to make the most of every day she was lucky enough to live. All she knew was that her future no longer included clawing her way higher up the corporate ladder.

As she neared the tiny structure she'd be calling home for the next week, Jade had to chuckle at the unexpected turn of events. Not only had she overpaid for the cabin, but almost every plan she'd made had to change now that she was here on her own. She walked up the stairs to the porch and looked at the turquoise-and-white chevron-patterned mat where the owner told her the key would be. If there wasn't one, she would have a good excuse to call and make sure she was in the right place.

She lifted the corner and found the key exactly where she was told it would be. "Damn it," she whispered.

After unlocking the deadbolt, she pushed the door open and poked her head inside the living space. Her frown deepened when she spotted the turquoise cabinetry. The brightly painted shelving filled the wall of the so-called kitchen, which was nothing more than a cubbyhole with a fridge and a stovetop. Funny how the blue-green accents had seemed so charming in the pictures. In person, they looked more like failed attempts at making this dump a cheerful place.

According to the listing, the cabin could sleep up to six people. Looking around, Jade couldn't quite figure out how six people would even fit comfortably inside the living room. Standing in the middle of the room, she noticed a built-in ladder attached to one wall. Her gaze followed the wooden structure to a loft. Ah. There were likely beds crammed up there for extra sleeping space.

Slowly spinning, she took in the strange mix of décor. The turquoise cabinets stood out against the scratched and dented white fridge. In the dining area, a pine carved table and benches were directly under a chandelier made of deer antlers. However, a vibrant turquoise that matched the cabinets with a retro atomic pattern that had been popular in the 1960s covered the cushions on the two benches. That fabric had also been used for cloth napkins ornately displayed on the tabletop and two pillows on the faux leather sofa.

Jade tilted her head as she wondered if the odd mixture of *The Jetsons* and *Little House on the Prairie* decor was intentional. She determined the space had to be in the midst of a transition, but she couldn't decide if it was being turned from mid-century modern to mountain lodge or vice versa.

"Cozy," Jade muttered, recalling the listing. "I guess that's a word for it."

Tempted as she was to call the owner and dispute the amount he'd charged her, Jade pushed the thought away. Yes, the ad had been rife with half-truths, but she should have done more thorough research. Fighting over accommodations wasn't at the top of her list of things to do on this vacation. She'd been through enough in the last year. This was her break from reality, her chance to recharge, realign, and restart her life. Her intent was to spend time walking the beach and learning to paddleboard.

Out of habit, she ran her fingers along the ends of her pixie cut. Her fiery-red hair used to reach beyond her shoulders. When the strands grew back after the chemo, her once full hair fell flat. She hoped as it grew, the natural waves would return. But until then she was stuck with poker straight strands that, for the first time in her life, needed products and equipment to add lift and style. She hadn't quite mastered how to do that, so her hair tended to be limp.

She used to take so much pride in her hair. Now, she was simply happy to have hair.

So, no. She would not call and complain. She was going to embrace this little cabin as a part of the adventure she had planned for Life 2.0. When...*if*... Nick could join her, they'd laugh together over the unexpected arrangements and remind themselves they were in Chammont Point to leave the last year of stress and medical scares behind them.

Jade was healthy now. She had a second chance many with her illness never got. She was going to take it, and she wasn't going to kick off her new life by whining about how manipulative the owner of this cabin had been in the listing. Her reboot vacation was one week. She could stay in this mismatched shack for seven days.

Though the cabin was small, there was a second door in the kitchen area. She had to yank twice before it opened, but when she stepped outside, she found herself on the balcony with a view of the lake rather than the cove. Her smile returned. Though the larger body of water was far from the view the images had led her to believe, Chammont Lake shimmered in the distance. She could walk to the nicer beach within a few minutes. The sun sparkled down between the blowing leaves of the sassafras and red oaks, creating a canopy that helped her connect with her budding sense of peace. Like the interior of the cabin, this wasn't what she'd been expecting, but she could definitely make do.

As Jade inhaled the lake air, her stress and disappointment continued slipping away. She was here for the water, the hiking, and the slower pace of the small town. The cabin was just a place to sleep.

She walked to the banister and rested her hands on the

cracked and weathered wood. There wasn't a single car horn or airplane or siren to be heard. Birds chirped happily, bugs buzzed, and if she listened closely, she could hear the faint sound of water lapping the shore.

Hoping to get a better look at the lake in the distance, she leaned forward and bent at the waist to see under the branches. Her nice, relaxing, meditative breath came to a startling end at the sound of cracking wood. A scream of surprise surged from Jade and echoed around the cove as the banister gave way, sending her hurtling toward the ground.

Like some kind of surreal survival instinct kicking in, her mind flashed to those action movies her sons watched so often. In the seconds between falling through the banister and crashing to the patchy grass below, she decided the only way to come out of this unscathed was to do one of those rolling landing things she'd seen Angelina Jolie do a thousand times on-screen.

Jade managed to get her hands and feet in place, expecting to flip over and somehow land in a pre-sprint pose that would magically absorb the pain. If she were a stunt double in Hollywood, she might have nailed it. Instead, she landed hard, twisting her left ankle and bashing her face into the patchy grass. Since she didn't roll, or even come close to it, her chest smashed into the ground as hard as her cheek had. The oxygen pushed from her lungs in a painful rush, leaving her in a gasp, and her left ankle instantly started to throb.

She lay there, too stunned to move, trying to figure out exactly where she'd gone wrong with her landing and if anything had been seriously damaged in the process. *Damn it.* This hadn't exactly been a stellar start to her vacation.

Every attempt at breathing she made felt like a weight pressed on her chest. The wind had been knocked out of her and her ankle hurt like hell, but Jade was certain the only thing broken was her intent to make the best out of this stupid vacation.

"Don't be dead," a woman said from what seemed like a million miles away. "Don't be dead." Then she said something in a language Jade didn't understand. She thought it might have been Spanish, but the voice was so far away and the ringing in her ears was so loud, she couldn't be sure.

Seconds later, someone grabbed Jade's shoulder and flipped her onto her back. She barely had time to process what was happening before a woman dressed in a blindingly incandescent yellow shirt leaned over her. Firetruck red hair had been curled into victory rolls on top of the woman's head, making her look like a comic book throwback to the 1940s. The woman's eyeliner flared out into long wings, and her lipstick matched her hair.

Jade squinted her eyes, mostly out of confusion. Perhaps she'd hit her head harder than she'd realized.

"Don't worry. I know CPR," the woman announced and then took a deep breath.

Jade tried to explain that she didn't need CPR, but she hadn't caught her breath yet. Her protest came out soundless. Not even a whisper left her lips. However, she swatted the woman's hand away before she could pinch Jade's nose.

As Jade attempted to sit, the colorfully dressed woman pushed her back, hands planted hard on her shoulders, and stared into her eyes.

"Don't move," the woman warned with a dire tone. "You could have internal bleeding."

"I don't," Jade said, though her words were barely above a breathy hiss.

"You don't know that," she insisted.

Jade took another deep, painful breath. Though her diaphragm still wasn't working right, she got enough air into her to say, "I'm fine. Who are you?"

The woman pressed a hand with long red fingernails to her chest and said, "I live next door. I was on my way over to introduce myself when I saw you fall. You looked like a baby bird testing out your wings. Except they usually fly, you know. You just kind of..." She slapped her hands together to demonstrate Jade's far from graceful landing.

Jade scowled and turned her attention to her palms. More specifically, she focused on the sand and blood speckled scrapes she'd earned from her impact with the ground. Her right wrist was pulsating, but she could make a fist without too much struggle. Moving her exam down to her knees, she tentatively touched the scratches intermingling with the spatter of freckles on her pale knees. However, it was her left ankle that really caught her interest. Rotating the joint made her jolt with pain.

"Oh my God," the stranger said, her voice once again filled with panic. "It's broken." Rising onto her knees, she called out, "She's broken her leg."

Jade turned to see who she was talking to, expecting a crowd. There was no one. They were alone.

"Don't worry," the woman continued, returning her focus to Jade instead of...whatever...she'd been talking to a moment ago. "Chammont Point has a wonderful hospital. Real doctors and everything."

The thought made Jade cringe and her entire body shiver.

The last thing she wanted to see on vacation was a doctor with icy hands and needles. "I don't need to go to the hospital."

"You could have busted your spleen," the woman informed her.

Jade stopped examining her wounds to look at the caricature in front of her. "*What*?" She shook her head before the insanity could continue. "I didn't hurt my spleen."

The woman sank back and lowered her eyes. "You might have." She slowly lifted yellow-painted eyelids with unbelievably long false lashes. Though she looked like a bag of candy-coated chocolates with all her bright, clashing colors, she had the puppy dog eyes thing down. She pouted her red lips slightly and tilted her chin, and Jade's frustration fizzled. "You could have serious injuries that haven't manifested yet. Like a concussion or..."

"A ruptured spleen?" Jade finished.

"It could happen. I saw a TV show once where—"

Jade cut her off with a firm shake of her head, not wanting to know what medical advice the woman had gotten from television. "I'm fine. I promise."

"I guess we'll find out," she said and then smiled.

Jade turned her head enough to tune into the growing sound in the distance. As soon as she identified the wailing of an ambulance, her stomach bottomed out. "Did you call 9-1-1?"

"Yes, and it's a good thing I did," the woman said, placing a hand on her chest. "You've clearly broken your ankle."

Jade focused on the joint as she moved it from side to side, despite the pain the motion inflicted. "It's not broken.

11

Probably just sprained." Jade gave her neighbor her well-practiced disapproving-mom frown.

The blaring siren stopped, and Jade watched medics hop out of the ambulance. "This really wasn't necessary," she muttered.

"She's here," the woman yelled, as if the medics couldn't figure that out on their own. "Hurry! Hurry! She's hurt!"

"I'm okay," Jade countered.

The woman gestured to the balcony above them and explained how Jade had fallen. She even flailed her arms and did that hand-smacking demonstration again. Jade hadn't considered how ridiculous she must have looked flying through the air until then. Heat settled over her cheeks as a medic crouched next to her. He asked what hurt and how much as he flashed a light in her eyes.

"This is *really* unnecessary," Jade said.

"Maybe," the EMT responded. "But Darby is right—"

Jade blinked and leaned away from the EMT as she recalled the name on her rental agreement. "Darby?"

The man kneeling beside her blinked as well, but then he jerked his head toward the absurdly dressed woman. "Darby."

Jade tilted her head up and, as her mouth hung open, pinned the woman with a narrowed stare. "Darby *Zamora*?"

The woman smiled and shrugged slightly, as if she'd been caught with her hand in the cookie jar. No wonder she'd been so concerned about Jade's fall. She owned that dump.

Jade jolted when pain shot through her leg.

"You need X-rays," the EMT said.

Scowling at the slumlord, Jade said between gritted teeth, "I'm not going in an ambulance. Ms. Zamora can drive me."

Though the cabin's faux leather sofa wasn't long enough to accommodate her, Jade managed to make herself comfortable while resting her ankle between a pillow and a bag of frozen peas. The pain was considerably less after several hours of resting and a heavy dose of painkillers, but the throbbing continued even as the day went on. After another round of icing her ankle, she hoped the pain would decrease enough to move to one of the chairs she'd spotted on the rock patio overlooking the water.

A few hours into babying her ankle while reading the vampire romance novel she'd found in the bedroom, and this so-called vacation was already starting to wear thin. Nothing about this trip was going as planned. First her kids canceled, then Nick had a conflict, and then she'd taken a literal flying leap and injured herself. Despite her determination to look at the bright side, she was starting to feel like this trip wasn't meant to be.

Jade tossed the book that had failed to catch her interest aside and rolled her head back. Right above her, a water leak had left a stain on the ceiling. The shape reminded her of an image that might be flashed in a Rorschach Inkblot Test.

And what do you see here? a therapist might ask.

Cancer cells, she'd answer, *slowly eating away at my insides until there's nothing left.*

Jade closed her eyes, lowered her head, and rubbed her fingertips into her temples. She'd spent far too much time over the last year in doctors' offices and clinics and operating rooms. As determined as she was to put all that behind her and focus on the future, the fear was there. Sitting in the emergency room earlier hadn't been nearly as traumatizing as fighting cancer. But still, her anxiety had been triggered and continued to linger in the back of her mind.

Her doctor had told her fear was normal, healthy even. To an extent. She couldn't let it ruin her life or cripple her. However, she should always be aware that, as a survivor, her chances for a relapse were elevated. "But don't *live* in fear," she'd been told.

Easier said than done.

Jade glanced at the phone sitting on the coffee table beside her. She'd called Nick on her way to the hospital to let him know she'd fallen and then again on her way back to the cabin to let him know she had a minor sprain. He hadn't answered either call. While she and Nick had never been the clingy type of couple, over the last year, she'd come to realize how much she needed him. They'd always operated independently of each other to a point. He had his life, she had hers, and they'd come together in the middle for family time. Having cancer, however, had brought her to her knees, and she didn't know how she would have made it through if not for the love and support of her husband.

That had changed their relationship in a lot of ways. The biggest, for her anyway, was how much she'd come to rely on his encouragement to get through. They'd been together for so long, she'd started taking him for granted. But having him by her side had reminded her how lucky they were to have each other. If it were possible, she'd go so far as to say she'd fallen in love with him all over again. He'd been her anchor in the storm, the lighthouse in the harbor, and she'd never known how much she'd counted on him until her diagnosis.

She'd also never needed pep talks before her health had taken a bad turn. However, she could use one now. Her mind was spiraling into the darkness of the what-ifs that haunted her post-remission. Hearing his voice, even through the phone, would be a welcomed distraction from the frustration looming over her.

Jade was thinking anything would be a welcomed distraction when the door swung open.

"Knock, knock," Darby sang as she poked her head in without actually knocking. Nor did she wait for Jade to invite her in before entering. She held out a plastic container from the grocery store and lifted a bottle of wine. "I thought you might need these. I hope you like mint brownies and red wine."

Jade had always adored both. However, she'd completely altered her diet after her diagnosis. She'd never been a heavy drinker, but as soon as she'd read that alcohol and junk food increased the risks for the type of cancer she'd had, she'd cut those indulgences from her life. She hadn't had either in over a year. "You didn't have to do that."

After easing her offerings onto the table, Darby faced Jade. "Yes, I did. I am really glad your ankle didn't get hurt worse. That's definitely worth brownies and a moderately priced bottle of Malbec." She grinned. "And..." She opened the door again, reached out, and then spun dramatically. "Look at these." Darby beamed as she held up two gold-painted crutches covered in gems of varying size, shape, and color. "I dug them out of my closet for you to use as long as needed."

Jade widened her eyes as she stared in shock. Gaudy was an understatement. The display before Jade was *atrocious*.

"Wow," Jade said for lack of any other words. "Thanks."

"I, too, sprained my ankle once." Darby set the crutches against the coffee table and within Jade's reach. "You should never do cartwheels on a stage. While wearing vinyl platform boots. And drinking heavily."

"*Yeah*," Jade said, drawing the word out a bit. She didn't have to think too hard to see the image Darby had created. "That sounds like it would be a bad idea."

"Speaking of drinking, let's get to that wine." Darby turned toward the table where she'd left the bottle.

"Oh, thanks, but I don't drink," Jade said.

Darby stopped, frozen in time for a few beats, and then spun around and cupped her ear as if she hadn't heard. "I'm sorry, what?"

"I don't drink. I had... It's bad for my health. I'll take a glass of water, though." Jade could almost see the gears in the other woman's brain spinning as she processed the information. Jade had almost slipped in the bit about her cancer, but sometimes the words still stuck deep in her chest like a fist not ready to release its hold. The ability to share her struggles as freely as she'd heard others with major illnesses do was not something she'd mastered. She suspected she'd get there, but that was a skill she had to work on.

"You don't drink? How do you get through the day?"

Jade giggled as Darby stared with obvious confusion. "Slowly."

"I can't imagine," Darby said as she again pressed a hand to her chest.

Earlier, while lying flat on the ground and then again while sitting in an exam room filled with anxiety, Jade had been too distracted to consider how much effort Darby must put into presenting herself. Not only styling her hair and however long she'd spent putting on her makeup, but the style and colors of her clothing were such a clear representation of the person inside. Jade had always gone for boardroom executive on the inside and outside. Her practical hair, makeup, and clothing had represented her well. Until recently.

So much had changed in the last year, and Jade's mind was reeling from it all. She never would have thought she'd admire the confidence of an eccentric decade hopper. She wished she had the strong sense of self that Darby radiated. Part of Jade suspected Darby's outlandish style was a form of attention seeking, but she had the confidence to pull it off, and confidence was definitely something Jade had been lacking in recent months.

She watched curiously as Darby set two stemmed glasses on the counter and worked on removing the twist top from the wine. She filled one glass but added several ice cubes to the other and held it under the faucet. She glanced at Jade, as if to confirm, before turning on the tap.

As Darby carried the glasses into the living room, Jade couldn't help but ask, "How did you settle on this look?"

"What look?"

"Your clothes, your hair, your makeup."

Darby glanced down at her outfit and then smirked slyly at Jade and held out the wineglass of ice water. "This isn't a look, Mama. This is a *lifestyle*."

A lifestyle? Unlikely. Darby's appearance was a statement.

The type of show she was putting on was usually someone's attempt at making fun of themselves so other people didn't have the chance. The class clown survival mentality. *I know I don't fit in, and I'll be the first to say it so you can't.*

Since Jade was taking up the couch, Darby sat on the coffee table next to her. Once again, her overly made-up face turned into a sad pout. "Listen, I really have been meaning to get this place fixed up. I was hoping to make it through the summer. Give me some time to make a little..." She rubbed her thumb across her fingertips in the universally accepted sign of money. She dropped her hand to her lap and let her shoulders sag. "Being in the rental business is a lot harder than I thought it would be. People keep demanding refunds."

Jade tried to bite back the words, but the truth rushed from her lips. "Because your ad is deceitful."

"I wouldn't say deceitful as much as...slightly overstated."

"The pictures show a clear view of the lake," Jade pointed out.

Gesturing in the general direction of the larger body of water, Darby said, "You can see the lake from here."

Jade used that disapproving mom look again. "I almost broke my leg trying to see the lake from here. Your pictures lie. Your *ad* lies. The reason people want refunds is because you aren't giving them what they paid for."

A frown tugged at Darby's red lips. "Everybody lies in advertising, Jade. Do you really think buying a pair of tennis shoes will turn you into a pro athlete or diet soda will make you skinny? It won't. Trust me. I tried."

"That's a little bit different than selling this place as having a lake view when you have to squint through the trees to see it."

"Well, in the autumn, when the leaves fall—"

"Darby," Jade said firmly and shook her head. "You could still rent this cabin without all the false advertising. It is on the water and it *is* cozy. People who want water access without the crowds would like this. But you have to be straightforward about what they're getting."

"Are you going to request a refund?"

Jade widened her eyes. "Are you serious? I fell through your porch. You had to take me to the emergency room."

A pleading look fell over Darby's face. "I'm going to get the banister fixed. But...I kind of... I won't have the money if I have to pay you back."

"Darby—" Jade started.

"Jade, please," Darby said. "Please. I promise I'll make sure you have the best vacation ever, but...I can't give you a refund *and* fix the porch."

Though she was certain she was being played, Jade's resolve crumbled. Darby was a grown woman, yet she appeared to be completely unprepared for adulthood. As an executive, she'd had little patience for staff who couldn't fulfill their obligations. The kind of ineptitude Darby was showing had always been a trigger for Jade, but she was softer now. Maybe too soft, considering that the cabin wasn't simply a disappointment, it was dangerous. She had every right to demand her money back. But Jade didn't want the hassle of pressing Darby for a refund.

"Okay," Jade said, "I won't ask for my money back, but you have to reschedule my stay. I don't want to spend a week sitting on your couch. I'll go home and talk to my husband to figure out when we can reschedule."

Darby held out her hand, indicating she expected Jade to

seal the deal with a handshake. Instead, Jade held up her hands and showed Darby the scrapes on her palms. Darby switched from a handshake to a solitary pinky and waited until Jade entwined their little fingers.

"Deal." Darby didn't let go when a normal person would. Instead, she tightened her pinky around Jade's. "And you won't sue me, right? Because it was an accident."

Jade pressed her lips together. There was a difference between an accident and negligence. However, she suspected suing Darby wouldn't be worth the effort. She only had a sprained ankle and some scrapes, and Darby couldn't even afford to fix the banister. Even if Jade wanted to sue for damages, Darby wouldn't be able to pay.

"No. I won't sue you, but when I come back, that banister better be fixed."

"It will absolutely be fixed."

Jade couldn't help but laugh when Darby squealed as they sealed the deal like they were teenage girls.

TWO

JADE HAD TRIED to reach Nick several times before giving up and heading back to Fairfax. She understood how all-consuming hiccups on projects could be—she'd experienced her share during her career—but she was starting to get concerned. Nick had been working hard to keep his business thriving while also nursing her through her illness. As frustrating as it could be that he wasn't answering his phone, she did understand. But part of her couldn't help but think he should have at least texted her by now. She didn't want to think something was wrong, but fear had started to nag her.

Cursing at her clumsy movements, Jade stumbled into her and Nick's house on Darby's flamboyant crutches. She hadn't wanted to take them, but Darby had insisted. As she tried to hobble from the cabin to her car, Jade had reluctantly admitted she needed them. Without the gem-covered crutches, she wouldn't have made it. Even though they hurt her scraped palms, walking hurt more, so she'd chosen the lesser of the two.

Jade closed the front door and called out to Nick but

stopped at the shock of what she was seeing.

The bookshelf along the far wall was nearly empty. There were photos missing from the wall, and the portrait of Nick's grandfather, which Jade had always found creepy, was gone. Next, her gaze landed on a stack of boxes labeled with black marker in Nick's crappy handwriting.

Books. Pictures. Painting.

Jade furrowed her brow as she staggered farther into the half-packed living room. They had been discussing doing some light remodeling now that the boys were in college. She'd spent the last few months of her treatment gathering images for inspiration. She'd saved them to an online board that she'd shown her husband time and time again. Maybe the project that had kept Nick from joining her in Chammont Point was supposed to be a surprise.

But why were pictures of *her* family and *her* books still sitting out? Why would he separate them by owner? Her stomach twisted in on itself. Her mind was coming to conclusions that her heart didn't like. His belongings were no longer adorning the room. His belongings were inside labeled boxes.

Hers were not.

She was taking in the scene when he walked out of the kitchen with a beer, excitedly talking about something. Jade couldn't hear him over the thumping of her heart. Right behind him, a woman laughed. But she froze at the sight of Jade supporting her weight on crutches. Nick froze too. Then he cursed and blew out a big breath.

Time seemed to stand still as Jade and her husband stared at each other. Her stomach suddenly felt like an empty void into which her heart just kept falling and falling with no end in sight. Her chest, still sore from her crash landing earlier, grew tight, and her mouth went dry.

Jade thought she should say something, but she had no idea what. The tension in the room flared to a point where there was barely any oxygen left to breathe. Though she tried to deny what was obvious, her heart shattered, and the acidic burn of tears filled her eyes.

She opened her mouth, intending to demand an explanation, but the words lodged in her throat.

She didn't need to ask what he was doing. She already knew. The evidence was clear. He was leaving. For the woman standing next to him. He hadn't joined her in Chammont Point to begin Life 2.0 because he had no intention of taking part in her new life.

After what seemed like an eternity, Nick looked at the woman next to him. "Would you wait in the kitchen, please?"

She didn't hesitate to dart away. Relief seemed to fill her eyes as she rushed out of the room, leaving Nick and Jade to sort out whatever the hell was happening. Once they were alone, Nick set his beer down and shoved his hands into his pockets. He met Jade's eyes with a pitiful gaze.

"Use a coaster," she said. The words came out cracked and barely loud enough to be heard. But he did as she said and moved his drink onto the ceramic circle meant to protect the table's surface.

As he did, Jade chided herself for the stupidity of the demand. She'd just caught him in the process of leaving her, and the first thing she said was to use a coaster. His belongings were packed, there was another woman in her home, and she was worried about rings on the table. *Really*?

"How's your leg?" he asked.

"Apparently better than my marriage."

He looked away and blew out his breath again. That was his go-to move when he was anxious. Over the course of her treatment, he'd sat beside her, lost in thought, heaving those breaths thousands of times. Every time, she'd offer him a weak smile, a squeeze of his hand, and soft reassurances that they were going to be okay.

Clearly, she'd been wrong.

"I, um…" he started. "I…"

Tears burned her eyes as she narrowed them at him and said through clenched teeth, "What?"

He frowned and gave her another sorrowful look. "I didn't want you to walk in on this."

"What is this?" she asked, though the answer was obvious. She'd already done the math. She'd already solved the puzzle. But the answers weren't making sense. Knowing the truth and understanding it were miles apart in her mind. Part of her still insisted she must be misunderstanding.

"I'm leaving," he said with the confidence of a man who had a plan. A man who'd thought things through. This wasn't a rash decision or a spontaneous moment. He'd been planning this. For how long?

The uglier side of reality was something Jade had faced far too many times since hearing the word *cancer* slip from her doctor's lips. She had the scars and a patchwork body to prove it. Now, apparently, she had a lying husband to add to the list. A husband who had spent weeks at a time by her side in the hospital, holding her hand, drying her tears, reminding her how much she had to live for. She had assumed he was including himself in that list. But he'd told her to live for *this*. To watch him leave. With someone else.

"Why?" she asked. "After all we've been through. Why?"

At least he had the sense to be ashamed. He looked down and raked his fingers through his dark hair. When he lifted his head again, his eyes were sad. She'd seen that look while lying in a hospital bed, when her hair had begun falling out, when the reality of her deteriorating health had hit him. The look was a mixture of hopelessness, fear, and defeat. The look had broken her heart when she'd been sick, but seeing it now lit a spark of anger.

"Why?" she screamed as tears pricked her eyes.

"Jade." He closed his eyes and shook his head. "I..."

"Don't you dare tell me how sorry you are," she seethed.

"I..."

Marching across the room toward him likely didn't have the same impact since she was using crutches. But she stopped right in his face. "You're cheating on me?"

"Jade... I... I *am* sorry, but I'm not in love with you anymore." Once again, he blew out his breath. This time, however, he didn't look like anxiety was getting the better of him. This time, he looked like the weight that had been holding him at the bottom of the ocean had finally released him and he could escape. "I love you, but not like a husband should."

His words, which clearly brought him relief, felt like a thousand knives carving out her heart. She was glad she had Darby's horrid crutches to hold her up. Otherwise she might have crumpled at Nick's feet.

"I deeply care about you," he said. "I always will. We're family. But... I don't want to stay married to someone I'm not *in* love with. I don't want to keep pretending I'm happy when I haven't been for a long time."

"I've had cancer for a year, Nicky. I don't think that's a good gauge of happiness for anyone."

He lowered his face, and her knees once again grew weak as understanding dawned on her.

"You were cheating before then," she whispered.

"I was going to leave after Owen graduated. I wanted him to get through school, but then you got sick..."

Jade's diagnosis had been handed to them five months before their youngest son finished high school. Seeing him graduate had been one of the goals that had given Jade the strength to keep going. Living the rest of her life with Nick, being a better couple, being more attentive to each other, and focusing on their happiness rather than their careers, had been the other.

"How long have you been screwing her?"

Nick looked away.

"Oh my God." Angry tears filled in Jade's eyes. "You coward," she whispered with trembling lips. "You fucking coward. You've been screwing around while I was fighting for my life, and then you couldn't even leave me to my face? I had to catch you?"

"I was going to tell you, Jade. I wasn't expecting you back for a few more days. You're supposed to be on vacation," Nick said.

"So are you," she responded softly. "We were supposed to go together. That was *your* suggestion, remember?" A lump formed in her chest, making it even more difficult to breathe. "Oh God, Nick. This was your plan all along, wasn't it? To send me away so you could pack your belongings while I was gone. Oh, you really are a chicken shit." She laughed bitterly. "Deny it. Please, deny it. Please tell me that you didn't send me away so you could move out behind my back."

"I can't," he said as the shame on his face returned. "That was my plan. I didn't want to put you through watching me go. I was... I was going to go to Chammont Point at the end of your vacation and tell you so you were prepared when you came home. I thought that would be less painful for you."

"Oh, that's so noble of you. If you knew you were leaving, why did you spend so much time talking about what we were going to do when I was healthy? If I ever was healthy." Another one of those ugly reality slaps hit her, and she scoffed. "You were just... You were just being nice. You didn't mean it."

"Jade."

She glared at him. "Stop saying my name like I'm a child who just found out there's no Santa Claus. Jesus, Nicky. I deserve better than this. I deserve better than to have you sneaking out like a criminal."

"I'm sorry." He sounded sincere; she'd give him that. And the sorrow in his eyes seemed real. "I never wanted you to find out like this. I wanted to be kinder when I told you."

"Are you sure about that? Are you sure it was about me? Or did you stay because only assholes leave their cancer-stricken wives, and God forbid you ever look like the bad guy?"

A flash of anger lit his eyes. One of the ongoing fights they'd had as a couple was that Nick was always the one to pacify the kids, while she was the one who had to enforce the rules. If Nick didn't want to say no, he told them to ask Jade. If Nick didn't want to go out with their friends, he made an excuse that put the blame on Jade. He'd always made her out

27

to be the naysayer. She was his scapegoat. She had been for years.

"I stayed because I would never leave you to fight for your life on your own," he stated. "I might not be in love with you anymore, Jade, but I do care about you, and I never would have walked out when you were sick."

"Aww, that's sweet. You want a gold star for that?"

His shoulders sagged. "Don't do that."

"Don't do what?"

Nick shook his head at her like he was *so* disappointed. Jade couldn't remember a time when she wanted to kick him in the balls as much as she did right then. He was slipping out of their marriage like a thief in the night, and he had the nerve to look at her like she was being unreasonable.

"I don't know when you got so hard, Jade," he said, taking her aback, "but you did. I don't know when the job and the status and having the biggest, best accounts at the firm began to mean more to you than our marriage, but they did. And that changed you into someone I don't want to spend my life with anymore."

Once again, his words were like a knife. Another slap of that ugliness life seemed to be throwing at her in abundance lately. He wasn't wrong. She had clawed her way to the top of the marketing firm. She'd fought hard to become an executive. She'd worked long hours and missed so much of their lives. And she *had* changed. She *had* become hard and distant like he'd said. But then she'd gotten sick and realized how far from her old self she'd gotten. She'd seen the truth, and she had told him she was going to be better. And all the while, he'd known he wasn't going to stick around for that. He'd lied and let her make a fool of herself.

However, Nick seemed to have forgotten that part of the reason she'd had to work so hard was because of his big dream. His aspiration was to own a company, to be a businessman, and she'd supported that, not just by being a cheerleader, but financially as well. Someone had to work to support him and the kids while he spent years building his dream from scratch. She'd done so gladly, because she'd wanted his dream to come true too.

"You know it's usually the men, right?" he asked with a sad smile. "The men become so focused on their careers and working their way to the top that their wives feel neglected and unloved. It's the wives who need someone to make them feel worthy. This is just an old cliche, but the roles are turned."

"I had to work—"

Nick nodded. "To provide for us. I know. I know," he said gently. "You did have to pick up the slack so I could build my company. I know that. You did a great job, Jade. You provided us with a great life and gave me and our kids amazing opportunities."

"And you cheated on me because of it." She waited, but he didn't argue. She blinked, hoping to stop her tears, but they fell anyway. "That's great, Nick. I'm glad I gave you that opportunity too."

He flinched but recovered with a shake of his head. "I wanted us to have this life we created, but... You left me a long time ago, Jade. You chose your career over our family a long time ago."

"Don't you dare blame me for this." Anger boiled deep in her belly and sent heat to her cheeks. "You could have talked to me. You could have helped me fix this. You could have told me you were unhappy and given me a chance to be better. You chose to lie and deceive me. You chose to screw around. That was *your* choice."

He nodded. "I know."

"And then you tried to run out behind my back. I deserve better, Nick. Even if I wasn't the wife you wanted, I deserve better than this."

"Yes, you do. I wanted you to have a few months of recovery time after all you've been through."

"Ah. Giving me a breather between cancer treatment and divorce court. How courteous."

Instead of responding to her jab, Nick took the high road and said, "You're right. I was being a coward. I'm sorry."

God, how she wanted to punch him for that. She would feel a lot better about unleashing her anger on him if he got down in the mud with her, but he was restraining himself. He always had been the one to fight with a soft voice instead of letting his real feelings show. He had a way of being passive until she felt guilty for allowing her feelings to flow freely. Not this time. She wouldn't feel bad for giving him hell this time.

"I want us to find a way to work through this," Nick continued. "The boys are grown, but this will still impact them. I want us to..."

"Be friends?" she asked with a sarcastic lilt to her words.

"Yeah." He nodded. "Someday I want us to be friends again. Because I do care about you, and I want you to be happy. We haven't been happy for a long time, Jade. Neither one of us."

"*You* haven't been happy, Nicky, and you should have had the courage to tell me. You should have let me try. You're just walking out." She hated how her tears resurfaced and her voice cracked. She was losing everything she'd fought so hard to stay alive for. "You're not even giving me a chance. So go ahead, pat yourself on the back for holding my hand when we thought I was dying. Give yourself credit for suggesting I take a long vacation to give you time to slink away. Tell everyone how you nursed me back to health and stayed for the kids and all the other things that make you feel better. But at the end of the day, Nicholas, you're a liar. Just like your father."

Nick reared back from the emotional grenade she'd hit him with. His father had left. He'd started a new life and was rarely heard from again. Nick had become the so-called man of his house at the tender age of seven. That wound had never healed, and she'd just intentionally poured salt on it. She didn't even feel remorse. She wouldn't *allow* herself to feel remorse because she was so close to cracking, but she wouldn't give him the satisfaction.

For a moment, he looked like he was going to retort, and she silently dared him to.

"I hurt you," he said in that annoyingly calm voice he always used when they argued. "You're allowed to lash out."

She scoffed. "Stop trying to be the better person here. You're not. Not this time. I may have lost sight of us, of our marriage, but I never lied. I never cheated, and I never wanted to leave. Even if I did, I *never* would have let you find out like this. I *never* would have destroyed the life we built like this."

The shame on his face returned. She'd hit the mark. Good.

"I don't want us to be like my parents," he said. "It may

31

not feel like it right now, but I do want what is best for you. I stayed with you because you needed me to. You don't need me anymore so I'm going to... I'm going to have the life *I* want now."

"The life you want? What about the business you built with the money I earned doing the job you resented? What about this house that I paid for because you had to reinvest in your company? I gave you the life you wanted, Nicky. And now I'm paying the price because you weren't man enough to tell me you weren't happy."

"Stop," he said putting his hand over his heart. His wedding ring was gone. He'd already removed it.

Bile rose in her throat. She had to swallow hard to force it back down.

"Please," he said softly. "Before one of us says something that can't be taken back."

"Oh, I think it's too late for that." She looked around the living room. Though she'd worked long hours and hadn't spent as much time in this room as he had, she had memories here too. Good memories. Laughs and tears and fights. A life. She'd had a life here too. Fuck him for destroying that.

He lowered his head and brushed his brown hair from his forehead. For a moment, she saw the boy she used to know, the one who had promised to love and cherish her forever. She really wanted to punch that boy in the face right now for being a liar. And most of all for being a heartbreaker.

Finally, he looked at her again. "I want a divorce."

She laughed lightly before sarcastically responding, "Oh, wow. I hadn't figured that out yet. I was hoping you and your girlfriend would want to stick around."

"I think we should sell the house and put the profits toward the kids' college expenses."

The house where they'd raised their family. The house where their life had been created. For a moment, she wanted to push back and fight him for the memory of what was. But as quickly as the urge came, it fled. What would she do other than wander the empty rooms and think about what had been?

"I'll take responsibility for the loans we took out for my business," he continued.

"You've really thought about this," she said as he went down his leaving-his-wife checklist.

Tell Jade I want a divorce. Check.

Tell her how it's her fault. Check.

Pretend to be concerned about her happiness. Check.

An emotional fist closed around Jade's throat, cutting off her ability to breathe or speak, as another ripped what was left of her heart from her chest. She did her best not to respond, but she was quite certain her already pale skin had lost even more color.

She'd believed his sweet words as he'd whispered through the background noise of machines and voices over the PA system in the hallway of the hospital. She'd found comfort in him as doctors and nurses floated in and out of her room like she was some kind of science experiment. She'd dried his tears when they'd been told they should get her "affairs in order." She'd fought for him. She'd fought for their family and the life she'd taken for granted.

And now he was walking away. Just like that.

Like the fight they'd won meant nothing.

The emotion that had filled Jade's throat left in a laugh

that seemed to surprise both of them. Even though she was laughing, hot tears fell down her cheeks. She glared at him and shook her head. "You know, as hard as you think I became, as distant as you think I was, you are and always will be the bigger asshole for throwing our marriage away without a fight."

She looked at the platinum and diamond rings on her finger and easily slid them off. She hadn't even been healthy long enough to gain back the weight for her rings to fit properly. She held them out and waited for him to take them. "Hawk them," she said. "You're going to need the money because your so-called business is going to fail without the safety net I've provided you, and you sure as hell won't be getting any kind of spousal support for you and your girlfriend."

"Jade," he said.

She gave him one resolute shake of her head. "I'm going back to my vacation. When I get home on Saturday, your things need to be gone. *All* of your things."

"I'm sorry," he said one more time.

"Fuck you, Nicky," she seethed before heading for the door.

Much like she had earlier in the day, Jade sat staring at Tranquility Cabin, wondering what she should do. The sun was sinking behind the trees and dusk was settling over the cabin, making it seem much more welcoming than it had in the light of the day.

She'd told Darby to cancel her vacation, and now she was

going to have to ask her to change the plans again. She didn't think Darby would mind. Somehow, Jade doubted the owner of the cabin was a stickler for rules and regulations. Once Jade explained that she didn't know where else to go or what to do, she was certain Darby would let her stay.

But she *was* going to have to explain. She was going to have to say words she wasn't sure she could. Putting it off wasn't going to make the confession any easier. Jade climbed out of the car. She kept her left knee bent so she didn't put weight on her sprained ankle while she got the crutches from the back seat.

With her heart in her throat, she took her time crossing the path to Darby's house. Getting up the stairs on crutches was not the easiest thing to do, but she managed. However, once she was on the porch, she couldn't bring herself to knock on the door.

She didn't have to. The door opened and Darby poked her head out.

Though several hours had passed since Darby had helped Jade into her car to see her off, Darby still had bright red lipstick pasted to her lips. She smiled brightly and let out a little squeal. "I thought that was you. You're back. Yay!"

Though Darby was excited to see her, Jade couldn't even manage a smile. As she expected, the words stuck in her throat. She couldn't say what she needed to say. Her mind flashed to piles of boxes, the realization that her husband was leaving her, and Nick's sad eyes as he tried to justify his decision. She pressed her hands to her face and tried to hide her tears, but she was too late.

"No," Darby said, sounding panicked. "No, no, no." She stepped outside and wrapped comforting arms around Jade, hugging her tight. Any other time, Jade might have pulled away from an unexpected embrace by a virtual stranger. But after the long drive back to Chammont Point doing her best not to break down, the hug was nice. Jade leaned into Darby and accepted the comfort as she sobbed.

"What happened?" Darby asked as she ran her hand over Jade's back.

"I walked in on... My husband was..."

Gasping dramatically, Darby leaned back, holding Jade at arm's length. "In bed with someone else?"

Jade shook her head.

"Hiding a body?"

She shook her head again.

Darby widened her eyes. "Drinking red wine and eating brownies?"

Jade chuckled. She didn't want to, hadn't meant to, but Darby's last guess was amusing. Jade sniffed as her smile fell. "He was with someone else, but they weren't in bed. They were packing his things to leave me," she managed to say between hiccupping breaths. Her tears returned as she looked at Darby. "He didn't come to the lake with me because he's leaving me."

Darby's usual peppiness faded as she wiped Jade's cheek. "Oh, honey. Come in." She held the door open wide.

As soon as Jade stepped inside, her problems fled her mind as she absorbed the bright colors and geometric patterns. Her question about the transition happening at her cabin was answered. Darby was definitely in the midst of replacing the country lodge feel with a 1960s vibe.

A half-dressed mannequin stood in one corner with Darby's signature style hanging from it.

"Darby," Jade said with her snuffly voice, "do you make your clothes?"

"Most of them. I have a shop online too. You should check it out." She glanced over Jade's shorts and fitted T-shirt. "I'm sure you could find something in your...*style*."

Jade didn't know why she was shocked, but she hadn't imagined Darby as more than the goofy slumlord who hadn't taken care of the cabin. Guilt tugged at her for so harshly judging a woman she didn't even know.

Nick was right. She *had* gotten hard.

She wanted to apologize, but she couldn't find the words to explain that she felt bad for having such low expectations of someone she didn't even know.

Darby sat on a bright blue sofa and patted the cushion beside her. Once Jade eased down, Darby asked, "Are you okay?"

"I don't know," Jade admitted. "I was shocked and then angry. Now I'm numb. I'm just numb."

"Can you tell me what happened?"

"I walked in and there were boxes. His stuff was packed. Then he walked in with this woman, and...they were smiling and laughing." Jade's voice cracked as she recalled how happy her husband had looked. "They were so excited to be moving him out. I could see it. I could see how elated he was to be leaving." Jade wiped her nose. "He's been planning to leave me for over a year. But then I...I was diagnosed with cancer and he thought he should stay. How did I not know?"

"You had cancer?" Darby asked sadly.

Jade nodded as Darby grabbed a box of tissues off the table and held it out for Jade. "He intended to leave me before I was sick. He stayed longer than he had originally planned because he didn't want me to die alone. I should have seen the signs."

Sympathy turned Darby's usual smile into a deep frown. "We don't always see the side of people we should. Sometimes we don't want to because the side they're hiding is more than we can bear."

The way she said that made Jade think there was a story behind the words, but she didn't have the strength to ask. She'd circle back to the source of Darby's secret wisdom later. "That's very insightful."

"Well, I'm more than a fashion icon with big hair."

"He wants a divorce so he can have the life he wants." Jade sank back against the sofa and looked down at her naked left ring finger. "I didn't realize I was holding him back so much."

"That son of a bitch," Darby whispered. The words weren't rife with the high drama she usually used. Her natural sarcasm was gone. In a flash, she jumped to her feet, startling Jade.

"I'm going to kill him for doing this to you. I'm going..." Darby grabbed a bright yellow light off the end table. "I'm going to smash him over the head and strangle him with this cord and...throw him into the tub and electrocute him. And... What other ways can I kill him with a lamp?"

Jade shrugged. "You could probably stab him with it if you took the shade off."

"Yeah," Darby said with savage enthusiasm. "I'm going to stab that asshole right through the heart." She practiced a jabbing motion several times before putting the lamp down and resuming her seat. "I was trying to make you laugh, but I guess it's too soon, huh?"

"A little."

"I really will murder him if you want. Nobody would know it was me. I swear. I can be incredibly stealthy when I need to be. Like a majestic homicidal ninja in stilettos."

Jade grinned, which was as close to smiling as she could get. "I appreciate the offer. I'll keep it in mind."

Darby brushed her fingertips across Jade's cheeks in a maternal gesture that didn't fit her outlandish appearance. "In the meantime, you stay in the cabin as long as you want, okay?"

"What about your other renters? Whoever is coming after me."

Darby shrugged. "I'm not really having much luck renting that place. Seemed like a good idea at the time. I have a lot of those ideas. They sound great until I do them, and then..." She showed Jade two thumbs down. "My big ideas never work out."

Rather than suggest Darby invest in finishing the decor or making the cabin a wee bit safer, Jade offered another weak attempt at a smile. "I'm sure things will turn around."

"Sure they will," Darby said. "For both of us."

The cloud returned over Jade as she flashed back to the feeling of her stomach dropping to her feet. She remembered the look on Nick's face as he explained that their marriage was over. The sorrow he had shown hadn't been for the end of their marriage, but for the way she'd found out. He didn't seem to have a single doubt about leaving her, and that made her heart shatter even more. "Yeah," Jade whispered as more tears fell from her eyes. "I'm sure."

THREE

THE PAINKILLERS JADE had taken were kicking in, but she still wasn't able to relax. She thought back on the day before and all the things Nick had said. He didn't love her anymore. Simple as that. Bottom line. After over twenty years together, he was leaving her for someone else so he could have the life he *wanted* instead of whatever hell Jade had thrust upon him.

The last thought she'd had the night before was that Nick was leaving her. The first thought when she'd awoken was that Nick was leaving her. And all her thoughts since then were trying to understand why. She was tempted to call him and once again ask why he was destroying their marriage but forced the need away.

But what if... Jade closed her eyes as the voice nagged at the back of her mind and forced the fears away.

"Stop it," she told herself, refusing to give life to the hope that was trying to lift her spirits. There was no "what if." He'd been in another relationship for over a year. There was no doubt in his mind that their marriage was done. As if she couldn't figure that out when she'd found a strange woman in her home, smiling at Nick like he'd hung the goddamn moon.

A choked sob pushed from Jade's throat, and her eyes filled with tears again. Darby had shown up bright and early with a box of tissues and a notepad so she could get a list of all the things Jade might need to get through the week. In the hour since she'd been gone, Jade had already piled the coffee table with used tissues. She snagged another as Darby opened the door with her signature flare.

However, as soon as she looked at Jade, she pulled her pink cat-eye sunglasses off and turned her lips into a frown. "Oh, look at you. You're a mess."

"Thanks," Jade said and sniffled.

Darby set the reusable shopping bag on the kitchen counter and grabbed the small white trash can from under the sink. She carried it into the living room and snagged a clean tissue to brush the used ones into the trash. Then she sat on the coffee table and gave Jade a weak smile. "Are you ready for me to dig a shallow grave for him yet?"

"I'm getting there. I just keep seeing how happy he was until he noticed me standing there."

"It was really unfair of him to do this," Darby said.

"I have to figure out what to do now."

"First thing we do," Darby cheerfully said as she jumped up, "is toast to your newfound, though somewhat unexpected, freedom."

"Oh, it's too soon for that, Darby."

"It's never too soon." She reached inside the bag she'd put on the counter and pulled out a bottle of cranberry juice. "I got your juice, but since you didn't specify what you planned to do with it, I bought vodka and tequila to leave your options open."

"I don't drink, remember?"

Darby eased the bottle down as some of her enthusiasm faded. "Wait. You weren't kidding? I mean I assumed this was a mixer, but you're just going to...drink it straight?"

"Yes."

"*Okay*," Darby drawled quietly and produced a bundle of leafy greens from the bag. "And this...stuff. What do you do with this?"

"I eat it."

Furrowing her brow, Darby stared at the kale. "But I didn't buy any salad dressing. Did you forget to tell me to get salad dressing?"

Jade did a quick mental recall of the list she'd handed Darby when the woman offered to go to the store. "Did you get the olive oil and balsamic vinegar?"

Darby leaned back. "*No.*"

"No, you didn't, or no—"

"You just put oil and vinegar on a bunch of leaves and eat it?"

Jade nodded.

Darby pressed her hand to her heart. "Do you... Do you count calories?" She whispered the last two words as if they were a dirty secret.

Jade chuckled. Darby was putting on a show, doing her best to distract Jade from her dark thoughts. The kicker was it was working. Darby's performance was spot on. "No. My diet is for health reasons."

Darby ran her fingers over the kale. "I don't think I've ever seen this in real life. It's so...green." She set the bunch aside and once again examined the bottle of juice. "Straight, huh?"

"With ice. Please."

"This feels wrong," Darby muttered. "Are you sure you don't want a little vodka or tequila? I've got some pineapple juice at home. I can make you a killer bay breeze."

"No," Jade said. "Just cranberry juice."

"Okay," Darby sang and cracked open the bottle.

"Thank you," Jade said, but just like every other thought that came to her mind, her appreciation for Darby's kindness brought tears to Jade's eyes. "For being so nice to me and letting me come back here. I thought about going to my mom's, but she's had a hard time the last year with my illness. I didn't want to dump this on her until I got my head around it first."

"What about your dad?" Darby asked.

"He lives a few hours away, and I... He's not really nurturing, so I'd rather not be there right now."

Darby crossed the living room and bowed slightly as she held out a glass to Jade. "One cranberry juice. Straight, no liquor."

"Besides," she said, accepting the drink, "I'm beginning to enjoy having a handmaiden."

"Oh, God," Darby said, scrunching her nose. "You won't make me wear one of those red robes, will you?"

"Not today," Jade said. "It's too warm."

"Good. And I won't be a vessel for your unborn children, either." Darby ran her hands over her sides and curvy hips. "I've got to protect my figure."

"My children are both in college. I'm done with that mess."

Darby tilted her head and lifted her dark brows. "You don't look old enough to have kids in college."

"Well, we started young. I was only seventeen when Xander was born. I guess that's why I worked so hard. We hadn't been able to prepare ahead of time. I wanted to provide for them. I didn't realize how much I was missing."

Sitting on the coffee table, Darby stared so intently, her dark eyes seemed to be peering into Jade's soul. "That kind of reckoning is usually saved for old men on their death beds."

Jade let a wistful smile touch her lips. "I've had some time to reflect on my life recently. I spent way too much time focused on my career. But that's in the past. You know, when Nick suggested this trip, I thought it was so we could reconnect and figure out where to go next. Now I have to figure that out without him. I've never had to make a life decision without Nick. I did plenty of that at work, but... Nick was always there to talk through life decisions. It's jarring."

"Well, I hope you work it out soon," Darby retorted. "I'm not sure how many more glasses of virgin cranberry juice I can pour. It's freaking me out." Her smile was sweet, lacking the sarcasm that Jade had already come to expect. She pushed herself up and went back to the kitchen to unpack the rest of Jade's groceries.

"So no kids for you?" Jade asked.

"Nope. Not happening. I'm wild and free and intend to stay that way."

"No significant other, then?"

Darby waved her hand as if to shoo away the idea. "Men are like fads. While they are fun for a while, they come and go. Some of them come around again, but they never stay too long. I wouldn't want them to. I can't be tamed."

Jade looked into her juice as she sniffled. "I can see that about you. You're better off. Trust me."

"Speaking of men," Darby said, peering out the window. "Here comes ours." She stood taller and arched her back. Her breasts nearly popped from the red-and-white polka dot halter dress she wore. She patted her updo as if to smooth down any strays.

Jade leaned to look outside but couldn't see who Darby was drooling over. "*Our* man?"

"Hmm. He's going to be shirtless and sweating in no time."

Seconds later, a muscular specimen came into Jade's view. He was heading toward the cabin with a clipboard. "Ah. The contractor." Jade wasn't sure if she was relieved or disappointed. For a split second, the idea of a shirtless, sweating man had appealed to her. She could certainly use the distraction. But if she were honest, she probably would have started crying again.

Putting her hand on Jade's shoulder, Darby said, "Sit tight. I'm going to go hire us some entertainment."

She strutted out the door to greet the handyman, and Jade instantly returned her attention to her phone. She hadn't been lying when she told Darby Nick had been her go-to person. They'd started dating when she was sixteen and had gotten married before Xander was born. He'd been her best friend—her *only* friend, really—for most of her life. She didn't even know where to turn without him there.

After several seconds of chastising herself for needing to call Nick, Jade turned the phone off and tossed it out of her reach. "Jesus," she muttered. She wasn't going to beg. She refused to beg. Not that begging would help anyway. She couldn't remember the last time she'd seen him smile like he had in that split second before her presence was known. There was no point in begging.

Jade wiped her tears when her favorite property *mis*-manager walked back into the cabin with a man on her heels. Jade's attention shifted from her own pity party to the way Darby's light had dimmed. There was no sparkle in her overly enhanced eyes, and her bright red lips didn't have a hint of a smile. In fact, Darby seemed to also be on the verge of tears.

Jade had known Darby for all of twenty-four hours, but the change in her demeanor was obvious. Something had happened. Something that had dampened Darby's annoyingly robust personality. Jade only needed a minute to figure out what had changed.

Listening to the Hunka Burning Contractor tell Darby that he would have to rip out the kitchen cabinets, wall, and floor caused about a thousand red flags to start flying. By no means was Jade an expert on construction, but she'd been on the receiving end of enough of Nick's rants about his competition to know there were plenty of shady contractors out there who were willing to take advantage of unsuspecting customers.

Not only did Darby scream *look at me*, but she practically had a neon sign over her head asking to be taken advantage of. The doe eyes, blank stares, and pouty lips might have helped her in some areas, but when dealing with men who likely thought she didn't know better, her self-imposed innocence could do more harm than good.

"How much is that going to cost?" Darby asked.

"Well, with labor and material...a couple thousand."

"Whoa," Darby said. That one word said so much more. The sound of discouragement filled the air. More than discouragement. Defeat.

It was also the sound of someone being taken advantage of. Rage lit in Jade. She'd spent a lot of time climbing those corporate ladders and ignoring how those around her were treated. She'd also spent a lot of time ignoring that she was capable of stepping on people herself. That was a bad trait that had filled her with shame when she'd realized she'd turned into one of "those" executives. Staring down death had cleared her head of a lot of things and made her see that she hadn't always been a good person. That was another item on the long list of changes she intended to make.

One of the promises she'd made God or Buddha or the Universe—whatever the hell was out there—was that if she recovered, she wasn't going to be that person any longer. More than that, she would speak up when she saw someone being taken advantage of. Darby was that person at the moment.

Jade stumbled to her feet and hissed as pain shot through her ankle. She sucked up the discomfort as she scrambled to grab the crutches. "Thank you." Putting herself between the contractor and Darby, she scowled at him. "Thank you for stopping by, but you can go now."

He creased his brow and looked at Darby.

"No." Jade stared him down. "You need to go."

"But..." Darby started.

"He's going," Jade insisted. "*Now.*"

The man held out his card, and Jade snatched it before Darby could. He lifted his hands as if he were giving up trying to talk sense into the madwoman before him. "I'll write up a quote—"

"*No*," Jade insisted. "We don't need your quote. Get out." She used the crutch to point toward the turquoise-painted door. "Go."

He hesitated, as if waiting for Darby to intervene. After several uncomfortable seconds, he muttered under his breath and left the cabin.

"What was that about?" Darby asked.

"He was lying to you," Jade said. "He could fix the damage to the porch without tearing up the kitchen floor."

"Oh, no. See the...support *things*...come all the way under the kitchen."

"I didn't fall through the *floor* of the porch, Darby. I fell through the *banister*."

"Yes, but..."

Jade lifted her brows, waiting for Darby to catch on. Darby opened her mouth, closed it, and opened it again. Furrowing her brow, Darby rolled her eyes back.

"He does not have to rip out the entire porch to fix the banister. He was telling you that you needed more work than you do," Jade explained, trying not to let the fury she felt for the handyman bleed out on Darby.

"But...if the banister is rotten, then..."

"Even if there is rotten wood on the porch, there is no way the entire thing needs to be replaced. Maybe a few boards, but not the *entire* porch."

As the reality of what Jade was saying sank in, Darby gasped and put her hand to her chest. "He... He lied?"

"Yes. You're not hiring him," Jade insisted. "He's a thief."

Darby looked out the window to where he was still

making his way to his truck. "But he has a nice bum. Doesn't he?"

Jade looked out at the man walking away. "Yeah. But do you really want to hire someone because he looks good in jeans?"

Again, Darby opened her mouth.

"*No*. You don't, Darby." After hobbling back to the couch, Jade grabbed her phone. "We're going to find you someone who won't take advantage of you."

Darby parked directly in front of the doors to O'Shea Construction. The office, located in Chammont Point's only strip center, had big, tinted windows that reflected the midday sun back into Jade's eyes. Getting in and out of cars was still something she hadn't mastered, and Darby's old Mustang sat low with bucket seats that practically swallowed Jade. Though Jade was slightly taller than average, sitting in the car was like sinking into a pit.

Darby rushed around the front of her convertible and grabbed the crutches from the back before opening the passenger door. After handing the crutches to Jade, Darby opened her arms as if bracing for impact should Jade tumble into her. Jade was hoping to have more help getting out of the bucket seat. But she decided she was likely better off figuring this out on her own. She planted her good foot on the ground, grabbed the frame, and braced herself for the struggle.

After several false starts, she held out her hand and gestured for Darby to come closer. Darby's smile spread, and she looked like she was about to start gushing. However, she kept her cool enough to take Jade's hands and pull her from the car. As much as Jade hated the crutches Darby held out to her, she gratefully accepted them.

"I feel like a mama watching her baby take her first steps," Darby said as she stepped back. She pressed her fingertips to her cheek, batted her eyes, and grinned. "Look at you, being so independent. You're growing up so fast."

"Watch yourself, Mama. I have a sprained ankle and a broken marriage. I wouldn't need much to convince me to beat someone with these crutches right now, and you are making it incredibly tempting."

"Oh. You're already acting like a rebellious teen. I might cry."

Jade made her way onto the sidewalk and waited for Darby to hold open the door to the office. Once they stepped inside, Jade realized why no one had answered her calls. The office of O'Shea Construction was practically bare. One desk sat in the middle of the room with one chair. There wasn't even a place for consulting or a lobby. The only other bit of furnishing was a table with a coffeepot against one wall.

"This is very chic," Darby said. "Very minimalist. I like it."

"I don't think that's what they're going for," Jade said. "They must be closed."

"You are correct" came a voice from behind them.

They turned as a woman walked in carrying an empty box. She bypassed them, not quite stomping, but she definitely had a mission. Her dark, straight hair had been pulled back into a ponytail that swayed with each determined step. Her gray cargo pants and white tank top made it clear she wasn't a member of the office staff, but Jade wasn't sure who she was.

"Excuse me," Darby said. "We're looking for Mr. O'Shea."

Jade lightly swatted Darby's arm. "Ms. O'Shea."

Scrunching her face, Darby turned her attention toward Jade. "*Ms.*? Are we hiring a female contractor?"

Instead of answering, Jade simply stared back. She'd already explained that they were. Out of all the contractors she'd looked at, Jade had chosen O'Shea Construction because the owner was female. Not that she was hating on male contractors, but in the last twenty-four hours, her contractor husband had ditched her and the eye candy Darby had been tempted to hire had tried to take advantage of her. So, she wasn't hating on men. She was simply fed up with their shit at the moment and wasn't going to suggest Darby hire one if she could help it.

Jade turned her attention to the woman who was now packing away the coffeepot and asked, "Are you Taylor O'Shea?"

"I am," the woman said, carelessly dropping a container of coffee grounds into the box.

"We have a project—"

"I'm not taking any projects." She lifted her free hand and gestured around her. "*Ever.* I'm closed."

Jade blinked several times before asking, "Why?"

Taylor tossed the box down carelessly and pinned Darby with a harsh stare. "Because I'm a female, as you pointed out. And nobody in Chammont Point will hire a *female* contractor." With a dramatic gesture, she extended her hand toward the big window at the front of her office space. "This town is so goddamn backward that even when I submit the most reasonable quote, I can't get a job. Even when I am honest about what needs to be done, I can't get a job. Even when—"

"We'll give you a job," Darby interrupted. "That's why we're here."

"Well, it's too late," Taylor said. "I'm done."

Jade shuffled closer to her. "We really need an honest contractor. Just this morning—"

"I'm done," Taylor said again.

Jade straightened her back and held Taylor's determined gaze. "Okay. I understand. I mean, if you've already gotten another job to pay your bills, we shouldn't stand in your way. That wouldn't be right."

As she expected, the frustration on Taylor's face eased and a hint of despair flashed in her dark eyes.

Jade casually shrugged. "I'm assuming you already have another job lined up, because you can't just close your company without a plan."

Taylor cursed under her breath. Planting her hands on her hips, she looked around the barren office space. She closed her eyes for a few seconds before frowning at Jade. "What do you need?"

Jade waved her hand. "Oh, no. We wouldn't want to be an imposition. Come on, Darby. There are other contractors we can try."

"Stop," Taylor called. She let out a dramatic breath. "I don't... I don't have another job lined up, so..." She shook her head and pressed her lips together. "These people are ridiculous. I've worked for contractors all my life. I know what I'm doing." She gestured at a framed piece of paper on the wall. "I spent three years taking online classes to learn how to run a business, and they won't give me a chance because I don't have a...guy part."

"We're here because you don't have a guy part," Jade said. "Guy parts aren't our favorite things right now."

"Speak for yourself," Darby said.

Jade ignored her and asked Taylor, "Can you replace the banister on her porch? You could be done in a day."

Darby shook her head. "No, Eye Candy said the entire structure is bad and the..." She rolled her eyes back. "The strippers are rotten because there weren't flashers."

The crease between Taylor's brows deepened. "I don't know what you're saying. Eye Candy?"

Darby nodded. "Oh, yeah, this contractor gave me a cavity. He was so sweet."

"And there were strippers and flashers?" Taylor asked, clearly not connecting the dots.

Opening her mouth, Darby hesitated before confirming. "Yes. Apparently, the flashers protect the strippers, and without them, the strippers go bad."

Taylor focused on Jade. "I'm getting nothing here."

"He told her the stringers were bad because there was no flashing," Jade clarified.

Widening her eyes, Taylor said, "Oh. *Okay*. That makes sense."

"That does make more sense," Darby said.

"Maybe," Jade said, "but what doesn't make sense is he told her he needed to tear out the kitchen to replace all the boards and fix this. Now, granted, I didn't do a full inspection, but the only damage I noticed was to the banister I fell through."

"Were you drunk?" Taylor asked.

Darby cupped her mouth and whispered loudly, "She doesn't drink."

Taylor cocked a dark brow and eyed Jade. "You don't drink?"

"No."

"Like the hard stuff or…"

"Nothing. For health reasons," she said, as if she owed anyone an explanation. "Are you interested in helping us or not?"

Taylor turned her focus back to Darby, pursed her lips for a moment, and said, "I'll take a look at your porch, but I'm not making any promises. If Eye Candy was right, and this requires tearing out the kitchen, I'm out. Got it?"

"Got it," Darby said.

When the other two women looked at Jade, she shrugged. "Got it. Let's go."

Within fifteen minutes, Darby and Jade stood in the shade of an old tree while Taylor inspected the decking and banister.

"Do you really think we should hire a woman?" Darby whispered.

Jade glanced at her. "Do you think we shouldn't?"

Darby frowned. "I was really looking forward to sitting in the shade with a drink while sweaty men pounded on my deck."

This time, Jade's laugh rolled from her, and Darby's lips curved up. Darby wrapped her arm around Jade's shoulders and giggled. "Aw, honey, you're getting over him already."

The reminder of Nick's betrayal flared in her mind, and Jade's smile faded. "I wouldn't say that. I just forgot for a few seconds. Thanks for reminding me."

Taylor brushed her palms together and crossed the yard. "There is some damage to the stringers, but they don't need replacement, and you definitely don't need the extensive work Eye Candy told you. I can reinforce them, add the flashing, and replace the banister. That will take care of the porch. But you do have some settling around the foundation you'll want to look into in the near future. I need to take some measurements and price the supplies before I give you a quote."

"Does that mean you'll do it?" Jade asked.

Taylor looked back at the cabin and then nodded. "Yeah. I'll do it."

Darby clapped her hands. "Yay! We need to celebrate." She rushed toward the cabin, talking about the brownies and wine she'd brought Jade the day before.

"So, um..." Taylor started. "What's her... What's up with her... Why does she..."

"Dress and act like a 1940s bombshell?"

"Yeah, that."

Jade shrugged. "I can't really say. I only met her yesterday. She's very sweet, though."

Taylor lowered her sunglasses to eye Jade. With her thin face and long nose, her dark eyes seemed more suspicious than curious. "You met her yesterday?"

"Yeah. I'm just renting the cabin for the next week."

Taylor leaned back as if she couldn't quite believe what she was hearing. "You fell through the banister of a rental and you're staying?"

"Well, I did go home, but..." She debated how much to share. "My husband is moving out."

Taylor's eyes softened. "Oh. I'm sorry."

"Being here made more sense. I don't really want to witness him leaving me. That seems...depressing." She managed to smile, but the effort was almost painful.

"Being here is better." Taylor looked toward the water in the distance. "The lake is great for calming the mind when the rest of the world seems to be on fire."

Jade thought there was more to that statement, but Taylor gestured toward the cabin where Darby was waiting for them. Much like Darby, Taylor held her arms out as if she would catch Jade should she fall. Jade appreciated the unspoken offer, but she managed to get up the stairs on her own. By the time she and Taylor got to the kitchen, Darby was pouring two glasses of wine. In the third, she added cranberry juice and a few ice cubes as she rambled on about how excited she was to support a local business.

Jade sat at the table as Darby fussed in the kitchen.

"She doesn't eat brownies either," Darby explained, drawing Jade's attention. "She's very healthy."

Jade ran her fingers over the scar on her chest where the doctor had placed a port prior to the start of her treatment. She fought the need to amend Darby's assessment with the word *now*. She was very healthy *now*. The raised tissue was a constant reminder of the treatment she'd received. She was healthy *now*.

Taylor slid a plate of fresh fruit and a glass of cranberry juice in front of Jade. "This is how you're celebrating?"

"Well, I like to live on the edge."

"Slow down. Let the rest of us catch up," Taylor said with a smile and went back into the kitchen. Moments later, she slid into the booth across from Jade with a large slice of the mint brownie and her wine.

Darby dropped down and held her glass up. "Here's to dessert and wine in the afternoon." She glanced at Jade's plate. "Here's to meeting new friends."

Taylor and Jade cast glances at each other before lifting their glasses and joining the toast.

FOUR

EARLY THE NEXT MORNING, Jade frowned as she once again clumsily climbed out of Darby's car. The gravel parking lot made using her crutches much more difficult, but Jade got her balance and took a few wobbly steps toward the entrance of the store.

As she tended to do, Darby held her arms out, ready to catch Jade should she tumble over. That would be reassuring, but Darby didn't seem to be faring much better, thanks to her high-heeled black-and-white Mary Janes. Her knee-length halter dress was cut like one from the 1950s, but the material was red with black teardrops and the bottom was lined with green tulle, making her look like a slice of watermelon.

No doubt that was the point, but Jade had no idea why. She stopped, closed her eyes, and blew out a slow breath. Her irritation wasn't with Darby or her spunky outfit. Jade's irritation was from the pain in her ankle limiting her activities and with herself for not realizing Nick's master plan sooner. Now that her shock was wearing off, her broken heart was hardening with the anger of humiliation from catching him leaving her like she had.

That wasn't anything Darby had done. Jade inhaled again, held the air, and then exhaled through her lips, doing her best to center and calm herself. When she opened her eyes after another deep breath, she actually smiled. The reality was Darby *did* look like a slice of watermelon. But who could possibly look at her without smiling? Who the hell was Jade to resent that?

"Are you sure about this?" Darby asked.

Jade let the last of her irritability slip away. "I'm positive."

"I think you should wait a few more days."

Jade shook her head and continued her journey across the gravel lot. "Nope. I am not wasting one more minute of this vacation. Come on."

The small shop across the street from one of Chammont Point's more popular beaches was empty. So empty, Jade had to wonder if Lakefront Rentals was open. Life vests, bathing suits, and water sport accessories filled racks and lined walls. Several spinning displays had sunscreen of varying brands and strengths. There was even a vintage ice chest filled with unopened soda cans and plastic bottles of water, but there wasn't an employee to be seen.

"Hello?" Jade called. When she didn't receive an answer, she turned to Darby, who simply shrugged. Jade hobbled through the store and out a back door to where rows of canoes, kayaks, and paddleboards were neatly stacked on wooden racks. "Anyone here?"

"Aye," a deep voice answered. A man poked his head around the stack of orange-and-yellow ombre canoes and blatantly looked them both over before meeting Jade's gaze.

He stared at her through bright gray eyes shaded by long, thick lashes that almost made him look innocent. *Almost.* The lashes were offset by a mischievous twinkle that likely wasn't noticed by many until it was too late to escape his allure.

"Hi, Liam," Darby practically cooed.

"You know him?" Jade asked under her breath.

Darby grinned and batted her eyes. "Everybody knows Liam."

"I bet," Jade said flatly.

"Nice crutches," he said with a tempting smile.

"Thanks," Darby and Jade said at the same time. Darby, however, sounded flattered, whereas Jade sounded unamused.

"Do you girls need something?" Liam asked.

Girls? Jade had managed to push her irritation away, but this man relit her fuse. Just seeing his handsome face made her want to beat him over the head. For no reason other than that he was handsome and seemed to know it. Nick had always known he was handsome, too. The bastard. "No," she deadpanned. "We just like to wander around rental places in hopes of finding unwitting men to enchant with our siren songs."

He stood up and widened his grin. "Must be your lucky day."

"I doubt it," she answered. "I was hoping you could tell me the least painful activity to try with a sprained ankle."

The man's smile spread, and Jade silently swore if he said one untoward thing to her, she'd shove one of her jewel-encrusted crutches right up his ass.

"I think he's flirting with you," Darby whispered.

"I think he flirts with everyone to increase his odds." Jade dismissed him with a wave. "Never mind. There has to be a dozen other rental places I can try."

"Two," he said. "There are *two* other rental places. Unless you want to go out of town."

"Maybe we will," Jade said.

A cocky grin formed deep parentheses around his mouth and crinkled the lines around his eyes. Jade didn't think that was age as much as time spent in the sun wincing and smiling at foolish females. She doubted he was much older than her thirty-seven years, and she had recently started to take notice of the way the lines on her face never fully faded.

Yeah. She definitely didn't like the way he raked her nerves.

"Running off more business, Liam?" a young woman asked as she came out of nowhere carrying an armful of bright orange life vests.

"Just being hospitable," he countered.

Jade tilted her head as she looked at Darby. "I think he was bordering on sexual harassment. What do you think?"

"Oh, come on, Jade." Darby smiled and batted her fake lashes in his direction. "He's cute."

The younger woman shifted the life vests to reveal a very pregnant stomach. "I'm sorry about him. He thinks women find him charming."

Liam smiled and winked. "Some women do."

"I do," Darby offered as she raised her hand.

Though he was adorable with his shaggy brown hair and suntanned skin, Jade wasn't exactly won over by his approach. Lowering Darby's arm, Jade said, "We need to work on your standards."

"But—" Darby started.

Jade shook her head. "Being cute and flirty doesn't make a man worthy."

"I'll second that." The younger woman hefted the life vests again and held her hand out. "I'm Parker."

"Jade," she said, shaking her hand.

Liam, the insufferable, approached with his arms out, causing Jade's defenses to spike. However, he didn't pay her and Darby any attention. His focus was on the armload Parker was carrying. He took the life vests from her as he frowned. "I told you I would take care of those."

"I'm pregnant, not broken," Parker said.

"And I'm the boss," he stated before walking away with the vests.

"How can I help you, ladies?" Parker asked.

"I'm only in town for another few days. I'd like to do something besides sit around, but..." Jade gestured toward the foot she'd been holding off the ground.

"How bad?"

"The doctor said I'll be fine in a few days. I just can't put too much weight on it."

"It's worse than she wants to admit," Darby offered.

Jade frowned at Darby's assessment, mostly because she wasn't lying. "I really don't want to sit around doing nothing. What do you suggest?"

Parker pointed toward the stack of sit-on-top kayaks. "That's probably your best bet. You can sit on this in shallow water without much trouble. That would make it easier to get in and out of."

Jade had really been looking forward to learning how to paddleboard, but as she'd feared, her flying leap off the balcony had put that goal on hold.

"Have you used a kayak before?" Liam asked, approaching them again.

"It's been a while." A while had actually been close to a decade, and even then, she had fallen out of rather than gracefully exited the craft.

His sly smile returned. "I'm happy to give you a refresher course."

"Has anyone ever told you that you're not as cute as you think?" Jade asked.

"No," Liam said at the exact moment that Parker said, "Yes."

Liam's sarcastic come-ons eased, and he sounded sincere when he looked down toward her ankle and said, "You really think it's a good idea to get out on the water with a bad foot? What if you tip over?"

"I'll wear a life vest."

"Damn straight you will," he stated, as if he had any control over her actions.

Jade turned her eyes away when she noticed the way his muscles rippled as he lifted a canoe off the rack. She feigned disgust and looked at Darby. But Darby had slid her bright cat-eye sunglasses down to get a better view.

Jade gently bumped into her and whispered, "Don't encourage him."

"I know you're bitter right now, but even you have to admit he's adorable."

"So are stray dogs," Jade said, "until you find out they have a bad case of worms."

After setting the kayak on the ground, Liam rested his hands on his hips. "Get in. Not you," he stated when Darby headed for the kayak. "Limps-a-lot."

Jade lifted her chin a notch and stared him down.

He shrugged as if her resistance meant nothing to him. "I'm not renting to you unless I see you get in and out of this without breaking your other ankle."

"It's not broken," Jade informed him. "It's a *mild* sprain."

"Get in," Liam ordered.

Jade was torn between marching off as indignantly as her crutches would allow and proving to the egomaniac that she could, in fact, get in and out of the kayak. Holding his gaze, she smirked as she put both crutches in one hand and lifted her injured foot over the kayak to straddle it.

"Wrong," Liam said.

She started to step in, but Liam released a sound that was an obnoxious imitation of a buzzer.

"Do you want to flip over?" he asked.

She turned her back to him and started to sit, but her ankle screamed out in protest. Damn it. She was going to suck up the pain and prove she could do this. She tried again, but the pain won out.

"Oh, now she's in trouble," Darby muttered.

Jade shot her a silent warning to be quiet. "I would do this in the water, like Parker said, which would make it easier."

"Then let's try it in the water."

Jade widened her eyes. "What?"

Without another word and with little effort, Liam lifted the kayak onto his knee and then rolled it onto his shoulder. With his free hand, he gestured toward the lake. "Show me how much easier it is in the water."

She looked to Parker, who simply stared, and then to Darby, who seemed to be solely focused on Liam's muscles.

When Jade didn't move, Liam asked, "You want to do this? Because if you do, come with me so I can show you how to get in and out of this thing without finishing off that ankle."

Jade and Darby followed Liam across the street and down two steps to a sandy beach.

"Hold these." Jade held out her crutches to Darby.

"Jade," Darby practically begged.

Unfazed, Jade pushed the crutches at her again. "Take them, Darby."

With a frown, Darby accepted the crutches. "I'm going on record as saying this is a bad idea, and I'm terrible at recognizing bad ideas."

Ignoring her, Jade put her injured foot into the sand. Not only did the hot granules instantly squish between her toes, but the soft ground did little to support her. She ignored the pain as she limped her way behind Liam to the water.

Though he was wearing canvas sandals, Liam walked right into the water and put the kayak down with ease. Jade stopped beside him and planted her hands on her hips, waiting for him to impart his wisdom.

"How'd you manage that?" he asked, clearly meaning her injury though he was looking her in the eye.

"Fell through a banister."

"Wow. Vodka?"

"Gravity. I don't drink."

The perplexed look on his face made her laugh.

"Is everyone in this town a lush?" she asked. "How can one person's aversion to alcohol cause so much controversy?"

He shrugged. "Small town. Not much to do."

Jade opened her arms wide as she looked around the

lake. "There are a million things to do here. Like"—she returned her attention to the kayak—"renting me one of these."

"Right," he said. "We'll see about that."

The light reflecting off Darby's bright red hair was like a flare signaling for rescue as Jade paddled into the cove. Since Darby's car didn't have a rack to take a kayak back to the cabin, Liam had offered to take Jade and the rental. Jade, however, had tapped into her defiant side and insisted that she could paddle back.

Despite his and Darby's protests, Jade said all Liam had to do was carry the kayak back across the road to the water and she'd be off. They'd both argued with her, but Jade's determination had won out. Darby had taken her crutches home, Liam had seen Jade off, and she'd silently cursed herself for the twenty minutes it had taken her to make her way to the cove.

What. The. Hell. Had. She. Been. Thinking?

Her arms felt like gelatin. Five minutes into her excursion and she'd been on the verge of giving up and letting the lake take her wherever the waves wanted. After ten minutes, she'd considered tossing away the paddle so she could wither away to nothing in peace. But after fifteen minutes, she'd recognized the cove in the distance.

She was even more relieved when she saw Taylor walking toward Darby, who had started waving her arms and calling out to Jade.

"Help," Jade answered as she neared the shore. She put

the paddle on her thighs and reached out as if Taylor and Darby could magically pull her from the water. Neither even moved. They watched from where they stood, several yards from the beach. In that moment, Jade hated them both for no reason other than that they weren't being more sympathetic to her self-induced agony. She'd made a lot of bad decisions in her life—like that time she started with an advanced spin class because it was *just* riding a stationary bike, or when she spontaneously took up rock climbing because she was certain it couldn't be *that* difficult—but this was definitely in the top ten of her bad choices.

"My arms," she called out. "They won't work. Help me."

Darby and Taylor headed toward the beach, but both stopped short of entering the water.

"What the hell is wrong with you?" Taylor asked. "Darby said you were paddling all the way here by yourself. Are you a masochist or something?"

"That creepy guy said he'd bring the kayak over since Darby doesn't have a rack on her car. I didn't want him here."

"Liam Cunningham isn't nearly as bad as he seems," Taylor informed her. "He's like a puppy. He begs for attention but doesn't actually want it. It's just a game to him."

Jade was probably as close to shore as she could get without having to crawl out of the kayak. She'd learned, thanks to said creepy guy, that she needed a bit of depth to get out without hurting her ankle. The water helped ease the jarring of landing on her foot.

At least he'd been good for something other than smirking like a freaking know-it-all as she struggled to prove that she was ready to tackle the kayak. Though she staggered and nearly fell on her face, Jade managed to get out of the kayak and stay on her feet. Now she just had to get to shore, where Darby was waiting with her crutches.

As she neared the beach, Jade frowned at the disapproving looks on Taylor's and Darby's faces. She could understand that look coming from Taylor since she seemed to be much more logical than anyone else at the moment, but Darby had no right to look so malcontent. Especially since she'd confessed to doing drunken cartwheels on a stage while wearing platform boots.

Darby was the winner, hands down, when it came to bad ideas.

As tempted as Jade was to ask for help again, she refused to when they were acting like that. However, as soon as she got to the beach and no longer had the water to ease some of the burden on her ankle, Jade gave in. "Guys," she whined. "Are you going to make me crawl?"

Taylor headed toward her with a scowl on her face. "You should know better."

Darby handed Jade the crutches while Taylor pulled the kayak onto shore so it didn't float away.

"You're not ready for this," Taylor said as she followed Jade toward the chairs. "Until you can actually walk, you should be sitting on your ass right here and enjoying the view."

"I'm on vacation." Jade tugged her life vest off and sagged into the chair. "I don't want to sit here doing nothing my entire vacation."

Taylor put her hands on her hips and shook her head. "You're going to make that ankle worse and have to use crutches for weeks instead of days."

Jade crinkled her nose and looked at Darby. "She's bossy, isn't she?"

"Apparently you need that," Darby said. "Even I'm not this reckless."

Jade cocked a brow and smirked. "I'm not sure I believe that."

Darby lifted her brow in return. "Would you like ibuprofen with a juice chaser?"

"Yes, please." Jade forced a sweet smile to her face. "Thank you, Darby."

Taylor sat next to Jade. "If you're going to be using that thing, you better be able to get in and out of it without falling."

"Did you start on the banister?" Jade asked to change the subject from her stubborn stupidity.

Taylor stretched her legs out in what seemed to be her uniform of gray cargo pants, a tank top, and work boots and said, "I ordered supplies. I just dropped by to check with Darby on when I should get started when she told me about your little expedition. We agreed I should wait for your return before leaving in case Darby couldn't get you out of the water."

Jade grinned, genuinely touched by Taylor's thoughtfulness even though Taylor seemed more annoyed than concerned. "Aw, that was nice. Thank you."

"Don't do that again, Jade. You seriously could get hurt."

Rather than admit that Taylor, Darby, and even Liam had been right, Jade once again changed the subject. "Are you going to have to replace the strippers and flashers?"

Chuckling, Taylor shook her head as she rolled her eyes.

"Just the flashers. The strippers are going to be fine. However, this place is a mess. She needs more than just a banister."

Jade peered back at the cabin. From where she sat, she noticed several spots where the shingles had started cracking and other areas that were dark from years of protecting the cabin from the elements.

"It's not an investment property if you can't make money off it," Taylor observed. "She should sell it while she can."

"Well, maybe you can talk to her about that. If it really needs a lot of work, she might not want to hang on to it anyway."

"Look what I made," Darby sang carrying three wine glasses and the brownie container on a tray. "Nonalcoholic for you, darling."

Jade accepted the glass. "Thank you."

"How does your digestive system handle that much juice?" Taylor asked.

Jade laughed lightly. "I, um, I had colorectal cancer, so... There's not much of my digestive system left, really."

Darby creased her brow and slid her sunglasses down her nose. "You had what?"

"Colorectal cancer."

"Butt cancer," Taylor offered. "She had butt cancer, Darby."

"Well, it was more like..." Jade gave up the idea of explaining the ins and outs of where her tumors had grown and spread and the various parts she'd had removed. She simply nodded. "I had cancer in my butt."

Darby swayed on her feet and dropped into a chair as if she didn't have the strength to stand any longer. "I didn't know that was a thing."

"Well, it is," Jade confirmed. "They removed a foot of my colon, and then I had to have chemotherapy. The cancer had spread before we caught it, so there were other things. But we don't need to get into them because you look like you might faint."

Darby put the back of her hand to her forehead and gasped. "Please. I don't want to know."

"Are you okay now?" Taylor asked, ignoring Darby's dramatics.

Jade nodded. "Yeah, or so I'm told. But that's why I don't eat junk food or drink alcohol."

Darby jerked her glasses off, sat up, and gawked, her dark eyes wide and her mouth hanging open. "Junk food *and* alcohol?"

Jade toasted her with her wineglass of cranberry juice. "Unhealthy diet, unhealthy body."

Darby looked at the drink in her hand and started to pour it out but then held up one hand. After taking several big gulps from her glass, she dumped out the rest. "Okay. That's it. Kale and cranberry juice. I swear by all that is holy, I will never drink again."

Jade was not the slightest bit convinced by Darby's solemn vow. She glanced at Taylor, who shook her head, clearly not buying into the weak promise either.

"Listen," Jade said, "before I got sick, I was the most uptight, career-driven person you'd ever met. I have a second chance, and I don't want to waste it. All those things I never did, never *wanted* to do, I'm going to do them now. I appreciate the two of you for being concerned, but I'm not going to let a sprained ankle get in my way. I want fun and adventures. I want to try new things. I can't watch life pass me by any longer. I have to start living. *Now*."

"Now?" Taylor asked. "Like right *now*."

"Yes," Jade stated. "Right now."

Darby toasted her with her empty glass. "That's my girl. You gotta grab life by the cajones and take it where you want it to go." She started to take a drink but then seemed to remember she'd tossed out her wine.

"There's a difference between living and being reckless," Taylor said. "Kayaking halfway across Chammont Lake with a sprained ankle was reckless."

"I won't do it again," Jade said.

Taylor nodded toward the cabin. "How old is that roof, Darby?"

Scrunching up her face, Darby shrugged. "I don't know. It was there when I bought the place."

"When was that?"

"Um, two years ago, I guess."

Jade furrowed her brow. "Your real estate agent let you buy it with that roof?"

"Oh, I didn't use a real estate agent. I bought it from the owner."

Taylor's eyes nearly popped out of her head. "Did you have an inspection?"

Darby wrinkled her nose. "A what?"

"Are you kidding me?" Taylor muttered.

"Didn't your attorney have someone come out and determine the value of the property?" Jade asked.

"I didn't use an attorney."

Jade's eyes widened slightly. "Well, didn't the bank require an appraisal for you to get a loan?"

Darby tilted her head and smiled with obvious pride. "I didn't take out a loan, Jade. I had the money in savings. I was planning to take a trip to Vegas and bet it all on that spinning thing."

"The roulette wheel?" Jade asked.

"Yes! *That*. But something told me that would be irresponsible."

"So you bought a rental property without an inspection instead?" Taylor asked.

Darby's face sagged. "Yeah."

"Did you get the deed, Darby?" Jade asked.

Her smile returned. "Yes. Notarized and everything."

"You two are too much. Do you know that?" Taylor rubbed her forehead like she couldn't handle one more irresponsible act from her new friends.

Jade giggled. She couldn't recall anyone ever being fed up with her for her *lack* of responsibility. She'd always been the so-called stick in the mud. She was happy to hand that title off to Taylor.

Darby looked back at the cabin. "The last owner was a sweet old lady. She was going into a nursing home, and her son sold it to me for cheap."

"Of course he did," Taylor said. "He took advantage of you, Darby."

Darby started to shake her head but then stopped. "That actually happens a lot. I tend to jump in without thinking things through."

"Well, you're in it now," Taylor said. "Mind if I take a closer look?"

"Um, I guess, if Jade doesn't mind."

Jade waved them off. "Go ahead."

She pulled her phone from her pocket and removed it from a waterproof pouch. She'd bought the pouch from Liam as he explained how it wouldn't be his fault if she drowned in the middle of Chammont Lake. In his opinion, she wasn't nearly as ready for water activities as she'd thought.

For about the millionth time, she started to call Nick before she remembered that she shouldn't. *Couldn't.* Checking in with him was a habit—one she was going to have a hard time breaking, though she hadn't been given a choice in the matter.

Tears welled in her eyes, but she gave her head a hard shake. She snagged her crutches and managed to stand without too much struggle. "Wait up," she called. "I'm coming too!"

FIVE

JADE DIDN'T WANT to point out that Taylor had arrived early that morning to put up the new banister, but they had somehow ended up sitting on the beach instead. Things in Chammont Point seemed to move at a much slower pace than Jade was used to. That wasn't a bad thing. In fact, she thought she needed to be away from the frantic life she'd had in Fairfax.

If she'd taken a little bit of time to slow down and listen to her body when things had started to go astray, her cancer treatment might have been limited to one surgery and a biopsy rather than months of poison being injected into her bloodstream.

"Earth to Jade," Darby sang.

Jade blinked and laughed off her lack of focus. "Sorry. What?"

"Taylor has offered to man the grill for dinner. Chicken or steak?"

"Um, chicken."

Taylor suggested baked potatoes for the side instead of

corn on the cob. She didn't like the way corn got stuck in her teeth. That comment spiraled Darby into a completely different direction that, surprisingly, Jade was able to follow. Even though she and Taylor occasionally cast confused glances at each other, Darby's random changes of topic were starting to make sense in some roundabout way.

Three days into her visit to Chammont Point, and Jade couldn't quite believe she was sitting by the lake, discussing corn with two women who, for all intents and purposes, were strangers. Yet she couldn't remember the last time she'd felt so at ease. There were no deadlines looming in her mind. She wasn't panicked over balancing her day-to-day life with the aftereffects of chemotherapy. And, unless she let her mind wander, she wasn't obsessing about Nick.

Sitting by the water with her new friends really did seem to have the calming effect Taylor told her it would. That should have been the first sign that her day was going to go to shit. The calm never seemed to stick around for long in Jade's life. The phone in her lap rang, and her heart sank to her stomach when Nick's name flashed on the screen. She hadn't spoken to him in two days. Even if she'd wanted to, she hadn't trusted herself to not make a bigger mess of things. Her emotions were a roller coaster peaking with all-consuming rage and then plummeting to bouts of crying and confusion, only to slowly start the rise again.

Jade wasn't sure if it was intentional or not, but Darby and Taylor had done a great job at keeping her distracted. Whenever depression started nagging at her, Darby said or did something ridiculous or Taylor started talking about what she might do next. Darby sold her clothes online and suggested Taylor find something she could sell. Taylor didn't think she had the skillset for that, but Darby insisted she had a million ideas for how to make money that didn't involve what most people would consider a "real" job, and she would help Taylor find her niche.

That had led into a long discussion of all the various jobs Darby had held over the years and even more laughs at her colorful stories. Jade's mind was never on Nick for too long thanks to their constant companionship.

That couldn't save her now, though. The second ring filled her ears, combating with the thumping of her heartbeat.

"It's my husband," she said numbly to Darby and Taylor.

"What do you think he wants?" Taylor asked with a sharp edge to her voice that seemed excessively protective given they'd just met a few days prior.

"I don't know," Jade said, and part of her didn't want to know.

"Are you going to answer?" Darby asked after the third ring.

"I don't know," Jade said again. "I guess I have to."

"Actually, you don't," Darby said.

The fourth ring.

"It could be about the kids," Jade said. "I should answer it."

The muscles in Taylor's jaw clenched for a moment. "You don't take him back without sufficient begging. He broke your heart."

Jade offered her a soft smile. "Somehow I don't think he's calling to tell me he's changed his mind."

Darby offered her a weak smile as she stood. "We'll be close in case you need something."

"Thanks." Jade drew a deep breath for courage before answering his call on the fifth ring, the last one before her voice mail would have picked up. "Hey."

"Hey," he responded, sounding just as uncertain as she felt. "How...how are you?"

Jade ground her teeth so the sarcastic response didn't leave her and ran through the other possible answers.

Fine? But she wasn't.

Okay? Nope, that wasn't true either.

Confused, hurt, and angry. Yeah, that was it. But she didn't think she should say that for some reason. Probably because admitting how she was really doing wouldn't do anything to change the outcome. His leaving was inevitable. Apparently, it had been for a long time.

So why did it matter how she was doing? Why did it matter that she felt weak and tired and depressed? Did he even care that she was mad as hell? He was doing this to her when she'd barely gotten her body on the right track. Did he really care that she was a mess? Probably not.

"How's the leg?" he continued.

Jade lowered her face and pressed her fingertips into her forehead. "Small talk, Nick? Really?"

Nick exhaled slowly, as he did when he was nervous. "Look, I don't like how we left things. You were so angry."

"Oh, gee. I'm sorry." She instantly regretted the snark. She wanted them to have an actual conversation, and they couldn't do that if she didn't contain her anger.

"I was caught off guard the other night," Nick said.

"Yeah," she said, forcing away the bite from her words, "so was I."

"I'm sorry about that, Jade. I really am," he said. "Amber felt terrible."

"Oh, I'm really sorry I upset *Amber*." Saying the other woman's name made Jade's stomach turn and her throat tighten. Jade hadn't even considered that she hadn't known the other woman's name. As many times as she'd caught herself wondering how much time that woman may have spent in her house, in her bed, with her husband, she hadn't once wondered what the bitch's name was.

She hadn't wanted to know.

Jade dug her toes in the sand and watched her bright blue nails disappear. In an attempt to cheer her up, Darby had carried over an entire mani-pedi set to Jade's living room early that morning. Resistance was futile. No matter how much she'd tried to avoid the pampering, Darby had insisted a new nail color would change her outlook. Once her nails were electric blue with little white bubbles drawn on them, Darby had used a curling iron and more hair spray than any one person needed to add volume to Jade's hair.

Darby had been right. By the time Jade's nails had dried and her hair was poofed up, she'd felt better than she had in days. However, she suspected that was Darby's nonstop chatter about her various careers, women who had vexed her, and all the other ramblings that took Jade's mind off Nick.

"I meant..." Nick continued. "Neither of us wanted to hurt you, Jade. We wanted to make this as easy as possible for you."

Her eyes started to fill with tears. "You knew I was going to be blindsided by this."

"I did," he said softly. "I wanted the conversation to be

more thought-out. I wanted to have a clearer mind on what I needed to say to you so this was easier for both of us. I wasn't prepared to face you yet, and I didn't handle it as well as I'd hoped I would. I'm so sorry. I saw how hurt you were and... I should have been more prepared."

What was she supposed to say to that? Was she supposed to apologize for screwing up his plans to break her heart gently? This was on him, and she wasn't going to let him make her feel guilty it didn't go according to his lousy plans.

"Are you even going to give me a chance to fix us?" she asked, hating how weak her voice sounded.

He was quiet for too long before saying, "We were together for a long time. We had a really good run, but it didn't work out, Jade. I don't want to fix this. I want to move on."

"You gave up without talking through this with me first. You decided that our marriage is over without even talking to me. This isn't fair to me, Nick. This isn't fair to our kids. We're a *family*." Up until that moment, until she'd spoken of their children, the feeling of raw desperation had been something buried deep beneath her anger and shock and betrayal. Until she reminded him about Xander and Owen, she hadn't allowed herself to fully feel the impact Nick's decision was going to have on all of them. "You're tearing us apart, and you never even gave me a chance."

"Jade," he said softly, "look at what we've been through in the last year. If my heart was going to change, it would have when you were sick. It didn't."

The fist around her heart tightened. "This isn't just about us," she said. "What about the kids?"

"They're grown."

"So it's okay to rip our family apart because they aren't little anymore?"

"I stayed longer than I wanted to," Nick said. "I stayed for Owen to finish school, and then I stayed to help you get healthy. But I have to leave for me."

His words were the final blow her heart could take. She pulled her sunglasses off and dropped them into her lap so she could press her hand against her face as her tears started. She did her best not to sob, but emotion churned in her chest until it forced its way out.

"I didn't want you to find out like you did," he said, "but there was never going to be a right way to tell you. I hate how much this is hurting you, but I don't know how to stop that."

"You've known for a while that you were going to leave me, Nick. You've had a long time to process what you were doing. Please don't act like this is painful for you."

"It is," he whispered. "It's not the same, but it's hurting me because it's hurting you and I don't want that. But I can't stop it. I hate that I can't make it easier for you. I don't want this to be harder than it has to be, Jade."

She sniffed and forced herself to swallow hard. "Look, divorce is permanent. Maybe we should separate and—"

"No," he stated. "I've thought about this for a long time."

"You've made that clear, but I've only had a chance to think about it for two days, Nick. And I can't wrap my head around why you are so adamant about ending things." Reality punched her in the gut and stole her breath. "Are you in love with her?" she whispered.

His silence said what she didn't want to know. Her husband was in love with someone else. Jade forced herself to swallow so she didn't break down while he was on the phone to hear her.

"We grew apart a long time ago," Nick said. "For years we've been friends living in the same house, raising the same kids, but not being together. Even when we were, we lived in two different worlds. I thought that was okay. I thought as long as we were happy, even if we rarely came into each other's orbits, that was normal. It's not. And it's not what I want."

"So why didn't you tell me that? Why didn't you give me a chance? You're walking away from everything we've built together without even trying, Nick. Do you understand how unbelievably selfish you're being right now?"

"I don't want to go down this road."

"What road?" she snapped. She hadn't wanted to be angry, but damn it, he wasn't being logical. He simply didn't love her after all their years together? So that's that. The end. Game over.

"You can be angry," he said.

"I don't need your permission."

He sighed into the phone. "The fact you didn't see how far apart we were says a lot about you, too, Jade. Your career—"

"Supported your business, paid for our kids to get braces, bought them a really nice house to grow up in, and is single-handedly paying for their education." Her intention to be calm and reasonable ended. This was the one area where she wasn't going to be blamed. They had made a decision *together*, years ago, that her job would be the financial backbone of their family unit. She wasn't going to be chastised for the hard work she'd put into making that a reality.

"Was more important to you than I was," he said. "And that started to take a toll."

"A toll that could have been repaired if you'd had the courage to point it out." She closed her eyes to stop another bout of tears from forming, but it was too late. Two streams fell from her eyes like a dam breaking. "I cannot believe you're doing this."

"Jade," he said, sounding as if he were barely containing his frustration. "You worked hard, you brought home the bacon. I know that. I appreciated that. But that doesn't make a marriage. We have a nice house, and the kids have straight teeth and are going to good schools. None of that means our marriage is good or solid. Or happy."

"Maybe not, but those are things you tell your wife, Nick. You say that something is wrong and needs to change. You don't decide one day that you want to leave without trying."

"It wasn't just one day. It built up over time until it was too big to ignore."

"So why didn't you *say* something?" Jade pressed yet again.

"Because you weren't around to hear it," he barked out.

"That is a piss-poor excuse for your unwillingness to save our marriage."

"Maybe," he said flatly, "but it's enough for me. When are you coming home?"

Wiping her face and sniffling, she again scanned the lake. "I rented the cabin until Saturday."

"Okay," he said. "I'll be out of the house by then."

She didn't reply. Once again, she didn't know what she was supposed to say. She had done all the pleading for a second chance she was going to do. There was no fight to be had. Besides, she was so very tired of fighting. She'd been fighting for too long. This was supposed to be her chance to start over. She couldn't force him to be a part of that if he didn't want to be.

"We'll talk next week so we can figure out when to tell the boys," he said.

Again, she had nothing to add.

"Bye, Jade." He hung up, and as much as she wanted to throw her phone into the damn lake, she simply dropped it into her lap with her sunglasses and covered her face.

Within moments, Darby and Taylor appeared at her side. She appreciated them hovering and making sure she was okay. Darby dropped down beside Jade's chair and pulled her into a hug.

"How the hell did this happen?" Jade asked, knowing they couldn't answer. "What did I do?"

"This isn't about you," Taylor said.

"He doesn't love me enough to try to save our marriage," Jade said. "It *is* about me. But I...I deserved a chance. Didn't I?"

"Of course you did," Darby said.

"And that's why I'm saying it isn't about you," Taylor insisted. "If he cared, not just about you but how it would impact your kids, he would have given you a chance before involving someone else."

"I'm not a bad person," Jade whispered. "I was career driven, but I did that to take care of them. I was the breadwinner. I had to work. I'm not a bad person."

Darby grabbed her hand. "No. You're not. Not at all.

You're so sweet." She wiped Jade's tears with a bright blue handkerchief that had been tied around her wrist like a bracelet. "Honey, he'd been screwing around behind your back and then asked you for a divorce, like, five minutes after you went into remission. I don't think this is your fault."

"Maybe it is," Jade whispered.

Taylor crossed her arms and shook her head. "No. It's not, Jade. This was his choice. He's the liar. Don't let him twist it around on you."

The anger in Taylor's voice took Jade by surprise. She sniffled and looked at Darby, who seemed to be just as shocked.

"Okay." Darby sat back and smiled at her. "I have a brilliant idea."

"Oh, shit," Taylor muttered. "We're in trouble now."

"Hey," Darby chastised. "You don't know me well enough to make that kind of assumption about my ideas."

Despite the misery in her heart, Jade chuckled. She squeezed Darby's hand tight. She didn't care what Darby's idea was—how terrible and possibly illegal it might be. Jade thought she'd probably agree simply because she so appreciated that these two were able to help her smile. Her world was crashing down around her yet again. She'd gladly accept whatever light Darby and Taylor could bring to her.

"I was going to say, before I was so harshly judged," Darby said, "that we should go hit up Harper's Ice Cream. Please tell me you eat ice cream."

Jade forced herself to swallow and sat a bit taller in an attempt to appear stronger than she felt. "I do today."

Dusk on Chammont Lake was beautiful. Jade paddled her kayak out of the cove far enough to see the sun starting to set but stayed far from where the heavier traffic on the lake tended to be. She needed the quiet of being on the water. She needed the peace of not having Taylor and Darby hovering over her. Though she appreciated their help and their concern, they hadn't stopped worrying about her long enough for her to fully comprehend the sudden and unexpected change her life had taken.

The last year had changed her. Nick had accused her of becoming hard. She had. She couldn't deny that, but she'd done what she thought she had to in order to succeed. Becoming a top executive hadn't always been on her career bucket list, but the closer she got to that particular feather in her hat, the higher she'd climbed, and the higher she'd climbed, the more focused she'd had to become. Putting her family second had never been her intention, and it had taken a terrifying diagnosis to show her she'd been wrong. So incredibly wrong.

But she'd learned her lesson, recognized her mistake, and she'd apologized. Nick had accepted her apology. Jade had thought they'd moved beyond that and had returned to the close and happy couple they had been years and years ago. Once again, she'd been wrong. Nick had been faking. For far too long apparently.

Her chest grew heavy as her tired eyes filled with tears. The world again felt as if it had been thrown off its axis. Nothing made sense. Everything was a blur.

Looking up at the vibrant streaks of oranges, pinks, and

purples painting the sky, Jade let out a sob. She'd been holding them in all day while Taylor and Darby had kept her occupied. After they'd left the ice cream shop, they'd walked around until Jade insisted she couldn't spend another moment on the crutches. Once they returned to the cabin, Darby had put a few chairs in the yard and they'd watched Taylor start assembling the new banister. No matter how much Darby rambled and Taylor explained what she was doing, Jade's mind kept wandering back to the call with Nick.

Finally, she told them she had to take a break. As she headed out to the lake, Darby said she would pick up whatever was needed for dinner—something green and leafy that went well with cranberry juice and grilled chicken—while Jade was out. When she returned, there would be food waiting for her. Taylor put her phone number into Jade's phone and insisted she call, even from the middle of the lake, if she couldn't make it back to shore.

Jade was lucky to have found such good people in Chammont Point. If it weren't for Darby and Taylor, Jade honestly didn't know who she'd turn to right now. Most of her friends, and she used that term loosely, had distanced themselves when her cancer had taken a turn for the worse. Being a cheerleader and support group sounded great until the diagnosis changed, and they suddenly feared they'd be planning a funeral and consoling a widower. They'd scattered like roaches in a spotlight once that news had started to spread. There was a saying about knowing who one's real friends are when the chips were down. Jade had found she didn't have any. She couldn't blame them for that. As Nick had so lovingly pointed out, she'd spent her time focused on her career. In turn, she'd attracted people who were also focused on their careers. Once Jade no longer served their purpose, they'd slowly disappeared until she had none of her so-called friends left.

Now she didn't even have her husband.

There was no doubt in her mind that once she returned to work full-time the following week and her cancer started to become a memory, those who had jumped ship would come swimming back. They'd be quietly expecting her to repay them for occasionally bringing flowers and carry-out dinners with a boost to their careers. Maybe she'd be more inclined to do so if they hadn't always looked like they were crawling out of their skin just being in her presence. Like her cancer might be contagious. However, all of those fake friends would once again slink away when word about her marriage started to get around.

So, here she was, relying on strangers for the kindness she should be getting from friends.

Jade's tears turned into borderline maniacal laughter as she realized she was getting exactly what she deserved. Oh, sweet Karma. She'd chosen a shallow life, and she had that in abundance now. Her life had gone from one mess to another, and her career might never recover. The thing was, she didn't care as much as she used to. She really had changed. She really had realized Nick and their boys were more important.

She pressed her hands to her face, roughly wiped her cheeks, and chastised herself. This was the price she had to pay for putting career goals over people. This was the consequence, the inevitable outcome. Crying wouldn't change it.

"Get yourself together, Jade," she muttered. "Make a plan.

You know how to do that."

She needed a list of tasks to go through to get from point A to point B. Right now, those two points were the difference between being married and divorced. After that, she'd think about the rest of the points in the alphabet.

Instead of complaining, she needed to remind herself how thankful she was to have this problem. She slid her hand under the neckline of her top and ran her fingertips across the raised bumps of scar tissue—the constant reminder of what she'd survived. She was fortunate enough to have had a medical center and a surgeon who could perform a laparoscopic colectomy. Rather than one long scar along the length of her abdomen, she had several smaller scars in various areas where cameras and tools had been inserted to remove the tissue that was trying to kill her.

Then she rubbed the scar just below her shoulder where the port had been placed for chemotherapy. She didn't want to think that her scars had anything to do with Nick's change of heart, but a nagging in the back of her mind was starting to take hold. Her scars wouldn't let her forget cold hospital rooms, doctor visits, long talks about what-ifs, and so many humiliating instances where she couldn't control her body.

For someone who claimed to not love her anymore, he certainly had been a trooper through some very ugly times. She'd give him credit for that.

And that was all the credit he was going to get.

Jade dropped her hand when she realized her thoughts were making her angry again. There was no way she could avoid that, considering they were about to engage in divorce proceedings, but she couldn't let that kind of negativity settle over her. Darkness had consumed too much of her life.

She needed light now. She needed peace. She needed her life to be calm, like the lake where she now found herself floating aimlessly in a kayak. Looking out at the water, she suddenly had the urge to dive in, to be surrounded by the calm that she'd been admiring.

Though she was wearing a T-shirt and a pair of khaki shorts, Jade only debated for a few seconds before sliding the paddle under the bungee cord along the side of the kayak. The boat wobbled and tilted, but she was able to turn and dangle her feet into the water. That was enough to convince her to take a quick swim.

Her exit from the kayak was far from graceful, splashing rather than slipping into the water as she'd envisioned. Jade held onto the kayak for a few moments before taking a breath and going under. When she broke the surface, she wiped the water from her eyes and floated on her back. Looking up at the sky, she let the colors fill her mind and push away the depressing and ugly thoughts that had been ricocheting around her brain.

The warm water enveloped her in a welcoming hug, letting her float lightly on the surface. The colors above her were a strange but beautiful blend of pastels and darker hues. She was trying to identify the shade of orange—somewhere between tangerine and pumpkin—when she heard a splash. Before she could right herself to find the source, a face broke through the water's surface right next to hers.

She squealed out with surprise as Liam, the flirty kayak instructor, looked at her with terror-filled eyes. He held her gaze for a few rapid heartbeats before shaking his head, sending droplets of water flying from his shaggy hair.

After dragging a hand over his face and exhaling again, he narrowed his eyes at her. "What the hell, lady?"

"You scared the crap out of me," she snapped back.

"Who gets off their kayak, fully clothed, to float in the lake?" He shoved his fingers through his wet hair to stop the strands from falling into his eyes. "Christ. I thought you were dead."

Holding on to her kayak so she could float more easily, Jade bit back her sarcastic response. He'd jumped into the water to save her, though she didn't need saving. She probably shouldn't be too angry at him, even if her heart was pounding like it could burst out of her chest.

"I'm sorry I scared you," she offered though part of her didn't think she owed him an apology. He could have simply called out to her.

He scowled. "Where the hell is that life vest I told you to wear?"

Lifting her brows, she pressed her teeth together, but nope, she couldn't hold back any longer. "I know how to swim."

"I don't care. I rented this to you under the condition that you wear a life vest. Get back in your kayak before you do drown."

Jade stared at him. Part of her was feeling defiant, but the other part was feeling foolish. She hadn't actually considered how she'd get back into the kayak without the support of the lake bottom beneath her feet. Damn it. Why did she have to realize that in front of this jerk?

He floated beside her and gripped her kayak. "Use your dominant hand to reach across and grab that handle," he told her. Once she did, he tapped the handle closer to her.

"Use your other hand to grab that and then pull yourself up until your stomach is over the seat."

Jade gripped the second handle but was certain she wouldn't have the strength to do what he was saying. Though she was in remission, her body was still recovering, and her muscle tone was not what it had been when she was going to the gym four days a week. The last year had taken a toll on more than her marriage. Her body was significantly weaker. Pulling herself out of the water and halfway over the kayak was unlikely. Even so, Jade held fast onto the handles as she tried to lurch out of the water.

"Kick your legs to give yourself some leverage," Liam advised.

She did, but her next attempt failed as well. Liam moved to her side and rested his arm over her kayak in the most annoyingly casual way.

Then that shitty smirk curved his lips. "I'll help once you admit you can't do it alone."

Jade frowned before trying again. And again. And again, until her muscles were trembling and she was out of breath.

Finally, as she pulled herself up, Liam put his hands on her thighs and gave her a boost.

"Hey," she panted as she managed to lie flat across the kayak like he'd told her. She glanced back. "Watch the hands."

He released his hold and held his hands up as if to show his innocence. His smile gave him away. "Can you flip over and get your butt in the seat? Slow and steady," he warned.

She did as he told her, slowly rolling over and easing into the seat.

"Now turn and put your feet in the braces."

She did so and looked at him. "I could have made it on my own."

Resting his hands on her kayak, he chuckled. "I'm sure you could have, but I felt guilty just sitting back watching. Kind of like watching a wounded animal instead of putting it out of its misery."

Jade glared at him but couldn't think of a good retort. No doubt she had looked like a flailing fish out of water with no way to save herself.

"Maybe from now on, you could make better decisions," he said reminding Jade far too much of Taylor's warning the previous day. "I'm not always going to be around. Unless you want me to be," Liam added with a wink.

"Does this act really work for you?" Jade asked with an angry edge to her words.

"What act?"

"The Summer Fling Seduction thing you have going on."

He shrugged as he smiled at her. "Some days are better than others."

"Well, let me save you some trouble. I'm..." She let her words drift off when she caught herself about to tell him she was happily married. Her chest seized and her lips trembled for the briefest of moments before she pressed them together to control them. "I'm not interested," she said, but the words were breathy and unconvincing. She tugged her paddle free. "There are better ways to get business than messing with women's minds, Liam. Find one."

"Hey," he said, holding on to her kayak so her attempt to paddle away from him was futile. He hung on like a stowaway. "I didn't mean to offend you. Most women appreciate a smile or two."

"Smiles are fine. It's the flirting you need to learn to control."

"Okay," he said and bowed his head. "I apologize."

Feeling guilty was stupid. He'd earned her assessment of him, but she still let his subdued mood affect her. "Apology accepted."

Crossing his arms on her kayak, he continued to linger. "Can I ask something?"

"Could I stop you?"

He nodded toward her hands. "Where's your wedding ring?"

She looked away. "Really? Didn't we just talk about your flirting?"

"I'm not flirting. I'm observing. You didn't say 'I'm married' when you poured cold water on my sparkling personality—"

"Is that what you call it?" Jade asked. "Because I could come up with a few other ways to describe it."

"So I took a peek," he continued as if she hadn't spoken, "and the ring you were wearing the other day is no longer there."

She lowered her face, looked at her bare hand, and shrugged. "My husband has since informed me that he'd like a divorce." She scoffed when she heard how clinical her words sounded. "He's leaving me."

"I'm sorry. Truly." Liam sounded sincere.

"Yeah." Taking a deep breath, she looked out at the lake as she let some of her anger at Liam go. "Well, I'm sorry I scared you. I got it in my head being in the water would somehow calm my mind. It made more sense before you thought I was in mortal danger."

"The water is calming. But maybe next time, you shouldn't be fully clothed and just floating there."

"Point taken," she said.

Awkward silence lingered before Liam said, "He's a fool."

Tears stung her eyes, and she shook her head. "No. That's me. Thanks for your help. Have a good night, Liam."

"Night, Jade," he said.

This time when she started to paddle away, he let go. She made it back to the cabin without further incident and was able to limp onto the shore and pull the kayak in on her own. Every day she was making progress, little by little. At least as far as her ankle was concerned. Her mind and heart were still absolute messes. She simply couldn't make sense of her new reality, no matter how much she tried.

"Jade," Darby called as she rushed from the table she was setting toward the sliver of beach. "What happened? Why are you all wet?"

"I'm fine," Jade said.

"Taylor!"

Jade shook her head. "No, I'm fine. I—"

Taylor turned from the grill to where Darby was overreacting. Setting down the tongs she'd been holding, she trotted toward the beach. "What's going on?"

"I went for a swim," Jade explained.

Taylor furrowed her brow. "In your clothes?"

"Yeah. I didn't think skinny dipping was a good plan, so..." She heaved a big breath. "How's dinner coming?"

Taylor glanced at Darby. "Um, about fifteen minutes or so."

"Cool," Jade said, grabbing the crutches she'd left by the chairs. She could limp a short distance without them but still needed the support to get from the water's edge to the cabin. "Just enough time for me to shower."

"She went swimming in her clothes," Darby whispered as Jade made her way toward the cabin.

"Shh," Taylor hushed. "She'll be okay."

Jade ignored the urge to respond. She wasn't sure if she wanted to yell at them or cry, but they didn't deserve either. They really were doing far more for her than necessary, considering they hadn't even known each other a week yet. Jade had no right to dump all her emotional vomit onto them. They'd carried more than their share already.

She set her crutches against the bedroom wall before moving into the bathroom and turning the shower onto hot. As the water heated, she peeled her wet clothes off and tossed them into the sink. Though she'd had plenty of bouts of crying over the last few days, she'd somehow held on to the hope that Nick would realize he was making a mistake. Part of her really thought he'd snap out of whatever phase he was going through and realize he wanted to make their marriage work.

She hadn't allowed herself to digest the reality of his affair and what that meant for them. She hadn't allowed herself to think about how that would impact any chance they had at a future together. Her mind had focused on the fact that he hadn't let her try. It was just like her to get so narrow sighted on one point that she couldn't see anything else.

That had been the problem all along, hadn't it? She'd been so focused on her job and the financial responsibility they'd agreed she would carry that she'd lost sight of everything else. And while she'd been working long hours to support their family and his dreams, he'd been falling in love with someone else. While she'd been facing death and apologizing for not being the wife he'd needed, he'd been having his needs met elsewhere. While she'd been promising she was going to appreciate him more, he'd been planning to leave her.

How pathetic was that?

Jade used the edges of the pedestal sink to hold herself up since her crutches were in the other room. She finally let the truth of what was happening hit her. She let herself feel the knife slicing through her, and a sob ripped from her throat. Her mini breakdown was interrupted when the sink pulled from the wall. Jade jumped back and gasped. Holding her breath, she waited, but the sink stayed standing.

The sink not crashing down and breaking both her feet was probably the best thing that had happened to her all day. A wry laugh left her as she grabbed a handful of toilet paper and dried her face. The mirror was starting to steam, but she wiped the moisture away and looked at her reflection. Her pale skin was starting to take on an ashen hue, despite her time in the sun. She'd been slathering sunscreen on and sitting in the shade as much as possible, but she should at least look sun-kissed.

She didn't. She had that familiar shade of underlying exhaustion. The skin under her eyes was dark like bruises, and she seemed to have aged in the last few days. She needed real sleep, but she didn't think she'd be getting that anytime soon. Every time she closed her eyes, she envisioned the night she'd caught Nick leaving. The scene played on repeat, over and over. And she feared if she didn't find a way to make it stop, she'd never find a way to let him go.

SIX

THE SENSE that someone was watching her pulled Jade from sleep. She blinked several times before making out a figure standing over her bed. A scream erupted from her as she sat up, but the fear only lasted a moment. Jade cleared her throat and then fell back into bed, pulled the comforter back over herself, and muttered, "Darby, just because you own this house doesn't mean you can walk in whenever you want."

"I was worried about you," Darby said. "It's almost noon."

"It is?"

Darby held up a bottle of wine Taylor had brought over the day before. "Did you drink this?"

The wine had been unopened when Jade's guests had left after dinner. However, once she was alone, she'd started feeling sorry for herself. Then the wine began calling out to her. At first, she'd ignored the liquor. But then she'd told herself she'd have one drink, which turned into two, which had turned into several more. The last thing she remembered was crying in the kitchen. She couldn't even recall getting into bed.

"Jade," Darby pressed, "did you drink last night?"

Jade nodded and instantly regretted the movement. Her brain felt like water sloshing around in a mold.

"Why?"

"Because my heart hurts," she said with a cracked voice.

With a maternal touch, Darby stroked her hand over Jade's hair. "I know it does, sweetie. I can't believe I'm going to say this, but alcohol isn't the answer."

"I can't stop thinking about him leaving. Whenever I try to sleep, I just... I needed to not think about him leaving."

"Oh, honey," Darby cooed. "Not like this. I don't care how much he hurts you. You can't drink, okay? It's bad for your butt."

Jade didn't want to laugh, but she couldn't help herself. "I won't. I feel horrible. My head is spinning and my stomach hurts."

"I'll get you something for that. You stay in bed as long as you need. I'll take care of you." Darby took the empty wine bottle with her as she disappeared from Jade's side.

Jade chastised herself for giving in to the urge to drink her problems away. That hadn't seemed to help anyway. The heartache was still there, and her head had joined the party. Every part of her was regretting her decision to have "just one glass" to help ease her mind.

Staring at the ceiling, she let her vision swim as tears found her. Nick was leaving her. Her marriage, the thing that had gotten her through the last year, had been a facade. Worse than that, it had been a series of lies to hide how incredibly miserable she'd made him. She didn't care if he'd faked his concern to protect her or help her or whatever the hell he'd told himself to make himself feel better. He'd been lying to her for too long. She deserved to be treated better than that.

"I brought you cranberry juice. Straight. With ice." Darby held out a glass as proof. "What do you want for breakfast? Raw kale? Birdseed? Grass?"

Jade accepted the juice and two pills. She took the painkillers and let out a long, miserable groan. "I don't want to eat just yet. My stomach isn't quite right." She listened to the silence for several seconds before creasing her brow. "Where's Taylor? I thought she was going to finish the banister today."

"She didn't want to start all that banging while you were sleeping. I texted her to let her know I was checking on you. She's on her way."

As if on cue, there was a knock at the door.

"Don't worry," Darby said. "If she tries to give you a lecture about the wine, I'll distract her by telling her all about that time I got arrested for streaking down Main Street during the Christmas parade."

Jade started to ask for clarification but then clamped her mouth shut. She probably didn't need to know more than she had just learned. Darby disappeared once again, and Jade looked out the window at the bright blue sky. The day was annoyingly beautiful. If she weren't so hell-bent on being miserable, she'd be out on the water by now. She'd be enjoying this... Could she even call this a vacation? It certainly didn't feel like one any longer.

The muffled voices in the other room were intelligible, but she didn't need to hear them to understand the conversation. Darby was relaying Jade's overindulgence to Taylor. They were probably talking about how pathetic she was and how she needed to buck up and face life. Jade closed her eyes at the bitter, unfair thought that had rolled through her.

Just because she thought she was pathetic didn't mean her new friends did. They'd been nothing but supportive and didn't deserve the wrath brewing in her mind. Her anger wasn't directed at them but at herself and Nick and...*Amber*.

Taylor appeared in the doorway with her jaw set and her shoulders rolled back. Her eyes weren't exactly hard, but she was clearly upset. "Have you had any water yet?"

"No."

"You need some. We need to flush your system out, then you'll feel better."

Jade struggled to sit. "I have juice."

"You need water. Come on. I don't care what Darby says. You aren't staying in bed all day." Taylor crossed the room and pulled the covers back. "You slept in your sun dress."

Jade looked down at the wrinkled lime green material. "It's kind of like a nightgown if you think about it."

Taylor shook her head and took Jade's hand. "Come on. Up and at 'em. We've got things to do today."

Jade swallowed hard when her stomach lurched. She closed her eyes to stop the room from spinning after Taylor pulled her to her feet. "Like what?"

"Like getting your head out of your ass." A bright smile broke across Taylor's face as she looked down. "Hey, check you out."

Jade followed Taylor's gaze to her feet. She stood without

the assistance of crutches or the shooting pain that had plagued her for days.

"Does it hurt?" Taylor asked.

Jade put a little more weight on her foot and tested the pain level. "Not too much."

"You should try walking on it some today. Keep your crutches close though. You might need them."

Jade suspected that once her head stopped aching and her stomach settled, the slight pain in her ankle would increase. The other aches in her body were muting that one, but she didn't expect it to last.

"Have you called an attorney yet?" Taylor asked.

Jade blinked several times. The question seemed to have come out of nowhere, and she had to think about why she would have called an attorney. Oh. Right. Nick. Her stomach rolled again. "No."

"Have you called the bank to prevent him from emptying your accounts?"

Jade opened her mouth as her mind started to connect with the concerns Taylor was tiptoeing around.

"Jade," she said in that gentle but firm tone that made her sound more maternal than friendly. "He could be walking away with everything you have right now. Get up. It's time to make a plan."

"A plan?"

"Yes. You've had two days to feel bad. Now you need to get up and start taking care of business. You have to make some calls to start protecting your assets."

Taylor disappeared, and Jade looked around the tiny bedroom as she tried to make sense of what Taylor was saying. Yes, Jade needed a plan. She'd considered that while out on the lake, but her plan had been about moving on, not protecting her assets. Nick wouldn't steal from her. She was sure of that. But then she considered that he'd been planning to leave her for a long time, and she'd had no idea. There was no way of knowing what he'd been up to. Or what he might be capable of.

"Shit." Jade rushed into the bathroom, certain that a hot shower would clear her head. As the water warmed, she reminded herself to tell Darby about the sink. Though the sink should have held her weight without pulling from the wall, she'd offer to pay Taylor to fix it. She wouldn't put that expense off on Darby.

Twenty minutes and a lot of panic later, Jade headed right to the kitchen and dropped onto a bench at the table. Darby set a cup of water and a bowl of cottage cheese with a few strawberries in front of Jade. Taylor sat across from her and slid a notebook toward Jade with a numbered to-do list written in small but neat handwriting.

"First thing," Taylor said. "You need an attorney. Unless you have one you intend to contact, we need to start researching." Taylor's raised brow meant this minute. Immediately. Right this *very* second.

"I-I don't have one," Jade stuttered out.

"Do you have a will?" Taylor asked.

Jade nodded, feeling like a deer frozen in the headlights.

"Is Nick the beneficiary?"

Again, she confirmed.

Darby dropped down onto the bench next to Jade and lifted the top of a pink laptop that had been covered in jewels, much like the crutches Jade had been using. "Who did you use for that?" Darby asked.

103

Jade had to think for a moment before the name came to her. Her mind was a jumbled mess, and it wasn't just because she'd consumed alcohol for the first time in over a year. Taylor was throwing too much at her too fast to process. Usually, Jade was the take-charge type, but she was still in shock from how drastically her life had changed over the last few days.

Darby started pecking away. Within seconds, she grabbed the notebook and jotted down, in big bubbly letters that contrasted Taylor's neat print, a phone number next to number two: *Change will beneficiaries to kids.*

"Do you know a divorce attorney? Or have a preference?" Taylor asked.

Again, Jade shook her head. "I can ask the attorney who did my will for a referral if he doesn't do that sort of thing."

Darby scribbled another note, adding to the to-do list before Taylor pulled the notebook back and began throwing more questions at Jade. She suddenly felt like she'd been caught in a tornado. Taylor pointed at number three: *Check bank accounts for unexpected withdrawals.* Darby turned the laptop toward her as if she expected Jade to check right that moment.

This all seemed so drastic, but Taylor was right. Jade had to go on the defensive. Nick had been planning his departure for over a year. He might already have an attorney waiting to pounce on their assets. They weren't rich, but they were well off because *she* had worked hard to build a successful career. She wasn't going to stand back and let Nick take all they had, and he could be planning just that. She wasn't going to get taken by surprise again.

Even so, this all felt overwhelming.

Jade shoved her untouched breakfast aside, collapsed onto the table, and rested her head on her forearms. "Darby, I need—"

"Cranberry juice, straight, no chaser. On it."

"No. Drink your water," Taylor said. "Until her hangover clears, she gets water."

"Stop being bossy," Jade said as she rubbed her aching forehead. "I don't like it."

As Darby ran her hand up and down Jade's back, she whispered, "She's right. About the water and about getting ready for this divorce. You should listen."

Jade sat up to read over Taylor's list again. *401K/Pension. Loans. Investments.* The list went on for too long. It was thorough, and Jade understood why she needed to do these things, but damned if she didn't feel like she was being buried in despair once again. "This is too much. I can't deal with this."

"You have to. He didn't leave you any choice."

Jade sat back and looked at Taylor. "You've been through this, haven't you?"

"I haven't been what you'd call lucky in love. I came to Chammont Point to start over." She frowned. "It hasn't worked out as well as I'd hoped."

"I grew up here," Darby said. "I've tried to leave a few times but always end up right back here. I don't fit in, but I can't seem to escape."

"It's not so bad," Jade said. "There are worse places to be."

"Says the girl who's going home in a few days," Darby muttered.

"To an empty house," Jade reminded her.

"Come on," Taylor said gently. "Let's get through as much

of this list as possible today so you can find time to relax before heading back."

Reaching across the table, Jade put her hand on Taylor's and then gripped Darby's. "Thank you. Thank you both. I can honestly say I don't know how I would have made it through the last few days without you two."

"You're welcome," Taylor said.

Darby put her arm around Jade's shoulders and hugged her close. "We got you, boo. We're not going to let this keep you down."

"One hour," Jade conceded. "We're giving this list one hour, and then we're treating ourselves to an adventure."

"Will there be naked men involved?" Darby asked.

"No," Jade stated at the same time Taylor said, "Maybe."

Standing beside her car, Jade scanned their surroundings. Beyond the gravel parking lot of the busy winery, there were rolling hills and trees as far as she could see. Peace. That was the word that came to her mind. Despite the crowd, this place was filled with peace. She really needed that after the week she'd had.

Darby climbed from the back seat and pulled a black hat onto her fire-engine red hair, which she'd worn in long barrel curls that cascaded down her shoulders and clashed against the lemon-yellow dress. When Taylor had suggested they go to a polo match at a nearby winery, Jade had been hesitant and reminded them that she no longer drank—other than the slight mishap that she continued to pay for.

Darby's excitement had won out. She'd started talking

faster than Jade could comprehend, but Jade had picked up on the fact that Darby had wanted to go to a polo match ever since she'd seen *Pretty Woman*. In true Darby fashion, she'd dressed to the absolute nines, which was over-the-top for a winery. Jade had hushed Taylor when she'd tried to tell Darby that.

"Let her have this," Jade had whispered.

However, now that they'd reached their destination and people were slowing their stride to take in Darby's outlandish outfit, Jade worried that perhaps they should have intervened. As Taylor got the picnic basket out of the back seat, she glanced at Jade. She was obviously thinking the same thing, though Darby remained blissfully unaware that her outfit was drawing wide-eyed stares.

Darby pointed at a horse in the distance as she beamed with excitement. "Oh my God! We're going to watch a polo match, you guys. I feel like Julia freaking Roberts right now. This is going to be so much fun."

Taylor shook her head and kept her mouth shut, as did Jade.

"You're going to break an ankle in those shoes," Taylor said as they headed toward the winery.

Darby slipped her sunglasses down her nose and eyed Taylor's sensible shorts, T-shirt, and shoes. "Nobody who wears open-toed sandals without a proper pedicure gets to talk to me about shoes. Understand? I am a professional at walking in stilettos."

"In the grass?" Taylor asked as they neared the big cobblestone building. There, Taylor and Darby would taste wine while Jade chose something from whatever nonalcoholic options they had. Once they decided on their drinks, they'd head out to the meadow to find a place to spread a blanket and let Darby live out her fantasy.

"At least *she* tried," Darby said, gesturing at Jade, who'd worn a lace-trimmed dark blue romper and ballet flats, since wearing wedges would have caused her even more regret than leaving her crutches at the cabin.

Jade could walk without assistance now, but her stride had a significant limp to it. Even so, she'd opted not to bring the gaudy crutches, despite Taylor's warning that she wouldn't be carrying Jade if her ankle gave out. Jade didn't want to be shuffling around the winery with bedazzled props under each arm.

"How are you doing?" Taylor asked as she opened the door.

"I'll make it." However, Jade ground her teeth together and silently cursed herself for letting her ego talk her out of using the assistance for one more day.

"Sit here," Taylor told her, pulling out a chair tucked beneath a small table. "We'll get you a drink."

Easing down, Jade rested her left foot on another chair and sighed at the beginning signs of swelling in her ankle. Okay, she might have jumped the gun by insisting she didn't need help walking. The good news was that once they found a place to sit next to the polo field, she wouldn't have to get back up for some time. The bad news was, she probably should have brought an ice pack.

As long as she stayed off her foot, she should be fine. She was distracted from her internal debate when her phone pinged, letting her know she had a text message. She pulled her phone from her purse. Her heart flipped over when she read Nick's name on the notification.

She glanced around the room and sought Darby and Taylor. She wanted to call out to them and tell them to sit with her while she read the text, but they were deep in a discussion with a wine steward as he held out a bottle to them. Holding her breath, Jade tapped the screen on her phone and opened the message.

Just letting you know I've moved out. My keys are on the table.

Jade read the message three times before closing her screen. She didn't know how to reply to that. Not that she owed him a reply. She didn't owe that lying, cheating bastard anything but a swift kick in the balls.

After dropping her phone into her purse, she returned her attention to the spacious room around her. The rustic room was perfect for weddings or receptions. Jade imagined they had a lot of ceremonies there. Her wedding had been rushed. They'd never had a reception. She'd always said she'd plan a big party for their twentieth anniversary, but she'd spent that day in bed, too queasy from treatment to celebrate.

Nick had brought her a small cake that she hadn't been able to eat. She'd thought that was so sweet of him. She still did, if she put her anger aside long enough to give him credit. Giving him credit wasn't something she was up for yet. She was too angry. Anger was good. Anger would keep her strong. She needed to be angry right now.

So he'd moved out. Likely living with his girlfriend. Happy as a fucking clam, and she was sitting in a winery with two women she barely knew who had somehow become the closest thing she had to friends.

How the hell had she fallen so damn far in the last year?

"Jade?"

She blinked a few times and looked up at Taylor, who was holding out a bottle of juice. "Oh, sorry."

Taylor eyed her. "You good?"

Jade nodded, but her friends simply stared at her. "Nick texted. He's all moved out."

"Are you okay?" Taylor asked. "Do you need to go back to the cabin?"

When Darby gasped, Jade gave her a weak smile of reassurance.

"No," Jade said. "We're staying."

"Good riddance to him," Darby said. "You'll be better off without him."

"I'm sure," Jade said softly.

"Are you ready to go watch some guys smacking balls while horses shit everywhere?" Taylor asked.

Jade chuckled at her description of how they were about to spend their afternoon. "Yeah. Let's do this."

Darby led the way, head held high, ignoring all the ogling eyes, until they found the perfect spot on the grass. Jade didn't want to voice how happy she was to sit on the blanket and take the weight off her foot. But she suspected by the way Taylor was eyeing her, she'd known Jade's pain was steadily increasing. Still convinced she no longer needed crutches, Jade decided to make time to buy a brace from the drug store before going back to the cabin.

"Did you bring aspirin?" Taylor asked as she opened the picnic basket.

"Yes."

"Take some, please," she said.

Jade opened her purse, pulled the small bottle out, and

rattled them at Taylor as proof she was doing as told. "You really are bossy."

"I care," Taylor said. "There's a difference."

"Not much," Darby offered, lifting a bunch of dark purple grapes from the basket.

Jade never would have guessed all the time she'd spent at fancy company parties would come in handy someday, but she'd learned enough about wine and pairings to help Darby compile an assortment of cheeses and accoutrements to go with her *Pretty Woman* polo fantasy. Darby took out a plate and started carefully placing the various items. When Taylor reached in and pulled out a plastic-wrapped pre-made submarine sandwich and a disposable packet of mayonnaise, Darby cast a not-so-subtle glare her way.

"Stop looking at me like that," Taylor insisted. "I'm hungry. Grapes and cheese are not going to fill me up."

"You don't eat subs with wine, Taylor. Even I know that."

"Which is why I told you I wanted a soda instead of wine."

Scowling, Darby said, "You're not drinking soda at a winery."

"She's drinking juice," Taylor said, gesturing toward Jade.

"Alcohol hurts her butt." Darby bounced a grape off Taylor's forehead. "Stop ruining my fantasy."

"Excuse me, Julia Child."

Darby's glare intensified. "*Roberts*. Julia Child is... someone else."

Taylor rolled her head back and laughed, but Darby continued to frown.

Jade chuckled too. "Did someone piss on your parade as a child, Taylor?"

Taylor finally said what she'd clearly been fighting ever since Darby pranced out of her cabin dressed like she was heading to tea with a colorblind queen. "Do you see how people are looking at you, Darby?"

Darby's smile returned. "Do you see how little I care what other people think of me, Taylor?"

"You're dressed like a freaking lemon. It's absurd. *You* are absurd."

Jade watched as a bit of the light in Darby's eyes dimmed. Jade's heart ached for her. She was sure Taylor hadn't meant to hurt Darby's feelings, but she had. Her teasing had crossed a line and hit a nerve. Jade put her hand on Darby's.

"Okay, Taylor," Jade warned. "We are all friends here."

Darby didn't seem to hear Jade's reminder. "Just because you need to conform to feel good about yourself doesn't mean I have to."

Taylor's mood didn't dim, like Darby's had. It sparked with an underlying hint of anger. "Being normal isn't conforming."

"I like this dress," Darby said. "I like my hat and my hair. And I like sitting on a blanket with a cheese plate and wine while people play horse croquet in the distance. I don't care what you think, you...serial killer of joy."

The air around them seemed to still. Darby's words felt like an ice-cold wet blanket had been dropped on their little party.

"Ouch," Taylor finally muttered and turned her focus to squeezing mayo onto the wheat bun.

"Horse croquet?" Jade asked.

Darby waved her hand. "I was flustered. I couldn't remember what game they're playing."

"Horse croquet is good," Jade said. "Nobody's trying to kill your fun, Darby."

"She is," Darby stated, grabbing an empty wineglass.

"I'm not." Taylor offered Darby a weak smile. "I'm sorry. Look, I don't have a lot of friends, but I'm very protective of the ones I do have. I don't like how people are staring at you. It makes me want to fight them."

Darby's pout lifted into a smile. "You'd fight for me?"

"Well, no because I don't want to get arrested, but I don't want people making fun of you."

"I don't care what they think, Taylor," Darby said sincerely. "It's sweet that you do, but you're going to have to get used to people whispering behind my back if you hang around me. I don't fit in. I never will. People make fun of what doesn't fit."

Taylor shrugged. "Being the center of attention isn't my comfort zone. I prefer to blend into the background."

"Which you do incredibly well," Darby said.

"Ladies," Jade said with a firm, motherly tone, "my life is utter shit right now. When I go home, I'm going to be jumping headfirst into a world I don't even recognize anymore. I need what's left of my vacation to be peaceful. I don't make friends easily either, but I feel like we've become friends already. I need that. I need you guys. But if you start tearing each other down, I can't be around you. Do you understand that?"

"Yeah," Darby said quietly.

"Yeah," Taylor agreed.

"I don't need any more negativity in my life than I already have, okay?"

"We'll be good, boo," Darby said as she patted Jade's hand. "I promise."

"Thank you." Jade opened her bottle of juice and filled a wineglass. She never would have done that before Darby had barged into her life. But just a few days later, drinking juice from a wineglass felt like the natural thing to do. Why hadn't she started doing this sooner? She, more than anyone else she knew, understood that every day was a gift. Juice in fancy glasses should be a given.

"I eat stuff like this all the time because I can't cook," Darby said, returning her attention to her plate. "My mom tried to teach me, but I wasn't really interested. She came to Chammont Point from Mexico City when she was eighteen. She always wanted to open a restaurant but ended up working for someone else until she died."

"Where's your dad?" Jade asked.

"He didn't stick around. What about you?"

Jade picked over the strawberries Darby had put on her plate. "My parents divorced when I was young. Both remarried. My childhood was pretty normal. Up until I got pregnant and married at seventeen, but that happens a lot, really. Where's your family, Taylor?"

She shook her head. "I was raised by my grandpa. He's been gone for a while now."

"I'm sorry."

"He worked in construction. We used to build stuff together. I never really learned how to be girly," she said with a slight smile. "I guess that's why I prefer a hammer over makeup brushes."

Jade sensed the topic wasn't one Taylor was comfortable discussing, so she turned the focus back to herself. "Well, I have two sons, both in college, and..." She laughed bitterly. "I almost said and a wonderful husband. I guess I can scratch that one off the list."

"Yes," Darby agreed, "but you're replacing him with us, and I think that's a much sweeter deal."

"Hear, hear," Jade said, lifting her glass of cranberry juice.

After they toasted each other, Taylor wrapped up her sandwich and pulled a plate from the picnic basket. As she picked through the variety of snacks, Jade glanced at Darby and smiled. While Taylor's willingness to eat grapes and cheese instead of a sandwich might not have seemed like a big deal, the compromise brought the light back to Darby's eyes. The woman was ridiculous on some level, but she radiated a kind of gaiety that Jade never had. Jade suspected she and Taylor were similar in that aspect. Jade's focus had been so singular for so long, she'd equated success with happiness. She hadn't quite figured out what was stopping Taylor from embracing life like Darby had learned to, but Jade hoped they were friends long enough to learn.

She hoped Darby was right. Jade lost the relationship she'd come to count on when Nick left, but the relationships she had found in return might have been exactly what she needed.

"Oh my gosh," Darby squealed out and pointed to the field. "Look! The match is about to start." Her laugh caused Taylor to grin.

Jade turned her attention toward the field, but in her mind, she was alternating between rereading Nick's text and replaying the night she caught him leaving her. She chastised herself for obsessing about the pain he was causing her.

Darby grabbed her hand and offered her a smile, as if

she'd read Jade's mind. "You're okay," she said softly. "We're right here. You're okay."

Swallowing her tears, Jade nodded. Though she was still processing her hurt, she thought that Darby was right. She was going to be okay...eventually.

SEVEN

JADE HAD WOKEN up every day for the last week with a cloud hanging over her, but this one had nothing to do with her marital status. This was her last full day in Chammont Point. Her last day of having new adventures with Darby and Taylor. Somehow, that depressed her as much as the idea of heading back to Fairfax the next morning. She was glad when Darby and Taylor showed up bright and early to drag her out of the house for one last day on the lake.

In what had become a normal part of her day, Darby bounced into the cabin before Jade could let herself get too caught up in self-pity. Jade reminded her about respecting boundaries. Darby dismissed her with a wave of her hand and made breakfast. As they were eating, Taylor had shown up, insisting this was the day she was going to finish the banister. However, before she could finish her coffee, Darby had convinced them to do something else.

An hour later, Jade looked out over the water as she tested how her ankle felt. She hadn't used crutches for two days, and Darby insisted that could only mean one thing:

time to level up. She now stood on a paddleboard, testing out her balance.

"Are you sure you're ready for this?" Liam asked.

She looked at him but then glanced away. For some reason, looking into his eyes made her feel vulnerable. His constant flirting was an annoyance, but he'd seen her on the verge of a breakdown, floating in the water like a fool. She wasn't exactly embarrassed, but his eyes had changed from teasing to sincere, which set her on edge. She didn't like that.

"Why wouldn't I be?" she asked.

"Your ankle," he said.

She put more weight on her left foot and barely felt a twinge. "It's better."

He stared, as if assessing her, but she suspected that had less to do with her ankle and more to do with her confession that her husband had left her. Instead of letting him look through to her broken heart, she turned her focus to Darby, who was still struggling to stand upright on her board. Taylor, on the other hand, had already started paddling out into deeper waters. She'd clearly done this before.

Darby held a paddle and practiced the movements as Liam directed her, making *whish-whishing* noises with each fake stroke. She only stopped play paddling and *whishing* when she nearly tumbled over. As soon as she did, Liam gently gripped her arm and helped her straighten up.

As soon as Darby grinned at him and whispered her thanks with an undercurrent of seduction, Jade started to suspect Darby was playing him. The way Liam winked made Jade think they were probably playing each other. Two natural born flirts fine-tuning their art. Yeah, Jade wasn't sticking around for that.

"I'm going to catch up to Taylor," Jade said and started moving forward.

Darby didn't even object, confirming what Jade had suspected. Darby was more interested in giggling at their instructor than actually learning anything. As soon as Jade was about halfway between where Taylor had dropped to sit on her board and where Darby was still pretending to need Liam's help, Jade stopped paddling.

She looked around the lake, the calm waters, and the trees in the distance. The sun reflected off the dark blue ripples dancing across the water's surface. Far in the distance, boats and jet skis skittered along. People and bright umbrellas dotted the beaches. The scene was peaceful. Serene.

Chammont Point was perfect. So perfect, it made her heart hurt. She shouldn't be so sad in this place. She shouldn't feel so broken and useless. However, as soon as she stopped moving, Nick's words slipped into her mind. Whenever she wasn't focused on the next thing to do or try, the hurt he'd inflicted flared up.

Taking a deep, cleansing breath, she told herself to let go of the anger, to not let it ruin her day. However, she couldn't ignore the fury building inside her. When she wasn't sad, she was so damn furious, she wanted to throw anything she could get her hands on.

Twenty years. Two children. One horrific battle. Countless tears and whispered what-ifs. So much time spent looking back and apologizing for not being a better wife, mother, and all-around person. So many promises to do better. And not *once* did he man up and tell her that he didn't love her anymore.

She didn't care if he thought it would have been cruel to leave her when she was sick. Giving her false hope—fake love—was not the answer. Letting her believe that he was going to be here when she started her life over had been callous. His intentions might have been good, but his actions had been merciless. Kicking the world out from under her when she was finally learning how to stand again was heartless.

She didn't care how many times or ways he said he'd stayed to give her strength. She was convinced he simply hadn't wanted to look like an ass. Because only an ass would leave his cancer-stricken wife for another woman.

He hadn't stayed for her or for the kids. He'd stayed for his pride. To save face. So he could look at himself in the mirror.

Asshole.

The anger that bubbled up in her was so overpowering and burning hot that Jade had no choice but to let it out. Leaning her head back, she screamed like the banshee that used to haunt her dreams. When Jade was a child, her grandfather had told her the old Irish folklore of how a female spirit would herald the death of a family member by wailing in the distance.

After her cancer diagnosis, she'd had nightmares of the creature screaming outside her bedroom window. The demonic howling echoed in her mind for months, even when she was awake. She could almost feel the banshee's presence, looming in the shadows, ready to take her.

Now, here Jade stood in the middle of Chammont Lake, wailing like that beast over her dead marriage. Her scream echoed back to her as she took a deep breath so she could let out another round.

"Jade?" Taylor barked.

Jade cut her screech short and looked at the woman who had paddled next to her.

"What the hell?" Taylor demanded.

Jade shrugged. "I needed to let that out."

Taylor yanked her sunglasses off and squinted at her. "Are you hurt?"

"No. I mean...not like...physically."

"Is she okay?" Liam asked as he neared Taylor, who was gawking at Jade like she'd lost her mind.

Taylor frowned. "I think she's just a little unhinged at the moment. She'll be fine."

Jade sniffled when the urge to cry sneaked up on her. "I think after all I've been through, I deserve a little breakdown. Don't you?"

Liam looked from Jade to Taylor and back again, waiting for someone to explain. Neither did.

"Where's Darby?" Jade asked after a moment.

They all turned toward the shore, where Darby had still been practicing her balance while using the paddles. There, lying flat on her stomach on the board, she used her hands to propel herself forward.

"Don't worry, Jade," she called out. "I'm coming."

Once again, Darby's antics won Jade over. She laughed, Taylor shook her head, and Liam continued to look confused.

"I'm fine. Go help her," Jade told him. Once he paddled away, she looked at Taylor. "I needed to get some anger off my chest. That's all."

"Feel better?"

"Amazingly so."

"Good, I'm glad." She looked back at Darby. "She's never going to make it back to the cabin. We should let Liam haul these things home for us before she hurts herself."

"Oh, let's give her a few more minutes," Jade said. "She's having fun."

They paddled several times before Taylor asked, "Are you okay?"

Jade voiced the thoughts that had led her to screaming at the clouds. "He should have told me he was planning to leave."

Taylor was quiet for a few moments. "That would have been really shitty of him, Jade."

"No. Letting me believe in something that wasn't real while he was fucking someone else behind my back was shitty."

"So you would have rather been lying in a hospital bed all alone, not knowing if you were going to survive? You would have rather had the psychological trauma of cancer topped off with the heartbreak of divorce? You really think that would have been better?" Taylor shook her head. "He's a dick for what he did, Jade, but on some level, he did right by you. A shitty level, but he did try."

Jade considered her words before shaking her head. "No, I disagree. He let me make plans for a life he knew he was going to walk away from."

"What would it have done to your kids if he'd ditched you in the middle of your treatment?"

Jade hadn't considered that.

"What would they have done?" Taylor pressed. "How

would that have impacted them? They were already scared, I'm sure. But having their dad taking care of you had to have given them some comfort. Right?"

Looking out over the water, Jade frowned. "Yes. They were both at school and terrified."

"Nick being there was important to them."

Jade paddled harder. "Can't you let me hate him? Please? I really need to hate him right now."

"Go ahead, hate him. I hate him for you. But don't lie to yourself. Him leaving now hurts, but if that had been compounded by your cancer, it would have been worse. He's still a son of a bitch, but like... One of those sons of bitches you don't mind buying a beer for because even though you hate him, you know he has good intentions."

Jade blew out her breath. "I'd spit in his beer."

"Oh, so would I. Without hesitation," Taylor said. "And I'd find some chewed gum stuck to the bottom of a barstool and rub that shit all over the rim when he wasn't looking."

Jade chuckled. "Good. Thank you. I appreciate that you wouldn't just slap him on the back and tell him he had no easy choice."

"Never. I'd *never* do that."

Silence fell between them again before Jade confessed. "I don't know what I'm supposed to do, you know. What do I do once I go home? That life doesn't fit me anymore. Getting sick made me realize I hadn't just neglected my marriage. I don't even have friends to turn to because my career was more important than having a life."

"Hey," Taylor said, "you have us. We're here. We're your friends."

Jade glanced behind them and was happy to see Darby

and Liam standing upright and paddling toward them. "Look at that. She's found her footing."

"All it took was a man giving her his undivided attention." Taylor's tone sounded cynical and judgmental.

"You know how some kids get in trouble because bad attention is better than no attention?" Jade asked.

Taylor glanced at her. "Yeah."

"I think Darby screws up so someone will notice and show that they care."

"I thought you were a marketing executive, not a therapist."

Jade stopped paddling to let her arms rest. "Owen, my youngest, turned into a class clown to get attention for a long time. Like I said, I worked a lot and wasn't around as much as I should have been. For a while, he spent more time than not getting into trouble to get noticed. It's not quite the same, but I think that's what she's doing. Trying to get noticed."

"She needs help."

Jade giggled. "Don't we all?" She let out a long breath as she looked around the lake. "I hate feeling so lost. I hate not knowing what to do. But...I just don't know how I'm supposed to get through this."

"You'll get through it," Taylor said. "I promise. We're going to be here for whatever you need."

Jade laughed when Darby grimaced at the salmon on her plate. For her last night in Chammont Point, she'd invited her two friends over for a goodbye dinner. This wasn't goodbye, however. Taylor and Darby reassured Jade they were one phone call and an hour's drive away. They were adamant that they'd stay in touch. Even so, the meal she'd made had a shadow over it. She was leaving the cabin and heading home in the morning. The dread in her heart from knowing she'd be going home to an empty house seemed to grow with every beat. But Darby's dinnertime antics distracted Jade from her problems.

"You don't have to eat that if you don't like it," Jade told Darby.

"No," Darby said, "You invited me to dinner. I'll..." She swallowed so hard, Jade actually heard the gulp.

"You'd think someone who grew up in a lake town wouldn't be so uneasy eating fish," Taylor said, squeezing a slice of lemon over her plate.

"I eat fish," Darby said. "When it's coated in batter and deep fried. I don't like my food looking at me." Darby stuck her bottom lip out at Jade. "You should have cut the head off the poor guy."

Taylor put a napkin over the fish's head. "There. Does that help?"

"I guess. But I still know his little eyes are there with that blank stare."

"You're hopeless," Taylor said with a laugh. "Just try it."

Darby sniffed the Mediterranean-style steamed fish and then slowly put it in her mouth. Jade and Taylor watched, waiting for Darby's verdict on the dish.

"Hey," Darby said, "that's not bad."

"I'm glad you think so." Jade's smile fell as she glanced across the table at Taylor.

She was thinking something. Jade might not have known Taylor for long, but she'd already learned that

Taylor tended to get quiet when she was debating what to say.

"Do you want us to go with you tomorrow?" Taylor asked.

For a moment, Jade almost agreed. She's been dreading the idea of walking into her home, knowing the life she'd had there was over. However, after a few seconds of considering the offer, she shook her head. "Thanks, but I'm probably going to be a mess. You guys don't need to see that."

"We don't mind," Darby said. "We talked about it, actually. Maybe you shouldn't do this alone."

"I appreciate you two so much," Jade said. "I think I do need to do this alone, though. I'm closing the door on a pretty big chapter of my life. It's going to be rough."

Taylor nodded, as if she had been expecting that answer. "We're an hour away. One phone call."

"Which," Jade said with more cheer than she felt, "means that I'm going to be visiting all the time. I want you guys to start thinking of things for us to do on the weekends. And we don't have to stay in Chammont Point. You guys should come up to Fairfax soon. I have plenty of room for you."

"We're going to have so much fun," Darby said. "I can't wait. I have been looking for a Thelma to my Louise forever, and now I have two. It's amazing."

"Let's hope any road trips we take go better," Taylor said with a laugh.

Thankfully, the conversation turned from Jade's trip home to plans of things to come. A canoe trip was in their near future, as well as a picnic lunch on the shore of one of the small islands on the west end of the lake. Jade wanted to learn rock climbing, which Darby wasn't excited about because she was certain it would ruin her manicure, but Taylor's eyes lit at the idea.

By the time they finished dinner and cleaned up the mess, Jade and her friends had a short list of trips they were going to take before the weather turned too cold. They even had a few ideas for what to do over winter. Snowshoeing was on the list, and Jade couldn't wait. She felt like she had to learn everything all at once and was excited she'd found friends willing to join her in the adventures.

After folding a towel and setting it aside, Taylor eyed Jade. "It's getting late. We should go so you can pack and get some sleep."

Darby stuck her lip out. "Are you sure you're okay going home alone tomorrow?"

"Yeah," Jade said. Taking their hands, much like she'd done the day when they started organizing her divorce strategy, Jade squeezed them tight. "I am so thankful that I've had you two to get me through this week."

"Not just this week," Taylor stated.

Giving Jade a sad smile, Darby said, "Call if you need us."

Jade hugged them both and walked out to see them off. The almost full moon lit the way for Taylor to make it to her truck and Darby to walk the path between the two cabins. Once they both were gone, Jade looked out at the cove. When she'd first decided to come to Chammont Point, she'd done so to kick off her new, family focused outlook on life. What she'd found instead were two unexpected anchors in *yet another* unexpected storm in her life.

She looked up at the orb in the sky and fought the urge to laugh manically. Whatever the universe had planned for her had better be good because all she'd managed to do so far was build a fake sense of security that had been yanked away from her without warning. Things wouldn't be getting easier anytime soon. In the coming days, she'd be going back to work in the office full-time, telling her children their parents were divorcing, and splitting her assets with a man who had left her long before he'd ever confessed to it.

Despite her newfound friendships with Taylor and Darby, Jade couldn't think of a time in her life when she'd felt so alone. She'd never been one to have close friendships, but she'd never been one to feel like she needed them. Now that she had been left to face an unknown future, she understood how distant she was from everyone in her life. She'd come to count on Darby and Taylor far too much in the short time she'd known them, but she really was tempted to call them both and tell them she'd changed her mind. She *did* want them to go to Fairfax with her. She *did* need them to hold her hands as she walked through her house for the first time since Nick had left.

That seemed like a pretty big ask from two women she'd only met a week ago.

Instead of begging for help, Jade filled her lungs with the moist air rolling off the lake and stared at the moon, reminding herself that she was a strong, independent woman and could handle anything life threw at her. She'd built a successful career, single-handedly supported her husband and two children for years, and had beaten cancer when the doctors told her the odds were not in her favor. She'd survived far too much to give up now. She would survive this too.

Jade walked to the water's edge and dipped her toes in. The water was warm and inviting, tempting her to go in farther. She didn't stop until the lake was lapping at the hem of her shorts. As it had a few days prior, the water calmed her, soothing the rough edges of her frayed nerves. Closing her eyes, Jade sank down until the warm water embraced her.

"One of these days," someone called from the shore, "you'll wear a bathing suit into the water."

Gasping, Jade stared at the silhouette. Seconds passed before she connected the voice. "Liam?"

He walked into the water but only to the edge of his shorts. The light shimmered off his teeth as he grinned. "What is it with you and going into the lake with your clothes on?"

"It is almost ten o'clock. What are you doing here?"

"You asked me to pick up your kayak," he reminded her.

"Tomorrow," she clarified as she stood. "I asked you to pick it up *tomorrow*."

"You said you were leaving early. I didn't think you'd miss it. I can come back in the morning."

Jade said, "No, take it."

"Are you okay?" he asked when she stopped in front of him, her clothes soaking wet.

"I'm fine. Why wouldn't I be?"

Liam looked her over. "Maybe you aren't aware of this, but it's fairly unusual to swim in your clothes."

"You are *really* hung up on that."

"It's *really* odd," he said.

"I'm going home tomorrow. I thought one last dip was in order." Gesturing behind him to the shore, Jade said, "Your kayak's over there."

He ignored her hint and skimmed over her shirt and shorts. "You're a strange lady."

Jade smiled, reminded of what Darby had said about not caring what other people thought. Darby didn't mind being looked at like she was strange, because she was happy. Just like floating in the lake made Jade happy—fully clothed or not. "I know."

Her wet feet gathered sand as she crossed the beach, not bothering to justify her actions. If Darby Zamora could hold her head up while dressed like a piece of fruit, Jade Kelly could hold her head up while swimming fully clothed.

EIGHT

THE TWO-STORY gray house used to feel like home. Staring up at her house through her bug-spattered windshield, Jade once again wondered how in the hell her life had fallen apart in such a short period of time. Then again, that seemed to be how it had happened. A little over a year ago, she had been certain she had stressed herself into some kind of digestive problem. Turned out she had cancer. A week ago, she had left this house under the impression that her marriage was getting a second chance. Turned out her husband was leaving her.

Now, the structure that used to welcome her felt like a foreign land. Nick no longer lived there. She didn't even know where he was living. Part of her wanted to turn right around and go back to Chammont Point. She could paddle out into the middle of the lake and ignore the rest of the world. Maybe she could stay there forever, looking up at the sky while the soft lapping of water lulled away her worries.

Jade dropped her head against the headrest of the driver's seat, closed her eyes, and pictured the water and that crappy little cabin. She chuckled as she recalled how she'd fallen through the banister and landed flat on her face, terrifying Darby. How had that only been a week ago?

Now, she was coming home to an empty house. She couldn't avoid facing the space forever. At some point, she was going to have to go inside and see the voids on the bookshelves and the empty side of the closet. Jade started to reach for her phone, tempted to reach out to Darby and Taylor for courage, but she hesitated. Nothing they said could make this easier.

With one last breath for courage, Jade climbed from her car and took the bag from the back seat. Once inside, she simply dropped the bag at her feet and kicked the door shut behind her.

From the doorway, she scanned the living room. Big windows let in an abundance of sunshine, brightening the light blue walls and off-white carpet. The furniture, which Jade had always loved, somehow looked too stiff to be comfortable. The room appeared to have been staged by a world-renowned real estate agent. Everything was in its place. Perfectly matched. Colors and patterns chosen to be the most aesthetically pleasing. All the surfaces were clean and tidy. Other than the now disorganized bookshelf where Nick's missing belongings left gaps, the room appeared to be untouched. Cold. Hard. And yes, unwelcoming.

When she'd left for her vacation, this place and all of these things had offered her comfort and a sense of security. Now, they seemed unfamiliar.

Feeling like an intruder in her own home forced Jade to realize how much of a facade this life had been, not just for Nick but for her as well. This house might have suited the old Jade, but she had changed. Nick might not be willing to see that, but she knew, in her heart, that her career-climbing former self was gone. The colder version of herself had been cut out with her cancer and whatever had remained had been decimated by the treatment that had broken her down to the core.

She was different now, and this house no longer fit the life she wanted. She might not know what that life was yet, but this certainly wasn't it.

Jade walked into the kitchen, and a thousand memories flooded her at once—from the time the boys were young, insisting they didn't like whatever had been served for dinner, up through Nick trying to get her to eat just a little bit more to keep her strength up. The fridge used to be covered with stick drawings and sports schedules. Now the surface was empty. There were no longer piles of junk to be sorted or snacks left half-eaten before rushing off to some school event.

There would be no more bustling around in the morning, trying to align their schedules to see who could pick up groceries or drop off dry cleaning. That life, those messes and rushed mornings, were gone now. For all the complaining she'd done about them in the past, she'd give anything to have them back.

Wasn't that always the way?

Standing there, remembering how things used to be, started to drain her energy. Her spirits sank more with each passing heartbeat. This was taking a toll on her, and it had just begun. She couldn't imagine what the actual divorce proceedings were going to do to her. She'd be broken before they even started.

Opening the cabinets, one by one, she assessed what was missing. One of the sets of dishes. Half of the glasses and water bottles. Several pans, but he'd left the silverware and most of the utensils.

After leaving the kitchen, she walked through the home office. His desk was gone. He'd left the file cabinet and wall hangings, but all that remained of the bookshelf were indents in the carpet.

In the den, she stared at the space where his recliner used to sit facing the now empty wall. He'd taken the big-screen television, but she didn't mind. She rarely watched it anyway.

She walked back to the living room, gathered her bag, and carried it upstairs. In the master, she stared at the king-size sleigh bed, trying to remember the last time she and Nick had even touched each other there. Colorectal cancer had certainly given them both a good excuse to avoid sex. She'd thought that was valid, but now...

God, she'd been so blind to the signs that had been there for so long.

She sniffled as she emptied her bag onto the bed. After scooping her dirty clothes up, she turned to drop them into the wicker basket, but it was missing.

"Of course," she muttered and opened her arms, letting the pile drop to the floor.

She took her bag to the closet, gave herself one second to brace herself, and opened the door. As she knew it would be, Nick's side of the closet was empty. She stared at the empty hanging bars for a long time before putting her bag on the shelf above her designer blouses and tailored slacks. Most of those clothes were too baggy on her now.

Like her old life and her old way of living, the clothes didn't fit her anymore.

She wished she knew the words to convince Nick of that. If he'd stuck around for a little bit longer, she thought he might have seen that. Maybe he would have even come to love her again. If that was possible.

She turned to look at her reflection in the full-length mirror and replayed the words Darby had said over and over.

You are worthy. You are loved. To hell with that prick for making you feel like you aren't.

Jade chuckled as Darby's voice echoed around her mind. Her amusement faded quickly though, and a wave of loneliness washed over her. She turned her attention back to the empty side of the closet. Her tears fell, and the ache in her heart consumed her. The cloud of depression hanging in the back of her mind started to grow.

She couldn't be here, in this house. In this museum of a life that no longer existed. Jade practically ran from her room like the ghosts were chasing her. She trotted down the stairs and grabbed her purse as she headed for the door. Her heart pounded when she gripped the knob. Before she opened it, a realization slapped her square in the face.

She had nowhere to go.

She had no friends to run to because her work friends weren't really friends and the people she socialized with were the wives of Nick's friends. They weren't *her* friends. She had no one. Her parents, she supposed, but she still hadn't told them.

Jade released the doorknob, took several steps back, and sat on the stairs as her chest started to tighten with the rising sobs.

How had she gone so long without seeing how alone she was?

God. Nick was right. She was cold and aloof and self-centered.

Darby's affirmation ran through Jade's mind again, but she realized she couldn't add the part about Nick making her feel unloved. She'd done that to herself.

She took her phone from her purse and didn't hesitate to call Darby. She'd told Jade a dozen times to call her if she needed anything.

"Hey," Darby answered. "It's Jade," she called.

"Hi," Taylor answered in the background.

"What are you guys doing?" Jade asked.

"Taylor's making me stain the banister," Darby said, sounding disgusted. "My manicure is shit now."

"Did you make it home already?" Taylor asked.

Jade had to swallow. "Yeah."

"Are you okay?" Darby asked in that now familiar maternal tone.

"No," Jade confessed as her tears welled. "I'm not."

"I knew we should have gone with her," Darby said quietly, as if Jade wouldn't hear.

"Want us to come up?" Taylor asked.

"Please," Jade said in a cracked voice that sounded like a wounded bird. "I'll text you my address."

"Oh, honey," Darby said, "I have that on your rental agreement. I've already mapped out how to get there."

Taylor chuckled. "Need us to bring anything?"

"Do you have cranberry juice?" Darby asked. "I think we should take her juice."

"We'll pick up something to eat too," Taylor offered.

Jade didn't have the words or the strength to argue. She quietly thanked them and ended the call.

When they arrived just over an hour later, she was still sitting on the stairs, trying to figure out what she was supposed to do next. The front door opened, and Darby stuck her head in, causing Jade to grin. Apparently, Darby didn't just walk right into Tranquility Cabin. She walked right in wherever she was going.

Her bright red hair was like a ray of sunshine in the storm that had been hovering over Jade. "Oh, honey," Darby cooed. "You look awful." She stepped in carrying several large bags.

"Be nice," Taylor chastised, coming in behind her with both her hands full as well.

Jade tried to remember their conversation. She knew they were stopping at the store, but they had to have bought enough food to last the three of them for a week. "What is all this?" she asked, standing to greet them.

"We had no idea what kind of comfort food you eat," Darby said.

"We got a little bit of everything," Taylor said.

Darby whistled as she looked around the living room. "Nice digs, boo. I'm moving in with you."

Taylor scanned the room as well, but her eyes weren't as wide and in awe as Darby's. "Who did your crown molding?"

"Nick."

"Well, he didn't put much effort into it, did he? It's a mess."

Jade looked at the room that seemed to have mocked her when she first entered her house. "It doesn't matter. I'm selling it," Jade said. "I can't live here anymore."

Darby and Taylor shared worried glances before Taylor said, "Don't decide that just yet. You're still upset."

"I know that I don't want to be here anymore."

With a frown, Taylor firmly stated, "Don't agree to anything until you have an attorney involved. That's how people get screwed in situations like these. You just bite your tongue and hold your horses. Let the lawyer figure out the big stuff."

Jade hadn't asked, but she suspected Taylor had been through an ugly breakup or two in her past. She'd get to the bottom of that another time. For now, she led them to the kitchen and listened as Darby once again *oohed* and *ahhed* while Taylor put food away. Jade sat and watched Taylor move in this space like she'd been there a thousand times before. Jade didn't have the energy to do more than sit and watch.

"Are you hungry?" Darby asked, opening one cabinet and then another until she found a glass.

"Not really."

"You have to eat." Taylor held out a tray of sliced meats, cheeses, and vegetables. "Usually, this is when I'd whip out chocolate and alcohol, but this will have to do."

"It's good," Jade said. "Thanks."

They all sat at the island as a heaviness settled over Jade. She ate a carrot and a slice of cheddar before saying, "Even if I wanted to stay, this house is ridiculously large for one person."

"I told you I'm moving in," Darby said. "You're adopting me. I'll get the paperwork ready so all you have to do is sign."

Jade's shoulders sagged. "You'll regret it. I was a terrible mother."

"This is not a pity party," Taylor informed her.

Jade sniffled and asked, "What is it?"

Darby examined a celery stick and dropped it back onto the platter. "Sweetie, how long has it been since you've had a bad breakup?"

"Never. Nick and I have been together since I was old enough to date. He's the only man I've ever been with."

"That explains so much," Darby said. "She doesn't know."

"I don't know what?" Jade asked.

"The breakup ritual." Taylor started counting the steps off on her fingers. "First you are shocked, then you are sad, which turns into anger and you talk shit about him."

"We've done all that," Darby said.

"Then you cry again," Taylor explained.

Giving a resolute nod, Darby added, "Which you've done in abundance. So, now we do a makeover."

Jade touched the ends of her hair. "Oh, I don't think..."

"This is part of the process," Darby informed her. "It has to be done."

"We'll start small," Taylor told her. "Let's rearrange the furniture and get a few new things for your wardrobe."

Jade pictured her closet. "I need a whole new wardrobe. Nothing I own fits."

Darby's eyes lit. "Where is the closest mall?" She held up her hand when Taylor started to speak. "Do not ruin this for me. I have lived my entire life waiting for a moment like this."

Leaning on the counter, Taylor held Jade's gaze. "The trick to the breakup ritual is balance. Go too far, and you regret it. Don't go far enough, and you cling to the past. An entire new wardrobe might be going too far."

Jade slid off her stool. "Come with me." She led them upstairs and opened her closet.

As soon as Darby stepped inside, she gasped and fell back with her hand pressed against her chest. "My God! How many power suits does one woman need?"

Despite her misery, Jade giggled. Running her fingertips over the sleeve of a designer blouse, she said, "Well, I'm a very powerful woman when I'm not sick or losing my husband. Powerful and neglectful of my family."

"Hey," Darby said in that maternal tone, "nobody has all their shit together, Jade. Nobody. You can't be everything all at once. All anybody can do is try. Don't cut yourself down because Nick wasn't happy. That's on him."

"Yeah," Jade whispered. "I know, but I still feel like shit."

"That's where the makeover comes in." Taylor sorted through the blouses and slacks. "You don't have to replace all this, but I do think—and I can't believe I'm saying this—you could use a little color in your wardrobe."

Darby's smile was almost blinding. "Oh my God. This is the best day of my life. No offense, Jade. I know you're miserable, but...Oh my God. We're going shopping *and* Taylor wants to buy something colorful." She wrapped one arm around Jade and the other around Taylor, pulling them into a big hug. "Best day ever."

"He's right," Jade said without the slightest hint of emotion. Despite a trip to a salon to dye her hair a dark auburn, buying more clothes than she'd likely wear, and ordering updated living room furniture, the excitement of the makeover step was fading and she felt empty. Her emotional roller coaster had bottomed out. She pulled a marshmallow from the fire they'd built in the pit in her backyard and blew out the flame. "I really wasn't a good wife."

"Screw that," Taylor said. "Don't let him get into your head."

"I'm not," Jade countered as she squished the melted ball between two chocolate-covered graham crackers. "But he is right. I put my career above my family. I don't know why I didn't see this coming sooner. Actually, yes I do. Because I was self-centered and obsessed with my job."

Taylor waited until her marshmallow was black before blowing out the flame. "That doesn't excuse what he did. He chose to lie to you about your marriage."

Since Jade enjoyed making the treats but didn't eat them, she handed her creation to Darby. "That's not what I mean. I know his leaving like this was wrong, but we didn't have the life he wanted. I didn't give him what he needed."

"Don't fall into that trap," Darby said. "Every woman falls into that trap. Men screw up, and we take the blame. You have to keep the house clean and the husband organized and the kids educated. And what does the man do? Work fifty hours and call it even. Bullshit."

Jade smirked. "That's the point, Darby. That's the role I was filling. Nick took care of the house and the kids. I worked more like sixty hours a week and came home too exhausted to be part of my family. I wasn't there. For him or the kids. He did all the so-called mom stuff that I wasn't around to do. There's something to be said for that, right?"

"I'll send him a cake," Taylor stated flatly.

"With arsenic icing," Darby added.

Jade smiled. Not because she wanted to poison Nick but because having friends defend her felt really nice. Suddenly, she was struck by something that caused her heart to nearly seize in her chest. Jade looked from Darby to Taylor and nearly started crying again. "Can I confess something to you guys?"

"Yes, those pants *are* awful," Darby said. "It's a damn good thing we bought you some new clothes."

Jade looked down at her sage green capris.

"Shut up," Taylor warned.

"Oh, were we not discussing her dreadful fashion?" Darby blinked, but the hint of a smile proved she was trying to lighten the mood.

"Says the lost extra from *Grease*," Taylor said lightly.

Jade had to bite her lip so she didn't laugh when Darby stuck her tongue out at Taylor. "I was going to say that I'm so glad I met you guys. You've stood by me when you didn't have to. I crashed today—coming home with his things gone made this real. You didn't have to come running to help me, but you did, and I really, really appreciate it. Thank you."

Darby sat quietly for a moment. "You would have come running for either one of us, Jade. I know you would have. You're one of us now."

"Welcome to Loserville, babe." Taylor lifted her glass in a toast.

Jade looked around her backyard. Recalling when the kids used to run and play there, she sighed. "I don't know what I'm going to do when you two leave. I'll be on my own."

"We'll be here for you," Taylor assured her. "Whatever you need."

"We're only an hour away, Jade," Darby agreed. "We'll see you all the time."

"I hope so," Jade said, suddenly sad at the idea of not seeing Darby and Taylor every day. "I'm sorry that my vacation has caused you both so much upheaval."

"Adventure," Darby clarified. "Never think of your life as challenging or messed up. Think of it as an adventure."

"Don't take advice from her," Taylor said. "I mean...look at her."

Darby tossed a marshmallow at her. "Hey!"

Taylor tried to hide her grin but ended up laughing. "I'm just kidding. She's right. We all needed this shake-up."

"Well, in that case, I'm glad I could help." Jade's attention was drawn to a moth. It hovered near the fire, likely drawn by the light, and pivoted at the last second when the heat became too much. The movement resonated with her. It was a great metaphor for what her life had been. She'd been so distracted by the light, she hadn't realized she was about to get burned. Though she wasn't sure if she'd managed to redirect herself at the last moment. She thought she had, but here she was, crashing. "I can't let this defeat me," she said.

"You *won't* let this defeat you," Taylor stated. "I know it's overwhelming at the moment, but once we get you an attorney and get the ball rolling on the divorce, things are going to feel easier to navigate."

Glancing over the fire at her, Jade said, "Have you been divorced before?"

"Yeah," Taylor said flatly. "After my grandfather passed away, I was... I was not in a good place. Other than a few cousins that I rarely saw, he was the only family I had. I met this guy while working a construction job and thought he

143

was great. I jumped in because I wasn't thinking clearly. Then he left. And our divorce was ugly because I was young and stupid and let myself get taken advantage of. He took most of my grandpa's tools and equipment, and the judge let him keep it because I couldn't prove they belonged to me. It might not sound like much, but I lost everything because I didn't protect what was mine."

"It sounds like a lot," Jade said softly. Though the sun had set hours ago, she could see the hurt in Taylor's eyes reflecting in the glow of the fire. "Those things were important to you. What they represented was important to you."

Taylor nodded. "I know you think Nick won't try to take you for all he can, but divorce changes people, Jade. You have to protect yourself. I don't care how nice he was when you had cancer or how in love you used to be. That's over now. You're not on the same team anymore."

Jade looked down as she rubbed her sticky fingers together. Finally, she grinned, "Is that offer to kill him still available, Darby?"

Darby toasted her with her drink. "Always. See, ladies, this is why I'm single. This is why no man can tie this old gal down. No, sir. I am free. I will stay free. Forever and always. Amen."

"You got dumped too?" Jade asked.

"Like a fucking hot potato," Darby admitted. "But really, I'm usually the dumper, not the dumpee."

"Come on," Taylor said. "Tell us all about it."

Falling back into her chair, Darby shook her head and looked up at the stars. "I had just moved to Richmond and landed my dream job tending bar at La Viva Voom."

"La what what?" Jade asked.

"La Viva Voom. It's a strip bar."

Jade perked up. "You worked in a strip bar?"

Darby twisted her lips into a pout. "Then I met Johnny Rakin. He won me over with blue eyes and big tips." A wistful smile played on her lips. "He liked one shot of rum and two cherries in his soda. I always got it right, and he'd blow me a kiss and slip me some cash."

"So what happened?" Jade asked.

"He asked me out, and we had a great time. Eventually one thing led to another and..." Her wistful smile turned back into a scowl. "Then one day, this crazy woman comes into the bar, throws a whiskey sour in my face, and accuses me of screwing her husband."

"Oh no," Jade mumbled.

Darby lowered her gaze. "I was the other woman. But I didn't know it. I wouldn't do that, Jade."

"I believe you."

"Not only was he married, but he had *three* kids at home. Including a newborn. I have no idea how I didn't know."

"You trusted him," Taylor said.

"I was an idiot," Darby insisted.

"Sounds like a world-class prick if you ask me," Jade offered.

Darby shrugged. "I guess."

"You guess," Taylor said. "He was banging you while his wife was home cleaning baby poop. There is no guessing. He was a prick."

"Anyway, I got fired, I lost my man, and I ended up back in Chammont Point. *Again.*"

"You know what," Jade said, not in the mood to continue

spiraling into depressing territory, "we've all been dumped. We've all been hurt. And we've all picked ourselves up—well, I'm working on that—but the point is, we don't need them."

"Hell no we don't," Taylor agreed and lifted her drink. "Screw 'em all."

Jade lifted her juice. "Screw 'em all!"

Darby raised her glass as well. They all drank before silence fell over them.

"How booked is the cabin for the rest of the summer?" Jade asked. "I think I'd like to start spending more time in Chammont Point."

When Darby responded by glaring over the fire at Taylor, Jade hesitantly asked, "What?"

"She made me cancel all my renters," Darby accused.

"Until that cabin is no longer a hazard," Taylor stated, "you will not be renting it to anyone."

"Except me," Jade said.

"No," Taylor said. "You could get hurt, Jade."

"I'll sign a waiver."

Darby toasted her. "There you go. Problem solved."

Taylor shook her head.

"I'll stay at my own risk," Jade said to Taylor.

"*Mi casa es su casa*," Darby said, toasting her again. "Come down and stay forever if you'd like."

Jade chuckled. "I just might."

NINE

JADE HADN'T SEEN her kids in weeks. As happy as she was that they were coming for the weekend, her heart ached knowing they would walk into their home only to find out their parents were getting a divorce. She looked around the living room that Taylor and Darby had meticulously rearranged and organized the previous weekend.

Jade was just getting used to the new look—not only in the house, but also her dark auburn hair and her brighter clothes. Though Jade had been hesitant, the makeover step of the breakup ritual had helped her mindset tremendously. Rather than walking in from her first week back at work with the past haunting her, Jade had been welcomed by a completely different feel to her home. One that didn't take her breath away.

Taylor and Darby had dragged Jade into a home store, and in a matter of hours, she'd bought a new area rug, two new chairs, and a new coffee table to fill the living room. The old furniture was moved into the den that Jade rarely used so she didn't have to see it unless she chose to. Just that change

—not seeing the furniture where Nick had spent most of his weekends—had eased her heartache so much.

Now, however, she wondered if she should have put that off. Nick would be in her home today, in her new space, and they'd be breaking their kids' hearts. Standing in the doorway of her living room, looking at her new belongings, she realized once again that this house wasn't her home any longer.

She was still looking over her furniture when the doorbell rang. The sound made her heart twist in her chest and plummet to her feet. Her boys wouldn't ring the bell, and she wasn't expecting anyone else besides Nick.

Jade stood unmoving except for the rapid blinking and the long breath she blew out to brace herself. She would be facing him for the first time since she'd caught him moving out.

"You can do this," she whispered to herself. "You can do this."

She swallowed hard and forced her feet to move toward the front door. In the back of her mind, she was desperate to slip out through the kitchen and make a run for it.

Opening the door, she tried to smile, but her lips wouldn't move.

"Hey," he said. The uneasy shift in his pose reminded her of years and years ago back in high school when they'd first started dating. He used to come to her locker, give that sweet smile, and move awkwardly from foot to foot. He'd never been the overly confident kind.

In fact, Jade had been the one who had pushed them to get more serious. She'd always been the one who took charge and moved them ahead. If she'd left it to Nick, he'd still be struggling to get his business off the ground. They'd probably be buried in more debt than just her medical bills and the kids' college expenses.

The first decision Jade could ever recall Nick making without her push was to divorce her. Figured.

She stepped aside and gestured for him to come into what had, until he'd left, been their home.

He pointed toward her hair as he came in. "You changed your color."

"Yeah."

"How's your leg?"

"Better. I'm not using those gaudy crutches any longer." She added the last part with a soft smile, hoping to ease the tension.

He laughed gently. "They really were terrible."

She wanted to tell him all about Darby and her crazy sense of style. She wanted to tell him how Taylor was an amazing contractor who, if she could find it in herself to not give up, would have a successful business. However, she couldn't quite bring herself to share her new friends with him. Though it might be foolish, maybe even childish, she wanted to keep what little strides she'd made toward making a new life as separate from him as much as she could.

"I, um," he started and then faded off. "I'm glad you're doing better."

"Thanks."

He stopped in the doorway of the living room and scanned the furniture. "You... Where's..."

"I switched things up a bit. I think we should sit at the table." She turned toward the kitchen to redirect his attention. He didn't belong in this house any more than she did. But for now, this was her space. She didn't need to justify the change she'd made.

"Do you want something to drink?" she asked, walking into the kitchen.

Nick huffed. "I know where everything is."

She turned and stared at him. She did not glare, but she wanted to make certain he heard her. "You're a guest here now." That harsh statement wasn't simply to poke at him but to remind herself that he no longer had the right to make himself at home. Because this wasn't his home. This was her home. Hers alone.

He sank into what had always been his seat at the table. "I don't need anything. Thanks." After a few moments, he stuttered, "I-I-I, um... I'd like to tell the kids about Amber later. If you don't mind. One thing at a time is best, I think."

She turned to get herself a glass. "It's your secret to tell. I'm ready to sell the house," she stated as she grabbed a glass from the cabinet. "I'll let our attorneys sort out what that means financially." She jerked the fridge open and grabbed the cranberry juice. The bitterness she'd been forcing herself to work through was beginning to surface. Knowing they'd be telling the kids about their divorce had been a constant distraction. She'd ended up leaving work early the last two days. She couldn't be productive, and she hadn't wanted her co-workers to see her mind wander constantly.

Closing the fridge, juice in hand, she glanced at him, silently hoping he'd challenge her decision so she could unleash some of her pent-up frustration.

He simply nodded and muttered, "Okay."

Rather than engage in fake conversation, she put the juice away and leaned against the counter as a tense silence filled the room. They didn't have to stew in the awkward silence for long. Xander called out from the front of the house. Since he was picking Owen up on his way, that meant both her boys were home.

Just like when Nick had rung the bell, her insides twisted around themselves. This was it, the last few moments before they shattered the illusion of family for their kids. She forced a smile as they came into the kitchen but couldn't stop her eyes from filling with tears. "Hey guys," she said.

Her sons instantly looked concerned, and Jade silently cursed herself. She hadn't meant to start crying and knew they immediately feared that they'd been summoned to get bad news about her health.

"Mom?" Xander asked, giving her a big hug. "What's up?"

She opened her mouth, took a breath, but didn't know what to say.

"Hey," Nick said as he hugged Owen. "How's school?"

Like his older brother, Owen focused on Jade. He had her red hair and pale skin. Where she'd managed to escape having a splattering of freckles across her face, his nose and cheeks were covered. Though he was an adult now, technically anyway, she still imagined him as a little boy.

Hard as Jade tried, she couldn't stop a tear from falling. She wiped it away and tried to force a smile for her kids.

"What's going on?" Owen asked as if he could read her mind.

She cleared her throat and shook her head. "Hungry?"

Xander, who looked so much like his father with dark eyes and hair, wasn't buying her act either. "Mom?" he asked softly.

MARCI BOLDEN

Owen's gray eyes were wide as he watched. Waited. "Are you sick again?" he whispered.

The fear in his voice was like a fist punching Jade in the gut. "No," she answered quickly. "I'm okay."

"Have a seat, guys," Nick said.

Xander and Owen focused on Jade as she sat at the table.

"Sit," she said.

Once they were all situated around the table, Jade looked at Nick. This was his stupid idea. He should take the lead.

"We have something to tell you," Nick started.

"Mom *is* sick again," Owen said, and his already pale cheeks lost even more color.

"No." Nick glanced at Jade, and for the first time, he seemed to regret his decision. No, not his decision. The *consequences* of his decision. "But we've... Well, I...I've moved out, guys. Mom and I are getting a divorce."

Their sons sat in silence. Xander ground his teeth, and Owen glanced from one parent to the other as if watching a tennis match.

"Why?" Xander finally asked.

Again, Jade didn't have the words.

"It's complicated," Nick said.

It wasn't complicated, and she wanted to call him on that. She wanted to tell him he was full of shit.

Not in front of the kids, she reminded herself. They'd always had a rule about fighting in front of the kids. That was unacceptable. Instead, she waited for him to confess his misdeeds.

"We've been through a lot over the last year," Nick said. "It takes a toll."

Xander creased his brow. "Mom almost died so you're getting a divorce?"

"I've heard about this." Owen shot an angry look toward Jade. "People almost die and so they want to change everything. Is that what you're doing?"

Jade shook her head and wiped a tear that fell.

"I asked for the divorce," Nick said. "I'm the bad guy here. Don't be mad at Mom. She, um, she was surprised too."

Owen turned his glare toward Nick. "So, Mom almost died and now you're leaving her?"

"Like I said, it's more complicated than that," Nick said.

"How so?" Xander pressed.

Nick shifted in that uneasy way he tended to do. "Look, I just..."

"Mom *just* recovered from cancer," Xander said. "Last year..." His voice cracked, and he let his words fade.

Jade blinked. "Last year was difficult, but, um, Dad didn't have to stay. He didn't have to help me through that. So, if he wants to go now, he should...he should go."

"Go where?" Owen asked.

Nick took a long breath. "I've moved into an apartment. I'll get you guys beds so you can stay over."

"We can stay here," Xander said.

"We'll be selling the house," Jade said. "I'll be getting something smaller, so if you want any of the furniture, just let Dad know. He can put it in storage for you." She wasn't dealing with that, and the frown on Nick's face implied he really didn't want to either. Tough.

He smiled, but it was obviously forced. "Yeah, no problem."

"Are you guys going to even try to work through this?" Xander asked.

"I've been thinking about it for a long time," Nick said. "And there just isn't anything to work through. We don't hate each other, we... *I* want something else now."

"This sucks," Owen said.

"I'm sorry," Jade told him. "I know it does. But we're not going to let this turn into something ugly. We're not going to drag you into this. You'll be okay."

"You say that now," Xander muttered. "Just wait until Christmas when we have to figure out how to split our time."

"We won't do that to you," Nick said. "We're not going to put you in the middle of this."

"Newsflash, Dad," Owen barked, "we're the kids. We are *literally* in the middle of this."

"Owen," Jade said, knowing he was about to storm off.

As she suspected, he jumped up and marched away. He was really good at avoidance. He'd run up to his room and let Xander get more information to break to him later. When Jade had been diagnosed with cancer, Owen had hidden himself in his room while Xander had spent hours researching the disease and various treatments. He'd researched the doctor and the surgery and her chances of recovery. Then he'd helped Owen cope when neither Jade nor Nick could.

It wasn't like Xander to walk away without all the details, but seconds later, he jumped up. "I'm out."

"Hey," Nick called.

"Let him go," Jade said when Nick started to stand. "They need some time."

When it was just the two of them, Nick frowned. "A storage unit, Jade?"

Standing, she said, "You're not sticking me with all the details."

He opened his mouth, but she pushed her chair in. "Good night."

"Jade—"

"*Good night*," she said, emphasizing each word. She took her glass to the sink and dumped the contents out. When she turned around again, he was gone. She didn't know if she was relieved or disappointed. He really didn't have an ounce of fight to give her. Not even when she poked him.

On one hand, that was great. On the other, his lack of spark proved how far removed he was from their relationship. She really had to have been blind not to see. Even if she had been sick, even if she had needed him, she should have seen how deeply unhappy he'd been.

But she hadn't, and now they were all paying the price. She wasn't going to take all the blame, though. She was still pissed that Nick hadn't had the guts to speak up. Who sits back in silence letting their marriage crumble without saying a word? Who watches his family slip through his fingers without even trying?

Jade sat back at the table and stared at the empty seat across from her. She tried to remember the last time they'd sat there, having a meal that wasn't dominated by both of them looking at phones and making random comments that the other clearly didn't care about. Honestly, it'd been too long. She hadn't noticed, not really. She'd been aware, but she'd explained it away with their busy schedules, or by saying they deserved a distraction from her illness, or that they were tired.

Apparently, they'd been drifting away from each other and she'd ignored the warning signs of their dying relationship as much as she'd ignored the warning signs her body had given about the illness that had tried to kill her. But Nick hadn't ignored the signs. He saw them and let them grow apart anyway. Pressing her fingertips into her forehead, she tried to stop herself from crying but her tears fell anyway.

"Mom?"

Jade tried to smile as she wiped her cheeks. "Hey, Xander."

He leaned on the chair Nick had vacated. "Did Dad leave?"

"Yeah, I think so."

"You okay?"

She and Nick had decided a year ago that their kids were old enough to hear the truth, no matter how harsh, so she shook her head. "Not really."

"You honestly didn't know?" Xander asked.

"Not until he told me."

He sat across from her and fiddled with the pepper shaker. "While you were on vacation?"

"He didn't go. He, um, he used that time to move out."

"He sucks," Xander whispered.

Jade pressed her lips together. "I'm mad. Really mad. And I'm hurt, and when I found out, I said some really mean things to him. But the truth is, I don't want him to stay if he doesn't want to be here, Xander."

"You guys are just giving up?"

"Honey, I don't think we could recover even if he decided

he wanted to stay. I'd always be worried he had one foot out the door. I'd always be doubting him. That wouldn't be a good marriage for either of us. I'm sorry. I'm sorry you guys had to come home to this."

"I'm sorry we didn't go to the lake with you. We should have been there to help you through this."

"I appreciate that, Xander, but that's not your job. You don't have to take care of me. How's Owen?"

"He's on the phone with his girlfriend."

"Wait," Jade said. "Since when does he have a girlfriend? I thought he was all about the video game club he was into."

Xander shrugged. "I think she's in the club. She's pretty cool from what he said, but I don't know her."

For the first time since they came home, a genuine smile tugged at her lips. "I'm glad you guys are close. That's nice."

"We're home all weekend," Xander said. "Maybe we can go to the lake tomorrow since we didn't go with you before."

Jade's smile widened. "That would be great. We would have a lot of fun. I learned how to paddleboard when I was there."

"Really? That's cool."

"It was. You want to learn?"

He nodded and smiled too. "Yeah. That'd be all right."

She pushed herself up, grabbed his hand, and pulled him with her. "Come on. Let's go tell Owen."

"Mom," Xander said, pulling her to a stop. He searched her eyes for a few seconds. Then he stepped closer and gave her a big hug.

Jade sighed as she hugged him back. She hadn't realized how much she'd needed that kind of affection until he'd wrapped her up. She leaned back and tried to fight her tears, but they fell anyway. She ignored them and put her hand to his face. "We're going to be okay," she whispered. "I promise. We'll be okay."

Xander nodded. "I know."

Jade parked in front of Tranquility Cabin, and an unexpected sense of relief filled her. She was back here in this peaceful place where she knew she'd find support if she needed it. That felt nice.

Xander stared out for several seconds before pulling his sunglasses down to the tip of his nose and looking at her wide-eyed. "This is where we're staying?"

Jade chuckled. "Yup."

"What a shit shack," Xander said.

"I know, but I grew fond of it while I was here. I like the owner. Besides, we're just crashing here for one night. We'll be headed home in the morning."

"If you say so," Owen chimed in from the back seat. He climbed out with his backpack in hand.

Jade and Xander grabbed their bags and headed for the cabin. As Jade got the key from under the mat, Xander looked out at the cove.

"Can we swim here?" he asked.

"Oh, yeah," Jade said, recalling how Liam had caught her floating under the moonlight. "It's great. The water's a bit warmer here in the cove than out on the bigger beaches. Makes it nice. It's quieter here too."

"Sounds good," Owen said.

As soon as they stepped inside with their bags, Xander let out a low whistle. "*Mom*? What the hell is this place?"

Jade looked around, remembering all too well how she'd initially had that reaction. "It's a work in progress."

"I can't believe we're staying here," Owen said. "Especially after you fell through the banister."

She creased her brow in question. "How did you know about that?"

"Dad told us," Owen said. "He was worried."

Jade had to remind herself of her determination to be a bigger person than she used to be. The snide comment about how surprised she was that Nick had cared tickled her tongue, but she swallowed it. She wasn't going to get bitter. She could be angry and sad, but she refused to let him make her bitter. "That was...nice of him," she managed to force herself to say.

Her boys both shifted—a nervous trait they'd inherited from their father. She looked from one guilt-ridden face to the other. Years of experience with these two let her know they were hiding something they hadn't yet agreed if they should confess. She'd seen the tell-tale uneasy movements and diverting of eyes plenty of times over the years. A broken lamp when they were in elementary, a fender bender during Xander's senior year of high school, and now whatever they were still undecided about when or how to share.

"You might as well spit it out," she said. "No need to look so nauseated all day." She focused from Xander to Owen— the one who always cracked first. "Get it over with. What do you need to tell me?"

"I think we knew," Xander said, sounding ashamed. "That Dad was...gonna leave. I think...We never *knew*, but I think we might have suspected. Mom, we think he's... We think he's been cheating on you. We think it's been going on for a while."

Jade's heart ached for her children and burned with anger at her husband. He had no idea about the hell he'd been putting his own children through.

Owen nodded. "After you guys told us you were getting divorced, we talked and..."

"It made sense," Xander added. "Dad was always so hard to get ahold of, and when we were home, he'd disappear for hours at a time and..."

"Guys," she said softly, "he has been. He confessed."

Her words lingered in the air like humidity on a hot summer day. She wished she had some words of wisdom to make it easier for them to digest, but she hadn't quite figured that part out herself. "He, um, he wants to be with her now and... That's what he's doing."

"What a dick," Xander muttered.

Owen sighed and looked at his hands. "We're sorry, Mom. We should have figured it out and talked him out of it."

"Hey," Jade said with a firm tone. "You're not responsible for Dad's choices. Neither of you. He wasn't happy. That wasn't your fault. He left me. Okay? He cheated on me. This is between me and Dad. We're going to do everything we can to keep it that way. Neither one of us wants this to hurt you."

"We're not kids anymore," Xander said.

"No, you're not. You're old enough to know that sometimes people just grow apart."

"And that's what happened to you and Dad?" Xander asked. "You just grew apart, so Dad started screwing around?"

Jade frowned at the anger coming from her son. She couldn't blame him. She was angry too, and as much as she'd love to rage against Nick and his shitty approach to their problems, she wouldn't do that to her kids. "I wish..." she started but then stopped to give herself a second to put her thoughts together. "I wish he'd told me that he was unhappy. I wish he'd tried harder. But sometimes, guys, there's just too much time and space. Sometimes people don't even know how far apart they are until it's too late."

"Aren't you mad?" Xander asked.

She nodded as she said, "I'm furious, and I'm hurt. But what am I going to do, Xander? Stomp my feet and scream about how unfair this is? That won't change anything. All I can do is pick myself up and move on."

Owen sniffed and dragged his palm under his nose. "At least he didn't ditch you when you were sick."

"When he told me he wanted a divorce, I was so mad," she confessed. "But then he told me he'd wanted one because... He says he loves her." She had to swallow the lump rising in her chest. "He stayed with me when I was sick even though he wanted to be with her. I still have a hard time with that, but at least he didn't... I don't know if I would have had the strength to get through treatment if he'd left me alone," she admitted. "He could have walked away, and he didn't. He stayed and he helped me."

"He was still lying," Xander said.

Jade heaved a heavy breath. "Look, the thing you both need to know, not just about Dad but about everyone, is that you can't control what they do. You can't control the choices they make or the way they behave or how they treat you. You can only control yourself, how you behave, and how you react. Some of the things your dad said when he told me he was leaving were hurtful but true. I spent a lot of my life focused on the wrong things. I got so caught up providing for us that I forgot you guys needed more than just *things*. You needed your mom to be around. I wasn't there as much as I should have been for any of you. I want you to know that I'm really sorry about that. If I could change it I would, but I can't. All I can do is try to be better now."

Both of her sons were quiet for a few moments before Xander spoke up.

"Somebody had to pay the bills, Mom," he said. "Dad sure as hell couldn't."

Owen nodded. "We might have been kids, but we knew you worked so much because Dad couldn't get projects for his stupid company."

"Dad worked," Jade said. She didn't feel the need to protect Nick as much as protect her kids from forming some harsh image of the man who had been an amazing father to them. They might be angry now, but she wouldn't stoke the fires of bitterness. "He worked hard trying to build up his business. He took really good care of you guys."

"You don't have to defend him," Owen said.

"No, I don't," she agreed, putting her hand on his shoulder. "But I wasn't everything I could have been, either. We both made mistakes," she said. "I really do wish he'd given me a chance to change, but he didn't. So, my chance with him is gone, but I can still be a better mom. You might be in college now, but it's not too late for us to be closer."

"You've always been a good mom," Xander said, and Owen nodded his agreement. "But it would be pretty cool if you took us paddleboarding."

"Yeah," Owen agreed, grinning widely. He laughed, and just like that, his anxious fidgeting eased.

Jade let her lips curve into a smile. "I can do that. Put your things away while I call and make sure the rental place has enough boards."

"Where's the second bedroom?" Xander asked.

Jade pointed toward the loft. "I haven't been up there, so I have no idea what you'll find. But I was told there are two twin beds and a nightstand."

Xander hefted his small duffel bag over his shoulder and started up the ladder, making it only about halfway before a board snapped. He let out a startled yelp as he jumped down.

"Oh my God," Jade gasped and rushed across the small room toward him while he examined his palms. "Are you okay?"

He laughed and shook his hands out. "This place is a dump, Mom."

"Yeah," she conceded. "It is. You guys just crash down here, okay? I'll have the owner bring over some blankets." She directed one to the bathroom and the other to the only real bedroom so they could change into swimsuits.

As soon as they disappeared behind closed doors, she called Darby.

"Are you here?" Darby squealed.

"I am, and as I told you on the phone, my boys are with me. They just tried to get to the loft."

"Oh God, what?" she moaned.

"The ladder broke. They're fine," she said, "but I'm not risking them climbing to the loft."

Darby let out a big sigh. "Can't they just scale the wall?"

"We're getting ready to go out on the lake," Jade said.

"Would you please bring over some spare blankets so they can sleep downstairs?"

"I hope they like pink sequins."

Jade chuckled and shook her head, not at all surprised that Darby's outlandish style would extend to her bed coverings. "They'll survive one night."

"Did you tell them?" Darby asked.

"Yeah. We told them last night."

"How are they doing?" she asked gently.

"Okay. They're actually doing okay."

"Good. I'll look for some blankets."

"Thank you." She ended the call and found the number to Lakefront Rentals. "Hey, Parker," she said when Liam's young employee answered, "it's Jade Kelly. How are you feeling?"

"If I don't have this kid soon," Parker said, sounding exhausted, "I'm going to need a wheelbarrow to get around."

"I remember that feeling," Jade said. "The baby will be here before you know it. Do you have three paddleboards I can rent today?"

"Yes, ma'am. I'll have Liam get them ready since I'm not allowed to lift anything heavier than the telephone these days."

"Please don't tell Liam I said this," Jade said, "but it's nice that he's looking out for you."

"I guess."

Jade thanked her as Owen walked out of the bedroom. She told him to give her a minute while she disappeared to put on her suit and wrap.

By the time they got to Liam's shop less than half an hour later, he had three paddleboards set out for instruction. That was definitely something—one of the few things—Jade appreciated about him. Though he did tend to annoy her more often than not, she noticed that he always seemed to take a few extra steps when teaching people how to use the equipment he rented.

She stood back, watching as Liam instructed Xander and Owen on how to paddleboard. Then Liam used her board to show the boys how to pick the board up and carry it and the paddle across the street to the lake.

"I got it," she said when he started to lead the way. "*Liam,* I can carry my own board."

His only acknowledgment was a quick glance at her. He headed across the street, still talking incessantly to her boys about the places on the lake they should see and where they should be extra careful. Once they were in the water, he put the board down and showed Xander and Owen how to get on, find their balance, and paddle.

"Don't be like your mom," he warned them, "and end up on crutches."

"Get off my board," Jade told him.

He hopped into the water. "I'll be in the shop if you need anything."

"We won't," Jade assured him. As soon as she climbed up and got her balance, she grinned at the boys. "All right. Are you ready?"

"Ready," they said and took off so fast, she'd never be able to keep up. She didn't mind. They were laughing and having a good time. That was more than enough for her.

"You okay?" Liam asked.

She looked down and inhaled slowly. "Yeah," she said honestly, "I'm okay."

TEN

THE FOLLOWING WEEKEND, Jade, Darby, and Taylor walked through a little grocery store in Chammont Point. Jade was treating her friends to a picnic on the beach to thank them for coming to Fairfax when she'd needed them. She'd told them to buy whatever they wanted—which led Darby to start a game of loading the basket with the most bizarre items she could find. In response, Taylor would, without fail, demand to know why in the hell she needed that. Every time, Darby and Jade would fall into a fit of laughter while Taylor did her best to look disgruntled.

Jade's smile faltered when she noticed Parker at the checkout counting change and shifting nervously. Though she wasn't close enough to hear the conversation, Jade understood perfectly. She remembered how, more than once when she was younger, she'd suffered the humiliation of not having enough money to buy groceries. Parker began looking over her purchases, no doubt debating what to put back. Jade shoved the basket she'd been carrying into Taylor's hands.

"Take this," she muttered and dug into her purse. She

opened her wallet and found a twenty-dollar bill. Folding it, she rushed to Parker's side and bent down as if to retrieve something. "Hey, Parker," she said and stood. She held the money out to the girl. "You dropped this."

Parker eyed the money. She shook her head, but Jade pushed the money toward her.

"I saw it fall out of your purse," Jade said.

Parker opened her mouth, so Jade pushed it even closer to her.

"You dropped this," she stated in a nice but firm tone. "I saw you drop it."

Parker stared at the cash for a moment before accepting the money. "Thanks," she said quietly before handing it over to the cashier.

Jade returned to where she'd left Darby and Taylor by a chip display. Her friends had grown quiet, and a sense of unease settled over them. None of them said the words, but Jade was certain they all felt a bit of shame over the game they'd been playing. Their superfluous shopping had been in fun. They'd been picking things out for entertainment rather than need.

The heartbreaking reality of Parker's situation was like a bucket of ice water tossed over them.

Jade glanced back in time to see Parker smile uneasily as the cashier handed her the change. Parker accepted two bags of purchases and looked down as she left the store. Jade's heart ached for the young woman, knowing she must have felt so defeated in that moment.

"I'm putting some of this stuff back." Taylor started sorting through the basket.

"Not the daiquiris," Darby pleaded. "I *really* do need those."

Taylor glanced at her as she pulled out a few items and then handed the basket back to Jade. "You guys check out."

Without a word, Jade headed to the counter and the cashier who had helped Parker. She emptied their purchases onto the counter as Darby stood beside her in awkward silence. Jade had just paid for the food when Taylor rejoined them.

The uneasy shift in the air around them wasn't something Jade wanted lingering. She hoped once they left the store, Darby would work her magic and lift their spirits, but for whatever reason, Jade handing out cash to cover Parker's expenses had sucked the joy out of the afternoon.

As they stepped out of the store, Jade slid her sunglasses on and started digging for her keys.

"Hey," Parker called, distracting her.

Jade asked her friends to give them a minute and gave Parker a warm smile. "Hi."

"That wasn't my money, Jade," Parker stated, not quite angry but with an edge to her voice. Defensiveness maybe. "We both know that."

"I didn't want you to have to put stuff back."

Parker shifted as if she didn't know what to say. "I'll pay you back."

"Okay."

As she glanced around the parking lot, Parker shifted again. "Could you... Could you not tell Liam? He helps me out a lot, and I don't want him to think he's not doing enough."

"It's our secret," Jade said.

Parker nodded, but she still looked embarrassed. "Thanks. Um, here's your change."

Jade accepted the bills and coins rather than insisting that Parker keep it. She didn't want to ask, but she assumed Parker wouldn't have a single dime in her wallet until her next paycheck without it. She'd rather Parker kept the money, but Jade figured she'd done more than enough to ding the young woman's pride.

After putting the cash into Jade's palm, Parker finally met her gaze. "I'll get you the rest as soon as I can."

Again, Jade was tempted to tell her to keep the money but simply smiled. Before Parker could walk away looking like she was on the verge of tears, Jade gripped her hand. "I was your age when I had my son," Jade whispered. "There might be times when all of this feels like too much, but everything is going to be okay. *You're* going to be okay."

For a moment Parker smiled and a little light sparkled in her eye, but the twinkle faded, and her underlying shame returned. "Thanks, Jade. I'll see you later."

As soon as Parker turned away, Darby rushed up and wrapped Jade in a big hug. "Oh my God. You're like a fairy godmother or something. That was so sweet."

Jade discounted the praise with a wave of her hand. "I'm happy to help her. I like her. Besides, I've been there before, not knowing which groceries to put away because you just can't stretch your budget any further. It's humiliating."

"But you're rich," Darby said.

Jade pressed the button on her remote to unlock her sedan. "I was pregnant and married at seventeen, remember? I might have financial security now, but back then, I was just another teen mom struggling to make ends meet, wondering how we were going to survive." She glanced to where Parker was getting into her beat-up car. "I remember how hard it was being so young and staring down so much responsibility. It's terrifying."

Since Darby had called shotgun—loudly as she rushed toward the car—Taylor was in the back seat. She hadn't said a word since putting the excess groceries away.

Jade adjusted the mirror to see her better. "Hey. You okay?"

Taylor nodded, but clearly she wasn't. The tension rolling off her was palpable and filled the car. Darby turned in her seat to look at their friend.

"What's up, Tay?"

"Nothing," Taylor said.

Jade turned as well and furrowed her brow. "Are you mad that I gave Parker money?"

With a quick glance at her, Taylor shrugged. "No. That was nice."

"Something's wrong," Darby said. "You're doing that brooding thing you do right before telling someone off."

Taylor glanced at them. "I'm not brooding, I'm..."

"Brooding," Jade and Darby said at the same time.

Looking out the window of the car, Taylor twisted her mouth into a frown and heaved a sigh. "One of the few memories I have of my mom was her screaming at the cashier because she didn't have enough money to buy all the shit she'd put in the cart. She accused him of overcharging her and made this huge scene." Much like Parker had, Taylor shifted as if uncomfortable in her skin. "It didn't happen once. She did that all the time. That was her way of getting them to give her the groceries to get her out of the store." She glanced at her friends. "She had problems. Drugs and stuff. Whenever she didn't have some guy hanging around to buy us food, she... She would pick a store, load up the cart, and throw a fit until they either kicked us out or gave her a discount to shut her up."

Jade glanced at Darby. They had wondered more than once what had happened to Taylor to make her so bitter. Now that they were getting a glimpse, Jade almost wished she hadn't. She couldn't imagine the pain and damage that had caused a young Taylor.

"Mom went to jail when I was six. Prison," Taylor clarified. "That's why my grandpa raised me."

Darby stuck her bottom lip out. "Taylor. That's tragic."

Taylor shrugged and smiled as if she were about to blow it off, but Jade shook her head, silently telling her she didn't have to.

"I'm sorry you went through that," Jade said. "I can't imagine how scary that was for a little kid."

"My grandpa was better," Taylor said. "He cussed a lot and raised me like a boy, but he was better. He worked hard and took care of me the best he could. I guess that's... I guess that's what's wrong with me."

"There's nothing wrong with you," Jade insisted.

Taylor rolled her eyes and gawked at her.

"Okay," Darby said, "you're a little cranky and could definitely use a makeover, but other than that..."

"Shut up," Taylor said playfully, obviously appreciating Darby's joke.

"But other than that," Darby said softly, "there's nothing wrong with you."

"Where's your mom now?" Jade asked.

Taylor shrugged. "I don't know. I never saw her again after my grandpa took me in. He asked if I wanted to see her, and I told him no. So he never made me."

"Do you want to know?" Jade asked. "Now that you're grown up?"

After a moment, Taylor shook her head. "No. I don't. I think she's done enough damage without inviting her to do more." She smiled slightly. "Are we heading to the beach or what? Darby's daiquiris won't stay frozen forever."

"Oh," Darby gasped, turning in her seat. "Pedal to the metal, Jade. My heart can't take melted daiquiris."

Jade looked at Taylor for a few more seconds before turning in her seat and starting the ignition.

Jade tucked a blanket more tightly around her as Taylor added a few more logs onto their little bonfire. Though the air around them lightened significantly once they'd reached the beach, there had been something hanging over them the rest of the afternoon.

Knowing Taylor, as well as she did anyway, Jade couldn't imagine how difficult opening up had been for her. She and Darby had known there was something in her life that had made her more cynical than most, but for some reason Jade had chalked it up to a broken heart and a bad attitude she'd never outgrown. Taylor's pain had run so much deeper than that, and Jade was embarrassed she hadn't seen it.

Though Taylor had smiled, laughed, and resorted to her customary dry wit as the afternoon went on, Jade sensed the cloud hanging over her. The episode at the store had cut open an old wound that Taylor was going to have to take time to close again.

The worst part was, she'd once again put a bit of a guard up between herself and her friends. Jade had debated more than once throughout the afternoon how to help Taylor understand that she didn't need to protect herself from them. Finally, she realized, she needed to confess something that had always weighed on her the way she suspected the truth about her mother had weighed on Taylor.

"We stole baby formula once," Jade blurted out. Heat settled over her cheeks. Darby stopped fidgeting, and Taylor stared wide-eyed at her from across the flames. "We were both working—I'd just started as a receptionist at a marketing firm—but we couldn't make ends meet. We couldn't stretch our dollars any further than we had. No matter how we juggled the bills, there just wasn't enough. Xander was hungry, and we… We didn't have formula, so we… We stole it. I'd never felt so horrible in all my life. Not just because we stole something but because I was failing. As a mother. I was failing. As we drove home with that can of formula hidden in Nick's jacket, I promised myself I'd do whatever it took to never have to do that again."

She blinked, refocusing on her friends, who sat quietly. "I think that's why I put everything I had into my career. Every day I saw these executives coming and going in their nice suits, taking vacations, eating at fancy restaurants. And there I was, barely able to feed my baby. I was beyond rock bottom emotionally. I felt like…nothing. I started working overtime, running errands whenever someone needed it. I did whatever I could to earn some extra cash. Some higher-ups took notice of my so-called initiative. I moved up quickly, and when I asked about moving from administrative work to marketing, they helped me go back to school to get my degree. Now I'm one of those executives in nice suits, taking vacations, and eating fancy foods. But I barely know my kids and I lost my husband. I became so determined to never feel like a gigantic failure ever again that...I feel that way for other reasons now."

"You're not a failure," Taylor stated firmly. "You've done everything you could for your family. You're *not* a failure."

"My mom came here from Mexico," Darby said. "She tried so hard to give us the American dream that she spent her life in someone else's restaurant. I loved her, but I resented her at the same time. As hard as she worked, I always had to wear hand-me-down clothes that never fit right. That's why I learned to sew," Darby said with a slight smile. "I was trying to make my clothes cool so the other kids didn't pick on me. It never worked," she admitted with a smile, though Jade could see a sheen of unshed tears in her eyes.

Taylor was quiet for a few moments before speaking up. "My grandma died before I was born, and Grandpa didn't really know how to raise a girl. He let me cuss by the time I was ten, and I learned to hang drywall instead of learning how to walk in high heels, but it was good. He was a good guy. He did the best he could. He was rough around the edges, like me, but he had a good heart."

"He'd be proud of you," Jade said. "For building a business."

Taylor scoffed. "My business is a disaster."

"It won't be forever," Jade said. "We'll help you."

"Yeah," Darby said. "I mean, I don't know how to hammer things..."

"But you know how to do social media," Jade said. "We'll get a page set up for O'Shea Construction and start some buzz around town. We'll get your business going. If that's what you want."

Taylor shrugged and stared into the fire. "I don't know what I want."

"I know that feeling," Jade added. "I really thought my life was going to be wonderful after beating cancer."

"It should have been," Darby said.

"It *will* be," Taylor stated. "We'll make sure of that. Won't we, Darbs?"

"Yeah. We're going to take care of you," Darby told Jade.

Jade smiled. "We're going to take care of each other."

Darby gasped as she sat straight up. "You guys. We're like friends now. Like *real* friends who bond over shit. We've bonded."

Jade laughed quietly before realizing Darby was right. Looking at Taylor, she saw the same realization dawn on her. They *were* real friends. "I want you guys to know that if you ever need me, I'd be there for you. Like you've been there for me. You just have to ask."

"Me too," Darby promised.

Again, Taylor stayed quiet, but a few layers of her outer shell seemed to fall away. "Me too," she finally said.

ELEVEN

FOR THE THIRD Friday evening in a row, Jade wandered the Chammont Point farmers market. She hoped to spend time on the lake this weekend, as the last few weeks, she, Taylor, and Darby had spent exploring the town and surrounding areas rather than kayaking and paddleboarding. She missed being on the water and she hadn't seen Parker since their run-in at the grocery store. Spending her weekends at the lake had become her new routine after realizing sitting around her big empty house was too depressing. The house had been listed for sale the prior week, and Jade hoped when she returned to Fairfax Sunday, she'd be greeted with the news that there was at least one offer on her house.

She hadn't decided what her next move would be. But the more time she spent wandering the market in a sundress and one of those borderline obnoxious wide-brimmed straw hats, the more content she felt. Chammont Point had come to feel more like home than Fairfax had for a long time. And that crappy little cabin, despite the repairs that needed to be made, welcomed her like a hug every Friday when she carried her weekender inside. However, summer was fading quickly, and Jade was uncertain what the change in weather would do to her commute.

"Hey, Jade," someone called.

Turning, she noticed Parker waddling toward her, weaving through the crowd.

When she got to where Jade was standing, she heaved a big breath and smiled uncertainly. "I owe you this." She handed Jade a ten-dollar bill. "Thanks again for...you know."

"You're welcome. How are you feeling?" She laughed lightly. "You look like you could burst any moment."

"I should be so lucky," Parker said with a laugh. "Not too much longer to go."

"I'm sure you'll be relieved."

The shift in her posture seemed to be more from embarrassment than the discomfort of pregnancy. "I guess." She glanced up but barely held Jade's gaze. "I wanted you to know that... Well, I've applied for assistance. You know...for when the baby comes. I'm going to be able to feed it."

For a moment, Jade was thrown back to the time when she and Nick had realized they had no choice but to swipe a can of baby formula if they were going to feed their son. Her heart ached for Parker. "I'm sure you'll be fine, Parker. But listen, I've been where you are," Jade said. "I know how hard it can be. If you need anything..."

Parker shook her head, as if she could stop Jade from saying whatever she was going to say.

"...*anything*," Jade emphasized, "I can help you. And I promise I won't judge or tell anyone."

A soft laugh left Parker. "I heard what Darby said at the

store. About you being like a fairy godmother or something. That's a nice thought, but you're not, Jade. So...I appreciate the help, but I'm going to be okay."

"I know you will."

"Nice hat," Liam said, interrupting the moment. He seemed to realize, belatedly, that he was butting in where he shouldn't have.

Parker put on a bright smile. "I was just telling her that." She looked at Jade with a silent plea in her eyes not to tell Liam the real reason they'd been talking. "I need to get home. I'm tired."

"You okay?" Liam asked, clearly concerned.

"Yeah. Tired, that's all. It was good seeing you, Jade. Later, Liam."

They both watched Parker walk away before Liam eyed Jade with concern.

Though Liam still wasn't her favorite person in the world, Jade had to admit he'd grown on her more than she'd expected he would. His genuine concern for Parker made him seem less like the selfish jerk she'd taken him to be. When he was looking out for Parker, he was almost...human.

Running into him didn't irritate her now as much as it would have a month prior. He'd gotten a haircut since the last time she'd seen him. Though his hair was still longer than many men his age would wear it, he'd trimmed away most of the sun-bleached strands, leaving his hair darker brown. He continued to look like a man desperately trying to hold on to his youth, but the shorter strands were one step closer to accepting he was nearer to forty than twenty.

She took a sip and smiled at the girl while Liam doled out compliments on their behalf. He was surprisingly sweet with kids, which reminded her of how he'd taught her boys to paddleboard several weeks prior.

"Is Parker really okay?" Liam asked.

"She's fine," Jade said. "Starting to feel the toll of pregnancy, I think."

"Maybe I should give her some time off."

Jade shook her head. "Not unless she asks for it."

He eyed her again, and she pointed to the hat. She'd bought it specifically to protect her pale skin while sitting on the beach, but this was the first time she'd actually worn it. This was the first time she'd felt relaxed enough to let herself look a little silly. However, in comparison to some of the other shoppers wandering the aisle between booths, her hat did nothing to make her stand out. Some were dressed in bathing suits, some in brightly colored tunics or caftans, and plenty were wearing big straw hats to ward off the sun. "Were you being sarcastic or giving me a compliment?"

He smirked. "Both?" As Jade laughed, he gestured toward her bag. "I heard you like kale, but that's ridiculous."

Jade examined her overflowing canvas tote before smiling up at him. "Have you tried kale?"

"I have. Can't say I'm a fan."

"So I guess you won't be coming for dinner anytime soon. Darn," she said sarcastically.

Liam laughed, and the wrinkles around his eyes deepened. "Well, I might be persuaded to change my mind. Please don't tell me this is what you're buying to feed your sons."

She looked at her bag. "They aren't here this weekend."

He dipped his head down and grinned. "So you're on your own?"

Rather than answering, she stepped around him and continued to the next booth.

Liam caught up to her. "Did they have a good time when they were here?"

"Yes, they did. They really enjoyed paddleboarding. Thank you for helping them with that." She skimmed over the various berries, selected a small basket of blueberries, and handed enough cash to the vendor to cover the cost. "I expect they'll find the time to come with me again before summer ends. They want to get a canoe and go fishing. They've never been fishing, so that should be interesting."

"I'll take them," Liam offered. "Teaching them would be fun. I know a great place. We can bring our catches back and cook them on the fire. What kind?"

Jade was confused by his question until she realized he'd guided her to a booth stacked with homemade pies. "Oh, no. I don't..."

"Seriously," Liam said. "Don't tell me you don't eat pie. That would break my heart."

Jade had to admit the baked goods looked delicious. She hadn't allowed herself to break the strict diet she'd put herself on. Though her doctor had told her that healthy eating was a priority, he hadn't told her to cut out sugar, alcohol, and caffeine. She'd done that herself, and she'd never regretted it. Until now. The golden, flaky crust settled over various fruit fillings made her want to shove her face into one of the pies like she was going for first prize in an eating contest.

She had to resist. She'd given in to Darby's offer to take her to Harper's Ice Cream the day Nick had called her at the lake. And she'd give in to the temptation of drinking her cares away the night she'd singlehandedly consumed the bottle of wine Taylor had left at the cabin. She couldn't continue down this path. She could *not* be tempted with baked goods.

"Sorry," she said, "but I don't eat stuff like this." She turned to leave, but Liam slid his arm around her waist and pulled her back.

"Do it for the kids, Jade," he said.

"I just told you my kids aren't here."

"They are in spirit," he said, causing her to laugh. "Come on. One slice. I'm buying. What kind?"

"No, Liam."

He didn't exactly pout, but she suspected the look he was giving her had won over many women in the past. She hated to admit he was softening her resistance. "Jade. It's *pie*. Homemade pie. Even you can't resist that."

She bit her lip. Her resolve faded as a breeze carried the scents to her. "Okay."

"Yes," Liam said.

"Just *one* slice. Apple."

"We'll take an apple," he said as he reached into his pocket. "You get one slice. I get the rest."

While Liam bought a pie, she mentally kicked herself. Not because she was tempting fate by eating pie but because she'd let him sway her. She was not going to fall for his charms. She refused. He was not the type of guy she would ever consider getting involved with, mostly because she doubted there was any "getting involved" with Liam. She suspected he was one hundred percent the love-'em-and-leave-'em type. She wasn't interested in that either.

He accepted a white box tied with twine before leading

her away, beaming with pride. "So what is it with your healthy food obsession?" he asked as they pushed through the crowd at the next booth. "It's not like you need to lose weight or anything."

Jade debated how to answer. She didn't need to lose weight. In fact, she was finally back to a healthy weight, and all her time spent on the water had given her a muscle tone she'd never had before. She didn't like the way people tended to look at her when they learned about her battles, but she felt comfortable enough with Liam. Something about him told her he'd faced his own wars.

"I had cancer," she said. As expected, the air around them filled with anxiety. "In my overzealous attempt to learn everything about it," she continued, "I did a lot of research into diet. I choose to not eat things that could increase the risk of cancer returning." She sighed when sympathy filled his blue eyes. "Don't look at me like that. I'm still here, alive and kicking...when I'm not on crutches."

He didn't even grin at her joke. "How long have you been in remission?"

"Five months now."

The muscles in his jaw worked beneath his scruff. He looked at the box in his hands. "Damn it. I shouldn't have bought this."

"I didn't say *you* can't eat sweets," Jade said lightly. "I just choose not to."

Liam looked around them at the booths and the people strolling by. He looked at anything but her. Yes, there was the discomfort that speaking of her illness tended to bring.

"I know that eating kale won't save my life," Jade told

him, "but it makes me feel in control of something that is uncontrollable."

Finally turning his focus on her, he shook his head. "That son of a bitch is divorcing you five months into remission?"

Jade jolted, surprised by his attack against Nick. "What does that have to do with my newfound affection for leafy greens?"

When he spoke, his voice was soft but held an edge. "You don't leave somebody so soon after what you've been through."

"Well, he did," she said and gave her best devil-may-care smile.

"What kind of asshole does that?"

"Hating him would be easy," Jade said. "But I don't want to live with that. Life is a precious gift that I took for granted for far too long. I'm not going to do that anymore. Hanging on to anger isn't healthy." She lifted the bag to show him the vegetables she'd been buying. "I'm kind of fixated on healthy right now."

"How about I hate him for you?" Liam asked with a surprising amount of tenderness in his voice.

Though he was usually the one who cavalierly tossed winks around, Jade gave him one as she said, "Darby and Taylor have that covered."

"Well, there's enough to go around."

Her smile softened. "Yeah, there is. Listen, I'm not going to say I'm not mad, because I am. However, I'm not going to let my anger toward him consume me. I have a second chance that pretty much every doctor told me I wasn't going to live to see. I haven't quite figured out what I'm going to do with it, but I do know I'm not going to use it to hate Nick for not loving me anymore."

"Good plan. However, I am willing to bet one piece of pie wouldn't throw your cells into turmoil."

"Oh, no, I agree. One piece wouldn't, but one piece leads to two, which leads to three, and before you know it, I've eaten all the sweets in Chammont Point."

A grin toyed at the corner of his mouth. "Maybe not *all* the sweets."

"I can't risk it," Jade said. "I'm weak and have zero self-control."

"Good to know." He winked, and his usual flirty, borderline inappropriate self returned. "So I should take this pie home with me?"

Jade looked at the box, tempted by the butter crust she'd been eyeing at the booth. "Yeah, I think you should." She glanced around at the crowd. "So nobody else needs to know I was sick, okay?"

"It's a secret?"

Returning her gaze to him, she shook her head. "Not a secret, just not something I want everyone to know."

"Are you embarrassed that you were sick?"

"No, but people get freaked out sometimes. Like it might be contagious. Illness makes people uncomfortable, except during cancer awareness month. Then I'm a miracle and a badass."

Liam brushed her short hair behind her ear and traced his fingertips along her jaw. "You're always a miracle and a badass."

He trailed his fingers down her neck and under the edge of her sun dress. Jade was about half a second away from slapping his hand away when he ran his finger over the scar where her port had been. For many months, that had been the place where harsh chemicals had been pumped into her body to kill the cancer that had invaded her.

She hated that scar. All her scars. She hated the reminder of the pain and suffering. But more than anything, she hated how her body looked like some kind of science project. Every slice and stitch had left a purple mark on her pale skin that would never go away.

"You shouldn't hide them," Liam said as he brushed his rough fingertips over her skin.

Jade pushed his hand away and patted down the neckline of her dress. "I'm not."

"You are. They saved your life, Jade. Don't be ashamed of them. Be grateful. *Thank* them."

She cocked her brow and smirked. "Thank my scars?"

"Yes." He was serious. The usual playfulness had disappeared from his eyes. "They're beautiful. They're life. They're a part of your story. Your scars are proof that you're a fighter, a survivor. They're badges of honor, letting the world know you beat something that a lot of people don't."

Jade had to pause to process his assessment. She'd never thought of her scars like that. Of course, she knew she'd beaten something that many people succumbed to. She'd fought hard, overcome the odds that so many doctors had put against her. She'd conquered more than she could have ever imagined.

They *were* badges of honor in a strange and confusing way.

A sly grin curved his lips, but it wasn't the usual annoying

I'm-so-sexy smirk she'd come to know. "Look at that," he said softly. "I finally found a way to shut you up."

This was probably the most sincere conversation they'd had, and it made Jade feel uneasy. She knew how to handle sarcastic and annoying Liam. Sincere Liam was an enigma she wasn't certain she was prepared for. "And you think I'm strange," she said, determined to return him to his usual coy self.

Liam chuckled. "I didn't say I thought it was a bad thing. I'm being serious."

"I know, and it's freaking me out a little," she admitted. "I appreciate your pep talk, but I'm not ready to thank my scars. They still terrify me."

"I'm sorry for what you went through," he said. "But you'll never stop being terrified if you don't learn to be grateful."

"Give me a break, huh? My life has been in a blender for over a year. I need a little bit of calm and steady to catch my breath. Then I'll be grateful."

"Life doesn't stop because we need a break, Jade. Life keeps going, even when it's in a blender."

She rolled her eyes. "You were a Buddhist monk in a past life or something, weren't you?"

"Possibly. I've been known to spout words of wisdom every now and again."

"In between batting your long lashes and flirting with tourists?"

He gave her that mischievous grin of his. "Part of being good with your soul is spreading that peace to others."

"By wooing every woman you see?"

"By making them feel good about themselves for a few

minutes. Come on, Jade, don't tell me having a handsome fella flirt doesn't give your ego a little boost."

"Find me a handsome fella and I'll let you know."

Liam laughed heartily. "That's it. That's the spicy side I've been missing lately. Welcome back."

"Thanks."

"You're welcome."

A little girl called out to Liam, and they both turned in time to see her wave him over. Jade stood back, watching as he answered her plea to buy lemonade from her little stand, which was set up next to a booth selling homemade candies. He dropped a few dollars into the girl's hand, took two cups from her, and gave one to Jade.

She took a sip and smiled at the girl while Liam doled out compliments on their behalf. He was surprisingly sweet with kids, which reminded her of how he'd taught her boys to paddleboard the weekend prior.

"I meant it when I thanked you for working with my boys on the paddleboarding," she said as they left the girl. "I appreciate it. You taught them much faster than I could have."

He downed his drink in one gulp and tossed his plastic cup into a recycle bin. "They're good kids. They're worried about you."

She creased her brow. Liam's time with her kids had been limited, and Jade had been there the entire time. Yet, she couldn't recall either of her boys saying they were worried. "Did they say that?"

"They didn't have to. I could see it in their eyes—the way they watched you to make sure you were okay."

A touch of pride mixed with sadness washed over Jade. "I

wish I could protect them from all this stuff with their dad. I know they're grown, but I hate this for them."

"They're okay. They're being strong for you. I could see that."

"They shouldn't have to do that."

Once again, he gave her that sympathetic look. For the briefest of moments, Jade felt herself falling for his charms. She looked away from him and chastised herself. Though she wasn't nearly as susceptible to his charms as others seemed to be, she was only human.

"I need to take my kale home."

"Hey," Liam said before she could walk around him. "Come kayaking with me tomorrow."

She was tempted, but she wasn't about to trust herself to be alone with him. Her heart had been broken, and hard as she was trying to move forward, she wasn't foolish enough to ignore how vulnerable she felt sometimes. Instead of sharing any of that with him, Jade simply shook her head and started around him. "I'm busy."

Putting his hand lightly on hers, he stopped her. "Come on, Jade. We'll have a blast. I can give you an unofficial tour of the best places on the lake."

She sighed. "I don't think that's a great idea."

He lifted his hands to show her his innocence. "I'm not asking for anything other than a few hours on the water. I know you're going through a breakup."

"A *divorce*. We weren't dating, Liam. I spent over twenty years of my life with that man."

"And look how he treated you."

Jade narrowed her eyes at him as if she could peel away

his layers and see what was underneath. "Are you trying to use my pain as a tool of seduction?"

"I'm trying to be your friend."

"Really?"

"Yes, and you aren't making it easy."

Standing taller, Jade stared at him. "Maybe I would make it easier if I knew whether or not I could trust you."

"You can trust me. We'll be in two separate boats. What do you think I'm going to do?"

"I don't think it would be wise for me to underestimate what you could do in two separate boats."

Liam laughed loudly. "All right. Suit yourself. I've already told Parker I'm taking a break and hitting the water around noon tomorrow. I'd like for you to join me. I think we'd have fun." He bowed slightly before turning into the sea of people navigating around the booths.

By the time he disappeared into the crowd, Jade already knew she'd take him up on his offer.

Jade set her bag on the counter at Tranquility Cabin and looked around the small space. She wasn't going to think of Liam's request as a date, because it wasn't. He'd asked her to hang out on the lake for a few hours. That wasn't a date. That was...hanging out on the lake. With a man who she figured would go kayaking with anyone willing. And she wasn't sure that statement was limited to actual kayaking. She also had no intentions of finding out for herself.

If that was the game he was playing, he would fail. Not only because she wasn't emotionally ready—or even remotely interested—in letting a man back into her life right now, but also because she wasn't ready on other levels. Her body may have healed, but her mind was still broken from the trauma of what cancer and the treatment had done to her. Liam could thank her scars all day long, but that didn't make her any more comfortable with them.

Even so, the excitement of exploring the lake with him caused a bright smile to cross her face. These types of adventures were not ones she'd ever had before, and she was really loving her time on the lake. Sure, she knew going out with Liam was likely to end with her rolling her eyes and setting boundaries he should be firmly aware of. But she also knew there were likely few people who knew as much about Chammont Lake as Liam. His time as a tour guide was definitely something she didn't mind taking advantage of.

She rushed from the cabin and headed next door to tell Darby about her plans. Undoubtedly, Darby would turn Jade's time with Liam into something it wasn't, or ever would be, but again, Jade didn't mind. Having Darby's lighthearted teasing was another aspect of being in Chammont Point that Jade had come to enjoy. Darby was quirky and strange, but even more, she was lovable. Jade was excited to have a friend to share things with, even if she would have to convince Darby her intent was not to have wild sex with Liam in the middle of Chammont Lake.

Imagining Darby's inevitable over-the-top reaction to the news she was about to share caused Jade to giggle. Darby had been trying to convince Jade to let her do a makeover. Jade expected this would give her one more opportunity to point out that Jade needed to update her makeup and hairstyle. She was climbing the steps when elevated voices came through the open windows. Jade's smile fell as she rushed up the stairs toward the entrance to Darby's cabin. Rather than knocking, Jade let herself in, as Darby tended to do.

Inside she found Darby and Taylor in a face-off. The tension in the cabin, which was only slightly larger than the one Jade was renting, was palpable. Jade practically felt the waves of anger surround her once she stepped inside. She had no idea what was happening, but Darby's bright red lips were set in a scowl as she narrowed her eyes at Taylor.

"I'm not doing it," Darby nearly shouted. "You can't make me."

Taylor threw her hands up in the air. "Well, you can't leave a broken ladder for your renters to climb, Darby, and you have to fix the roof before fall. It won't last another winter. These aren't things you can just ignore and hope they go away. They'll only get worse."

"I can't afford it, Taylor. You're going to have to find some other way."

"Ladies," Jade said.

She was ignored.

Taylor shrugged. "There is no other way, Darby. You can't rent a cabin that's a literal hazard to the occupants. You'll get sued. I guarantee you that not every tenant is going to be as understanding as Jade. You *cannot* rent that cabin knowing there are safety concerns."

Darby huffed and crossed her arms. "If I don't rent it, I can't pay to have it fixed."

"Poor financial planning on your part is not the concern of your tenants. That's on you to figure out."

"Taylor," Darby said as she stomped her foot.

"Welcome to the world of property management," Taylor

stated. "It's not all fun and games and terrible decorating decisions."

Darby's mouth fell open with her typical dramatic flair, and she pressed a hand to her chest as if she'd taken an arrow to the heart. "Bad decorating?"

"Terrible," Taylor stated. "I said *terrible*."

"Ladies," Jade said more forcefully, "what's going on?"

"She's no better than Eye Candy," Darby accused, pointing a long fingernail toward Taylor.

Jade needed a moment to remember that Eye Candy was the man who had given Darby a long and inaccurate assessment of repairs.

Taylor clenched her jaw and pressed her hands to her hips. "Darby, you never should have bought that dump in the first place. But now that you have it, you *have* to make the necessary repairs. Even if you don't want to."

"I don't have the money, Taylor. I can't do all that."

"Start small," Taylor suggested.

"Thousands of dollars for a new roof isn't small."

Taylor said, "Well, take out a loan like everyone else."

Darby pouted and let her shoulders sag. "I can't. I tried. My credit is too bad."

Taylor rolled her eyes and blew out her breath. "Then sell it before you get sued, Darby."

"Who would be dumb enough to buy that dump?" Darby asked and then blinked. "Oh. Me. Shit." After a few seconds, her pout switched to a kind of newfound determination. With a fierce shake of her head and a few muttered curse words, she grabbed the multipurpose lighter that was sitting next to an arrangement of candles on her counter. "That's it. I'm done with that mess. I'm burning it down."

"No, you're not," Taylor insisted.

"I have insurance. They'll pay to rebuild it. That will solve all my problems."

Jade blocked the door and held her hands up in a silent plea for Darby to be reasonable. "Not if you're in jail for arson."

Darby's red lips trembled as she looked imploringly at Jade. "I can't afford this."

Before Taylor could once again offer the insight that Darby never should have invested in the property, Jade blurted out, "I'll buy it. Sell it to me."

"*No*," Taylor practically yelled.

Darby's eyes lit with excitement. Behind her, Taylor waved her hands frantically and shook her head.

Jade ignored her. "I'm going to be here all the time anyway. I'll buy it. I'll do the repairs."

"Jade," Taylor warned, "you have no idea what you're getting into."

Darby threw the lighter carelessly aside, took two big steps, and grabbed Jade's hand. With a firm handshake, she smiled. "Deal."

"*Jade*," Taylor tried again.

"Sorry, Tay," Darby said as she draped her arm around Jade's shoulders. "It's done. We shook on it. Jade's buying the cabin *as is*. She can't back out. We shook on it."

"We shook on it," Jade said with a laugh as Taylor rolled her head back and screamed out with frustration.

"You are both preposterous," Taylor stated. "Do you know that?"

"We know," Darby said. "That's why we're the fun ones and you're *you*."

Taylor shook her head. "You have no idea what you're doing, Jade."

"Yes, she does. She's fixing it so we can be neighbors." Darby squealed and bounced excitedly. "*Forever.*"

Jade laughed and returned Darby's overzealous embrace. Taylor finally dropped her head down and eyed Jade with a blatant what-the-hell glare. Jade simply shrugged. This was her second chance. Life 2.0. Why not take a risk or two?

In fact, the idea of owning a cabin on the lake felt like the first right decision Jade had made in some time. Being in Chammont Point had been good for her. Getting out of her house and away from the reminders of the last year were turning out to be crucial breaks to keep her from spiraling into long bouts of self-pity. Owning the cabin was the next logical step in getting herself back on track with her life. Even if Taylor didn't agree, Jade was convinced this was the best option for all of them.

"I'm breaking out the champagne," Darby said. "Except for you, neighbor. You get cranberry juice." Darby rushed into her kitchen, and Taylor stepped into Jade's view.

"You cannot do this," Taylor said quietly.

"Taylor," Jade said calmly, "relax. I can afford to fix it up."

"It needs to be bulldozed."

Jade shrugged and said, "Well, I can afford to have it bulldozed and rebuilt."

Taylor shook her head. "I can't let you do this."

"Stop worrying so much," Jade said with a reassuring smile. "It's okay."

"It's not. This is a really bad idea, Jade."

Darby came out of the kitchen carrying three flutes. She hadn't been kidding about the champagne. "Here we go."

Taylor looked at the glasses but didn't take one. "I'm not toasting to this. This isn't a good thing."

"For whom?" Darby asked.

Taylor gawked at Jade for a few more seconds. "You're making a mistake, and I will not stand by and watch it happen," she said and stormed out, slamming the door behind her.

Darby twisted her lips and spat out, "If she's going to act like that, I don't think she should be my spare Thelma anymore."

"I'll talk to her," Jade said. "She's just worried about how much work the cabin needs."

"How much it needs for *you*. She doesn't care about me."

Jade accepted the glass of juice from Darby. "That's not true."

"Whatever." Darby drank the contents of one flute in a single gulp before toasting Jade with the other and shrugging. "I'm used to being the third wheel."

"You're not the third wheel," Jade insisted. "She's looking at this from the standpoint of a contractor. Once she calms down, I'll talk to her. It'll be okay."

The subtle dejection hanging over Darby wasn't something Jade was used to, and she wasn't quite sure how to bring back the woman's usual spunk. "I'm going out on the lake with Liam tomorrow," Jade said, testing to see if she'd get the excitement she was expecting.

Darby dropped down on her sofa and let out a dramatic sigh. "Wear sunscreen. And take extra water. It's supposed to be hot."

Jade sat on the coffee table and dipped her head to make eye contact with Darby. "Really? I'm going out on the lake with a man and your advice is to wear sunscreen and stay hydrated."

Darby shrugged and stuck her bottom lip out farther. "I'm not in the mood to tease you right now. Taylor hurt my feelings."

"Hey, things will work out with Taylor. She's just frustrated."

When Darby finally lifted her face to look at Jade, a sheen of unshed tears had filled her eyes. "This is why I don't make friends. They get fed up with me and leave."

"She's not going anywhere. We've bonded, remember?"

"Friends *always* leave," Darby said around her pout.

"I'm not going anywhere," Jade reassured her. She put her hand on Darby's and squeezed tight. "In fact, I'm moving in next door, remember? You're never getting rid of me."

Slowly, Darby's smile returned. "Yeah. That's going to be great."

"It *is* going to be great. We're going to have so much fun."

"Sleepovers and pillow fights in our jammies," Darby said.

Jade tilted her head but decided now wasn't the time to tell her that wasn't exactly what Jade had in mind. "Yeah. Sure."

Darby lifted her glass, sniffled, and blinked away her tears. "Congratulations, neighbor. Let me be the first to officially welcome you to Chammont Point."

Jade sat taller as a smile spread across her face. She clinked her glass to Darby's and said, "Thank you. I'm thrilled to be here."

TWELVE

JADE SHOVED her floppy hat on with one hand and carried a small cooler in the other as she followed Liam toward Chammont Lake. "I am capable of carrying my own kayak," she said.

"This is my job, Jade." He walked across the street with ease as if the kayaks on his shoulders weighed nothing. "I've got this. You don't have to worry about me."

"I wasn't worried. I was pointing out that I'm not helpless."

His tone was light with amusement when he responded. "That word would never cross my mind where you're concerned."

"Good," she said.

"However," he said as if he weren't even straining from the load he carried, "*stubborn* crosses my mind often."

Jade smirked. "Stubborn isn't the criticism that people seem to think it is. Being stubborn is actually a virtue."

"How so?"

They had just reached the water's edge when a bubbly

brunette smiled and practically cooed, "Hey, Liam," as she pranced by.

Jade's irritation immediately spiked. She rolled her shoulders back, set her jaw, and glared from behind her sunglasses. Venom raced to the tip of her tongue, but she caught it before enraged words could leave her mouth. For a moment, she was offended that this woman would dare to blatantly come on to Liam when he was clearly there with Jade. However, just as quickly, Jade reminded herself that, though they were standing together, they *weren't* together.

She had no reason to feel betrayed by him for responding to the attention of another woman. In fact, her response had been ludicrous. However, the flash of irritation was a strong reminder why she needed to steer clear of anything more than friendship with him, no matter how many times he batted his eyes and flashed his sweet smile.

Liam was a born flirt. Jade was in the process of divorcing her adulterous husband. Talk about pouring gasoline on a raging fire.

The hair-trigger reaction was also a reminder that as much as Jade told herself to let Nick go peacefully, as much as she told herself she had to simply keep moving forward, there were still red-hot embers of fury lingering beneath the surface. They wouldn't need much prodding to ignite something ugly inside her.

Jade wasn't setting herself up to get hurt again so soon. Instead, she made a mental note to picture herself throwing gas cans into a bonfire every time Liam tried to flirt with her. That would be a strong reminder of how things would end between them.

Blowing out a slow, measured breath, Jade forced the

unwarranted jealousy to leave her chest. As she did, she had a flash of Nick standing before her, looking half-ashamed and half-relieved that he'd told her he didn't love her anymore. The knife in her gut twisted.

Liam eased the kayaks down into the water and turned to smile at her as if he had proven some great point.

"Nice job, Hercules," she commented with more clip to her tone than intended.

His grin softened. "Are you okay?"

"Fine," she said.

He brushed his hands together as he glanced beyond her, likely at the woman sashaying away. Jade moved around him to one of the kayaks, hoping he didn't pick up on her ridiculous and unwarranted moment of jealousy.

"You were about to tell me how being stubborn is a virtue," he said.

"Oh, right. Being stubborn means I'm not a pushover. I can make a decision that is right for me or the situation and stand by it. That comes in handy."

He nodded. "I would agree with that."

Jade focused much more than necessary on pulling her paddle from the bungee cord. She'd done this plenty of times now. The movement was almost second nature. But she wasn't ready to look at Liam yet. She needed a few more minutes to clear her head. "Everyone thinks being stubborn means not willing to admit you're wrong or you refusing to budge. Sure, some people use the trait that way. But for me, it's the strength to put my needs above others when necessary." As soon as she said that, a hint of doubt kicked her in the gut. Wasn't that the reason Nick had left her? She had justified her willingness to put her career over her marriage because she was the breadwinner. Her job was the main source of income. She *had* to focus on her career—for her family. But maybe she was simply being stubborn. Self-centered. Single-minded.

Inhaling until her lungs couldn't hold any more of the fresh lake air, Jade forced the lingering question away. She'd apologized to Nick for that. While she'd been lying in a hospital bed recovering from surgery, she had sworn to him she would do better. She wasn't going to allow herself to spiral back into the cycle of beating herself up. Everyone made mistakes. Everyone had things in the past they'd like to change. She'd apologized to Nick and to her kids. Now she had to forgive herself and let that go.

Which, she was finding, was easier said than done.

Liam cocked his head ever so slightly. "Having a little internal debate with yourself there?"

"Don't try to read me," she warned.

"Because you're so complex?"

"I'm not complex. My life is right now." She pulled her sunglasses off and held his gaze. "This isn't going anywhere. You know that, right?"

"By anywhere you mean..."

"I'm not having sex with you, Liam. If that's what you're after."

Liam's chuckle was slow to rise, but when it did, his shoulders shook.

The heat of embarrassment started to creep up Jade's neck. His reaction made her wonder if she'd been thinking the wrong thing. Maybe Liam hadn't been flirting with her. Maybe he was just...obnoxious by nature. She didn't doubt herself often, but she'd done so twice in a matter of minutes and both times were because of him. Her dislike for him was beginning to grow again.

"I really admire how straightforward you are," he said. "You don't find that much these days."

The warmth settled on her cheeks. "There's no point in dancing around the truth. It comes out eventually, and lying only hurts people. Trust me. I know firsthand."

"I didn't bring you out here to seduce you. I just wanted to spend some time with you."

"Why?"

"I like you, Jade. I like how real you are. I don't know your story, not all of it anyway, but I want to."

She narrowed her eyes at him. "*Why*?"

Liam shrugged as he looked out at the lake. "Why not? Why do I need a reason to want to be your friend?"

"You don't. As long as you understand that I'm not looking for more than that."

"Understood." He took the cooler from her and set it on his kayak.

Jade put her sunglasses back on as awkward silence hovered between them. Part of her was sorry she'd rained on their trip, but she'd said what she needed him to know. She'd set the boundaries of their relationship and planted brightly colored flags so he didn't overstep.

Now that she was practiced at the art of getting into the raft, she was situated before he finished securing her cooler to his kayak. Within minutes, they were paddling toward the west side of the lake.

Several minutes into their trip, Liam asked, "How are you doing, Jade?"

"I'm keeping up."

"No. I mean, how are you doing with all the changes life is tossing at you?"

She considered his question. "I've accepted his choices, and I'm moving on the best I can."

He rested the paddle across his lap and focused on her. "That sounds absolutely clinical. How are you *doing*?"

She rested as well. "That varies day by day. Moment by moment, really. Taylor and Darby have been an unexpected blessing."

"Darby's something," he said with a smile.

Jade eyed him, waiting to see the meaning behind his words.

"When I first came to Chammont Point, she was into the eighties. Big hair and shoulder pads for days. I'm not sure what she's running from, but it must be something."

Jade shrugged. "We're all running from something, aren't we?"

The shadow of sadness in his eyes confirmed he was too. "That's life." With that, he started paddling again.

"I'm buying her rental cabin down in the cove," Jade said as she caught up to him. "The one where I've been staying. I plan on being in town a lot more. Renting doesn't make sense. I've been trying to decide if I want to buy a kayak or a paddleboard. I might do both. That way when the boys come with me, they each have something to take out on the water."

He glanced at her, and she suspected she still hadn't answered the heart of his question, but that was intentional. That was part of the boundary she'd set with him. Until she got her feet firmly on the ground, she intended to be careful around this man. *Any* man, actually.

"Sounds like you're keeping your chin up," Liam said.

"Well, the alternative is to crumble. I'm not willing to do that." She paddled harder so she was at his side instead of slightly behind him. "I fought hard to have this second chance at life. I'm not going to let my husband's bad choices ruin it for me. Besides," she said, looking out at a few birds diving toward the lake, "I don't want someone to stay with me out of some sense of obligation or because he pities me. It's better he moves on. As much as I hate him right now, I know once I'm able to finish processing my anger, I'll get to a place where I want us both to be happy."

"That's noble of you."

She grinned. "It's not noble. It's...realistic. Don't think for a minute I'll ever forgive him. I won't. His deception wasn't a spur-of-the-moment thing. He lied and deceived me, deliberately, for a very long time. I'm simply not willing to let my anger rule my life."

"That's a really good plan, but is it as realistic as you insist? How long were you together?"

"Over twenty years."

"That's a long time, Jade. The hurt he caused is going to linger longer than you think."

Digging her paddle into the water, she propelled herself forward faster in a purely symbolic motion. "I can't let it. I *refuse* to let it. I won't spend my life being bitter. What about you, Liam? What's your story?"

He gave her a lopsided grin. "I'm just a guy who owns a kayak shop on a beautiful lake."

Jade doubted his life was that simple but let his avoidance slide. He had a story, a past that had shaped him into the facade he presented to the world. Every once in a while, he dropped his sexy smirks and thin come-ons to reveal a genuine and kind soul. One that probably had as many dings and bruises as everyone else's.

Silence fell over them as Liam led them to the other side of the lake. As they neared an area with rocky cliffs, he told Jade about the landscape and history that had happened there. Rather than the heavier discussion of her divorce and current frame of mind, he recited facts like a well-learned tour guide. When they stopped close to a rock wall, he removed the bungee cord securing the cooler. In the shade of the sassafras tree branches hanging over the lake, he served the lunch she'd packed.

After taking a bite, he moaned his appreciation. "This is an amazing turkey sandwich."

"Thanks," Jade said with a smile. "It's my specialty."

"I thought that was kale."

She chuckled. "I have more than one."

He tossed a wink her way, and Jade sighed as she shook her head.

"You really need to stop falling back on that insufferable playboy persona. It's annoying as hell, Liam."

"Ouch," he said with a laugh. "And to think I just complimented your sandwich-making skills."

"I just mean...you don't always have to be on. You don't always have to be trying to woo people. I can see through your act, and it's starting to come across as sad."

He had the sense to look a little offended. "We all put on acts, Jade. You're putting on an act right now."

Creasing her brow, she asked, "How so?"

"Chin-up, march forward, pretend that your heart isn't crushed by your husband's betrayal."

"I'm not pretending," she argued. "I'm fully aware. But I

also know that my time in this world is limited. I'm not going to waste one precious day wondering why he did what he did. I know why. We'd grown apart, and he gave up instead of trying to make things better. I can't change that. I can't fix our marriage. Why would I cling to it?"

Liam toasted her with his bottle of water as his signature smirk returned. "Why, indeed? I'm glad you're so in touch with your feelings."

His sarcastic reply reignited the irritation she'd felt on the beach. She'd made a point in telling him she wasn't interested in a romantic relationship, but she was starting to realize she wasn't really interested in having a friend who constantly encouraged her to be angry either. She was trying to better herself, and being furious with Nick every waking moment was not taking her in the right direction. "You should try getting in touch with your feelings, Liam," she responded with the same flat tone. "Being honest with yourself is quite refreshing."

He capped his drink and met her gaze. "Are you being honest with yourself? Or are you ignoring your wounds, hoping they don't get infected?"

His words struck an unexpected nerve. Jade took a breath and sat taller. "I think you could ask yourself that question."

"I'm asking *you*," he said.

She was moments away from lashing out, but she exhaled and laughed lightly. This jerk had no right to question her mental and emotional well-being, especially when he was so obviously denying his own issues. No. She was not engaging in this conversation any longer.

"This has been interesting," she said, putting her

sandwich back into the baggie, "but I need to get out of the sun before I burn."

"Jade," he called as she dropped what was left of her lunch inside the kayak.

She ignored him and shoved her paddle into the water. He could easily catch up to her, but she didn't care. Getting into an argument with Liam wasn't on her list of things she wanted to do right now.

Or ever for that matter.

She'd admitted she was still processing her feelings about Nick's decision to leave her. She didn't need some faux Zen junkie telling her she wasn't doing that right. To hell with him for thinking she needed him to help her process her heartbreak.

Jade made it all the way to shore before looking back. Liam hadn't followed her. *Good.* She dragged her kayak the rest of the way out of the water, secured the paddle, and grabbed her lunch. She didn't have the smooth finesse that Liam used to lift the kayak, but she managed to carry it across the street without stumbling.

She dropped her kayak next to the rack just as Parker came out of the store.

"Where's Liam?" Parker asked.

"Burning in hell if I'm lucky," Jade snapped.

Parker didn't seem the least bit fazed by the response.

"How are you doing?" Jade asked with a softer tone.

Though Parker tended to avoid eye contact more than not these days, she diverted her eyes only for a moment before focusing on Jade again. "I'm okay. Thanks for asking."

"I'll see you later."

"See you later, Jade," she called as Jade headed toward her car.

She didn't make it far when she turned around and faced Liam's employee. "Hey. What is his problem anyway?"

"Who? Liam?"

"Yes, Liam. Batter of eyelashes and giver of smarmy smiles."

Parker giggled. "He's not as bad as he pretends to be. He's actually a good guy once you get to know him. I'm not sure what I would have done if he hadn't given me a job, even though I can't do much these days." She rested her hand on her belly. The way she waddled more than walked implied the baby would be coming soon. "You just have to give him a chance."

Jade glanced at the lake and saw Liam paddling toward shore. "Yeah, I did that. He still pisses me off. See you later," she said and left before she had to have another confrontation.

Jade set a glass of water on the counter and eyed Taylor, who had conveniently been examining the banister when Jade had returned to the cabin. However, Jade wasn't buying the accidental run in. Taylor had been waiting for Jade to return, and Jade was pretty sure she knew why. Taylor was horrified at the idea that Jade was buying this cabin and was going to try to talk her out of it.

Jade really wasn't in the mood for this, but with Taylor staring at her, clearly trying to find the right words, Jade knew she couldn't avoid the discussion. "I'm buying the cabin."

Taylor shook her head slightly. "You can't, Jade. Darby never even had an inspection. You have no idea what you're getting into, but I can tell you it's bad. It's *really* bad."

"I know."

"There could be mold or termites or plumbing issues," Taylor said, sounding desperate in her plea.

Jade sat at the table and gestured for Taylor to sit across from her. Once she did, Jade said, "I know this place needs a lot of work. I know it's a fixer-upper."

"It's way more than that. Darby has done nothing but put bandages over gaping wounds."

"I'll get an inspection," Jade assured her. "I'm not going into this blind, Taylor."

"But you *are*. You've already told her you'll buy this dump. She'll freak on you if you try to back out."

Jade shrugged. "I'm not going to back out."

Taylor sank back in the bench. "Whatever she tries to sell it to you for, it is too much. This place needs too much work."

Jade nodded. Everything about this place was on the verge of falling apart and while she appreciated Taylor's concern, Jade was frustrated Taylor wasn't giving her enough credit to understand what she was doing. "I can do it. I *want* to do it."

"No. Jade—"

"Listen," she stated firmly, "I like the location. I don't even mind how small this place is. The size is kind of refreshing, actually. I've lived in that big house for years. I don't want all that space anymore. It's too much. I want to start over with a more minimalistic lifestyle so I can focus on what's important. I want peace and quiet."

"There are dozens of other lakefront cabins you could buy."

"Yes," Jade said, "but I like this one. I like being on the cove where there aren't a lot of people. There aren't crowds in this part of the lake. I like that. And I like being next door to Darby. I've never had close friends before. I'm really looking forward to spending more time here with you guys. We've had some really good times, Taylor."

"Yes, but the roof—"

Jade scoffed at the amount of pushback she was getting. "I know. Look, when I get an inspection, if I'm told this place isn't worth fixing up, then I'll have it torn down and build something new. Right here, because this is where I want to be."

Taylor stared at Jade for a few seconds and gently said, "Jade, you're still reeling from Nick leaving you. You're feeling off-balance and uncertain. And you're making rash decisions. You need to take time to process all that you are going through before making any big decisions."

Jade frowned and sat back as she realized the heart of the matter wasn't the cabin. Nick. The issue was Nick. Just like Liam, Taylor thought her job was to tell Jade how to grieve for her dead marriage. Just like Liam, Taylor thought Jade wasn't *processing* things right.

"I am still reeling," Jade stated, trying to sound calmer than she felt, "but I have to start my life over. I can't wait until I come to terms with *his* affair. I refuse to waste my life hanging on to someone who doesn't want me. I have to start moving forward, and this is the perfect place to do that."

Taylor pressed her lips together, as if debating her next move. "What about your job, Jade? Your house? Your kids? You have to remember your decisions have ripple effects."

"I can commute to my job. I'm selling my house anyway. And my *fully grown* children know they can count on me, but they are adults now. I don't have to measure every decision I make on how it impacts them. Any other personal issues you'd like me to clarify?" she asked, letting her frustration slip.

Taylor sat back. "You're really getting mad at me for looking out for you?"

"No, I'm getting mad because you're treating me like a child who can't make her own decisions. And, to be frank, I'm a little pissy about how you're going about making your point. Darby thinks you're throwing her under the bus on this cabin thing."

Taylor crossed her arms. "Because I'm honest about what a shithole this place is?"

"Because she felt like you were choosing me over her," Jade snapped. "She's been hurt, Taylor. We've all been hurt. We need to be more careful with each other."

"I'm not going to let you get screwed over because she can't deal with adulthood."

Jade lifted a brow. "It's not your job to save me. I know this place is a dump. I'm going in with my eyes wide open."

"She's rubbing off on you," Taylor said softly. "You're making bad decisions without thinking them through. You're being reckless. You have to think ahead, Jade. You need to look at what you're getting into before you jump. You're being irresponsible."

Jade shook her head. "If I didn't have the ability to invest in the cabin, I would be acting irresponsibly. I can afford to fix the cabin or build a new one, if needed. I'm not being irresponsible, Taylor. I'm living my life for the first time ever. I'm making decisions for *me*, not for the children who don't need me any longer or a husband who has been secretly plotting to leave me for who knows how long. I only have to worry about myself. This is what *I* want."

Taylor looked at her with the same kind of pity Liam had when he'd found out she was in remission.

"Jade," Taylor said sadly, "you don't know that. You haven't spent enough time in Chammont Point to know if you want to live here. You might not even like it once you get here."

Jade stared across the table, not completely understanding where Taylor was coming from. Like Darby and Liam, she sensed there was more to the story than she was seeing. Maybe if the conversation didn't feel so tense, Jade would push and pry, but at the moment, she was simply tired of having to defend herself. "Well, if it isn't, then I'll leave."

"Just like that?" Taylor asked.

"Yeah. Just like that. I'm not hurting anyone."

"Except yourself."

Frowning, Jade lifted her hands to show her lack of concern. "At least I would have tried, Taylor. What else am I going to do? Go home to a big empty house and wonder why he didn't love me? Work countless hours for more things I don't want or need? Maybe I won't find what I'm looking for in Chammont Point, but I already know it isn't in Fairfax, so why shouldn't I try living here?"

Taylor twined her fingers together and looked at them for

a few seconds before lifting her gaze. "Is it true that you went on a date with Liam today?"

"It wasn't a date. We went kayaking."

"Do you really think that's a good idea? You're clearly feeling vulnerable."

Furrowing her brow, Jade repeated, "*Vulnerable*?"

"Jade, you're acting carelessly. You are not thinking things through. You're going to get yourself hurt."

Just like Liam had earlier, Taylor's words struck something raw inside of Jade. "I consider us friends. I really do. But you don't know me well enough to be dishing out this lecture."

"It's not a lecture."

"It is, and I don't appreciate it. Yes, I am going through a lot of changes right now, but I'm a big girl. I can handle making my own choices, and I *can* handle Liam, just to be clear."

Sadness filled Taylor's eyes. "You're going to get hurt."

"If I do, that's my business," Jade said more sharply than intended. "I'm not seeking your approval. On whom I see or what I buy."

Taylor shook her head slightly. Jade recognized that move. It was one of a parent fed up with trying to talk reason into a petulant child. Again, Jade's anger piqued. She inhaled slowly to stop herself from saying something she'd regret.

"Okay. You don't need my approval. But you *are* going to need a different contractor, because there is absolutely no way I'm getting involved in this mess. Good night and good luck." She slid from the table and headed for the door.

Jade considered calling out to stop her friend from leaving, but the words wouldn't form. She sat in silence, replaying her crap-tastic day over and over in her mind. She'd be leaving for Fairfax the next afternoon, and she didn't want to go home with two disagreements weighing on her.

At first Jade was too shocked at how the conversation had turned. But then she thought maybe Taylor was right, maybe she was being too spontaneous. She had been through a lot lately, and jumping into buying the cabin probably *was* a little bit irresponsible, but buying this place felt right. Jade leaned against the table and contemplated what had led to the argument with Taylor.

As she looked around the cabin, she wished she had someone other than Darby and Taylor to talk to about the things happening in her life. This would usually be a discussion she would have had with Nick, but she didn't think she should rely on him for that any longer.

What would she say? *Hey, honey, I had a terrible day. It turns out you leaving me for someone else is having a deeper impact on me than I've been telling myself, and apparently I'm spiraling out of control.*

A wry laugh left her, and she shook her head.

She really had screwed herself over by being so narrowly focused for so long. She could call her dad, but he was already worried about her. Ever since she'd told him about her impending divorce, he'd been pushing her to slow down and reconsider every step she made...much like Taylor had.

Her mom tended to get quiet and usually ended up crying. Jade didn't need that any more than she needed someone offering advice on how she should be dealing with her divorce.

Jade grabbed her phone off the counter, curled up on the

sofa, and scrolled through her contacts until she settled on calling her oldest son. She waited, expecting the call to go to voice mail as it usually did, but Xander answered.

After a few minutes of catching up, Jade ran her idea by him. She was going to buy the "shit shack" they'd rented in Chammont Point with the intent of remodeling. As soon as she finished her sales pitch, she waited, expecting him to tell her it was a terrible idea.

"That's cool," he said instead.

"Cool?"

"Yeah. Owen and I had a really good time on the lake, Mom. Once you get the ladder fixed so we don't risk our lives climbing it, we'll come visit. That'd be awesome."

Jade's smile spread and her confidence returned. Xander and Owen had enjoyed their time with her on the lake. They thought this was cool. That was all she needed to hear. She didn't care what Taylor said or what her father would say. She was doing it. She was buying Tranquility Cabin. "That would be *incredibly* awesome," she said.

"Have, um... Have you talked to Dad this week?"

Jade blinked a few times, surprised by his question. "No."

"Oh, um..."

"What?" she pressed.

"He called me and Owen to let us know he'd signed the divorce papers. I thought maybe he'd told you too."

Jade's heart felt like a boulder falling out of a plane. "Oh. I suppose I'll be hearing from my attorney soon, then."

"I'm still pissed at him," Xander said.

"I have my moments too, but that's not going to change anything."

Xander was quiet for a few seconds. "He wants us to meet her."

Jade held her breath. "He seems to care for her very much—"

"Don't, Mom. Owen and I have talked about it. We know we have to do this, but it's too soon. We'll meet her when we're ready. I just wanted you to know because... I don't know why, but I don't want to feel like I'm keeping his secrets from you."

Jade blinked. Tears started to form in her eyes. "I appreciate that, but this isn't your mess, kiddo. You aren't responsible for your dad's actions, and it isn't your job to protect me. I need you to know that. I don't want you to feel like you're stuck in the middle."

"It's kind of hard not to."

"I know," she said gently, "and I'm sorry for that."

Another lingering silence filled the call. Xander redirected the conversation back to the cabin, the lake, and wondering how soon they could visit again. Jade was thankful for the distraction, but the resentment she was so determined not to feel had started simmering in the back of her mind.

THIRTEEN

JADE HAD JUST TURNED on the shower to warm the water and wash away an absolutely horrid day when someone knocked on the front door of her cabin. Her first instinct was to ignore whoever had come calling so late in the evening, but then she recalled Darby's insecurity and Taylor's frustration. Whatever had brought one of them over at this hour likely needed to be addressed, and the sooner the better.

After turning the water off, Jade wrapped herself in her swimsuit cover since she didn't have a robe at the cabin and walked to the door. As soon as she yanked it open, her stomach clenched. "Liam? What are you doing here?"

He gave her one of his sly smiles as he held up her cooler. "You forgot this in the midst of your tantrum."

Jade narrowed her eyes at him and reached for the cooler. Before she could grip the handle, he pulled it from her reach. She crossed her arms, leaned against the doorjamb, and scowled at him. "You accuse me of having a tantrum and then play keep-away. I'm not sure you're equipped to accurately assess my level of maturity."

"Invite me in," he said.

She looked down at her knee-length wrap. Though the teal material covered all the essential areas, it barely did so. The area where the material crisscrossed left a precariously high slit between her thighs and, while the front of the top looked more like a sun dress, the back was open down to her waist. Though Liam had no way of knowing, Jade was keenly aware that she was naked underneath the thin material. "I'm not dressed for company."

"So get dressed." With that, he slid by her into the small living area of the cabin. "I'll wait."

She closed the door. "I didn't invite you in," she stated as she turned around.

Liam set her cooler on the counter and slowly took in the cabin. "We got off on the wrong foot when we met. I thought we were making progress toward righting that until you paddled away today."

"You know what," Jade said flatly, "I've been through a lot lately, and I simply do not have the patience to deal with someone who wants to cast stones to distract from their real problems."

He smirked. "Isn't that what you're doing? Pretending to pick yourself up and carry on as if your divorce is just one more hurdle to overcome."

God, he knew how to light her fuse. Jade inhaled slowly, determined to not go yet another round with him. "Nick made his choice. I can't change that, and I'm not going to wallow in something I can't change. My choice to pick myself up and carry on is the only *choice* he left me."

"Stop with the tough guy act, Jade," Liam said. "Having someone end a decades-old relationship is soul shattering. You don't just dust yourself off and keep going."

"Oh, really?" she asked with a sarcastic lilt. "What should I do, Liam? How should I behave to appease *you*?"

He put his hand to his heart and creased his brow. "You feel it, Jade. You were lied to. You were cheated on. That hurts. Let it hurt. Be angry. Cuss and throw things. But don't just smile, go on an adventure, and act like you're fine."

She leaned closer and blinked several times. "Wait. I told you my husband was leaving me. I never said he'd cheated. How do you... Darby," she said. "Darby told you. Why would she do that?"

He shrugged. "I asked."

"Why?"

"Because I was curious," he said as if that were the most obvious answer in the world.

"Well, don't be curious about me, Liam. It's not your place."

He cocked his head. "It's not my place? I didn't realize I needed permission to want to know more about you."

"If you wanted to know more about me, you'd ask me, not my friend. Getting to know someone is a two-way street. Otherwise it's just you taking a shortcut to get wherever the hell you're trying to get."

The muscles in his jaw flexed like he was biting back the words he wanted to say. "The thing I've noticed about you, Jade," he said after a few tense seconds, "is that you avoid the pain of your past like you can outrun it. You can't. It will be there. Nick's affair, your cancer, those things won't ever leave you. They are part of you now. You have to..."

"Thank them?" she asked sarcastically. "Thank Nick for breaking my heart and cancer for nearly killing me?"

"Not Nick. Not the cancer," he said softly. "Thank the lessons, Jade. Thank life for what you learned. Thank whatever force is pushing you, for the understanding that you've found, the strength you've found. Until you can do that, you aren't moving on. You're simply avoiding. That isn't healthy."

Jade heard his words, but she was too enraged to actually *hear* them. "Thank *you*, Liam, for teaching me that I should be more careful of the company I keep."

Liam stared at her as if he didn't know how to respond. Jade wasn't going to allow herself to be swayed by his puppy dog eyes and pouty lips. She'd fought with Taylor. She'd fought with Liam. She'd found out her husband had not only signed divorce papers, but he couldn't even wait for Jade to officially be out of his life before trying to introduce her kids to his girlfriend.

The unexpected prick of tears forced her to roll her eyes and look away. "You need to leave."

He sighed and raked his hand over his hair. "Jade, I don't know what I did to make you hate me—"

"I don't hate you."

"Well, you don't seem to like me very much."

"I've had a bad day...*year*... I don't need you confronting me because I'm not following your life mantras. You don't know me. You don't know anything about me. You don't get to tell me how to recover."

He lowered his face. His shoulders sagged. "I guess I misread you."

"I guess you did," she said and turned back toward the door to show him out.

He gently grabbed her arm and stopped her. "I thought you needed a friend. I wanted to be that for you. I know what it's like to have to start over with nothing. You're standing on the edge of a precipice, putting on a brave face, but I can see that you're terrified and hurt and all those other things that make a person feel weak. You're not weak, Jade. You're hurt. There's a difference. I wanted to help."

The tears she'd been fighting ever since her call with Xander filled her eyes and trickled down her cheeks.

Liam dragged his thumb across her cheek. "Let me help," he all but begged.

Jade ground her teeth together. How dare he put voice to the truth she'd been ignoring? How dare he shine light on the monsters hiding under her bed? That wasn't his place.

But he was right. To a point. She wasn't avoiding and ignoring her pain, but she was keeping the pain in a cage in the corner of her mind. Liam wiped another tear from her cheek, and in that moment, she didn't care if he was gasoline and she was fire and this was going to burn them both. As he looked down at her with concern in his eyes and tenderness on his face, her anger gave way to something else. Stupidity.

Jade threw her arms around him and pressed her mouth to his. She hadn't changed her mind about him. She still thought he was a womanizer who shouldn't be trusted with her heart, but she didn't care. Not when, once again, she felt like her world was crumbling around her.

Only a few seconds passed before Jade realized Liam wasn't reciprocating her kiss. She leaned back and met his wide-eyed gaze. Okay. She'd taken him by surprise. Now that he was expecting her advances, she tried again.

Liam put his hands on her hips and pushed her back. "This isn't why I came here."

"Oh really?" she asked with a disbelieving scoff.

"I was worried about you."

Jade's lips fell into a frown as once again she found herself feeling embarrassed in front of him. She didn't know why she'd kissed him, but his rejection was the last bit of bullshit she could handle. The irritation that had been brewing turned into raw anger—anger at Taylor for treating Jade like she was too stupid to know what she was getting into with the cabin, anger at Nick for leaving her, and absolute fury at Liam for toying with her for the last few weeks only to push her away when she reciprocated.

"I think we could be friends," Liam continued as she pulled away from him, "but I don't get why you keep giving me the cold shoulder."

"Because of this," she said with a tense voice. "I knew you were playing games with me."

"What games?" he asked, sounding like he had the right to be fed up with her. He was the one who had come here, well into the evening hours, smiling and wiping her cheeks dry.

"You've been coming on to me from the moment we met—"

"I've been nice to you," Liam corrected.

"Please don't act like you don't know how you treat women. Like we're disposable. Like we're toys you can play with and throw away when you're done." She poked his chest with her pointer finger. "You did not show up here at ten o'clock at night to bring me a cooler and tell me you want to be my friend. You're playing head games, and I'm not in the mood for them."

"Okay, this is..." he said calmly, "this is getting heated and I don't think it's all directed at me. I can take it, but you need to recognize that this isn't about me as much as it is about your divorce."

She wanted to tell him to go to hell, but he wasn't wrong. She wasn't going to admit anything, however, not when she was so angry. Her day had finally taken its toll, and she was close to erupting.

"Look," Liam continued, "I admit that I'm a flirt. It's who I am. But you...you have to know I'm not here to get you into bed. Don't you?"

Jade considered his words for a few moments. "You know what really bothers me about you, Liam?"

"Somehow, I don't think it's my endless charms and boyish good looks," he muttered.

"You're fake," she said, her words dripping with accusation. "Your smiles and your winks and your smooth approach... They're fake. *You're* fake. And I'm really not in a place where I want to be around people who lie as easily as they breathe. I spent a year fighting for my life while my husband talked about a future he knew damn well he wasn't going to be a part of. His lies might have had some noble intention, but they were fake, and I simply have no room for that kind of bullshit anymore."

Liam stared for several seconds before saying, "I didn't realize I offended you so much."

"Well, you do."

"Okay," he said softly. "Message received."

"Good." She walked to the door and opened it in a silent gesture for him to leave.

He made it all the way to the porch before turning around and holding her gaze. "Take some time for self-reflection, Jade. I'm not sure you're as real as you like to think."

Rather than responding, she closed the door in his face and turned the deadbolt. "Jerk," she muttered and headed back to the bathroom. She turned the shower on again, stripped down, and stepped in before the water had a chance to completely warm up. The cold water was a shock, causing her to gasp. As soon as the surprise wore off, however, the emotional outburst she'd had washed over her.

She heard Liam's words, saw the hurt in his eyes, and confusion filled her mind. Not just at her actions, but his. The mixed signals he'd been sending were too much. She couldn't sort them out when she was such a tangled mess herself.

Pressing her palms against the shower wall, Jade braced herself as a sob welled in her chest and burst forth. For about five minutes, she'd felt like she had her life together. For about five minutes, she thought she could pick herself up and move on. And why shouldn't she? Nick had moved on. Nick had moved on a long time ago.

And Taylor? Even though Jade cared about her, maybe it was best if Taylor walked away and left Jade and Darby to their unique friendship. Jade could find a different contractor to make the cabin what she wanted it to be. She and Darby could sit in the cove drinking juice out of fancy glasses and ignoring what the world thought of them.

And Liam? Liam could go straight to hell. She didn't need

someone, even a friend, who couldn't stop twisting and turning things around.

Despite telling herself all those things, another cry escaped Jade and misery filled her chest.

CHAMMONT POINT

Jade hadn't slept a wink. She finally rolled from her bed and wrapped herself in a blanket to sit by the cove as the sun rose. A layer of fog hovered just above the water as she put another log on the fire she'd built. The fire wasn't quite warm enough to ward off the chill of the morning, but she refused to go back inside. Every time Jade walked into the living room, she remembered what an ass she'd made of herself the night before.

She'd thrown herself at Liam. After accusing him of being a player, after accusing him of toying with her, she'd been the one to blatantly make a move. He was the one who threw cold water on the moment to stop her from doing something she'd regret.

God. What an idiot she'd been! What an absolute fool.

"You look cold," Darby said softly. "I made you some hot tea."

Jade smiled when she was offered a cup. "Thank you. You're up awfully early."

Darby shrugged. "I was worried."

"About what?"

Darby sat in the chair next to her and pressed her hands together. Even though it wasn't even seven in the morning, she'd taken time to put on a thick layer of makeup and curl her hair. Jade was beginning to wonder if she really did wake up looking like that.

"You're going to change your mind, aren't you?" Darby asked. "About buying the cabin. You're going to back out."

Jade offered her a soft smile and shook her head. "No. I'm not."

"Even though Taylor doesn't want you to?"

"It's not Taylor's decision, Darby. It's mine. The only thing I'm starting to second-guess is if I should move here. I might just use it on the weekends."

Darby looked at her hands. "Why? I thought you wanted to be here."

"I think I just..." Jade blew out a long breath. "Taylor's right about one thing. I'm not thinking clearly. Despite my determination to keep myself together, I'm kind of falling apart. I did something really stupid and embarrassing."

"What?"

Jade winced and pulled the blanket closer around herself. "I don't want to talk about it."

Darby sagged. "Come on, Jade. I'm the queen of doing stupid and embarrassing things. Maybe I can help you sort through it."

"Liam stopped by last night."

A dramatic gasp filled the air. "You shagged him?"

"*No*," Jade stated. "God, no. But"—she frowned as she considered how far things would have gone if Liam hadn't put an end to her advances—"I kissed him."

Again, Darby gasped with all the melodrama of a soap opera actress. "You didn't. *Jade*! Why? What happened?" She scooted her chair closer and tried to hide her excited smile. "Tell me everything."

Despite Darby's enthusiasm, Jade's mood sank a few notches. "Well, after going out on the lake with Liam, he pushed the wrong button and I paddled away like a defiant toddler. Then Taylor showed up and we had a few words about the cabin." She glanced at Darby. "Which is not your fault, so don't feel bad about that."

"If you say so," Darby muttered.

"Then I talked to my son and he told me that Nick signed the divorce papers."

"Oh," Darby said. "I'm sorry."

Jade sighed. "Nick wants our boys to meet his girlfriend."

"Yuck."

Burrowing deeper into her blanket, Jade frowned. "Yeah. So I was feeling really crappy and...Liam showed up at the cabin."

Leaning closer, Darby asked, "So you kissed him?"

"Well, I told him I didn't like him very much and we had a pretty heated exchange. Then I kissed him."

Darby's eyebrows shot up. "What did he do?"

Jade felt heat settling in her cheeks. "He rejected me."

"Liam?" she asked with wide eyes.

"I know, right?" Jade laughed softly. "I told him he was fake and made him leave. But, of course, after he did, I realized he was right. I have been acting like an idiot. I made a fool of myself, Darby." Rubbing cold fingertips into her forehead, Jade confessed, "I feel so humiliated."

"I'm so sorry, Jade. Just remember that you've been going through a lot. You're not thinking clearly. You acted in a way that lots of people do. I know that doesn't make it better, but sitting here beating yourself up isn't going to change it. It happened. All you can do is what you've been doing since you got to Chammont Point. You have to keep moving forward."

Jade nodded. "Yeah. Easier said than done. I was mean to him, and he didn't deserve that."

Darby ran her hand over Jade's arm soothingly. "We all have bad days sometimes. I'm sure he'll understand. Listen, I want you to know that if you decide not to buy the cabin, it's okay. You don't have to do that if you don't want to. I'll figure something out. I always do."

"I'm buying the cabin, Darby. That's the only thing I do have clarity on. I want to." Jade smiled at her friend. "My life has been hell lately, but you know what? Having you to talk me through it has been the best thing that's happened to me in a long time."

Darby smiled and wiped a tear from her cheek. "Me too. I'm glad you'll be my neighbor. If you decide you only want to spend weekends here, I'll keep an eye on the cabin for you."

"Thanks."

At the sound of a vehicle door closing, Darby and Jade turned toward the driveway. Taylor, with a bag and a drink carrier in hand, headed toward them. Her steps were slower than usual. She tended to take long, determined steps. But this morning, she moved hesitantly down the gravel walkway toward the sitting area.

"Maybe I should go," Darby said and started to stand.

"Stay," Jade insisted.

"I don't think she—"

"She has three drinks, Darby," Jade pointed out. "I bet one is for you."

Darby sat back, but her discomfort was obvious. Jade had

suspected Darby's class clown act was to hide her fragile feelings, but she hadn't realized how deeply those insecurities ran. Seeing her friend shrink like a flower wilting before her eyes made Jade's heart ache.

"Hey," Taylor said, sounding as uneasy as Darby looked, as she approached the sitting area. "You guys couldn't sleep either, huh?"

"Not much," Jade said. She looked at Darby, who had averted her eyes.

"I brought iced coffee for you, Darby. The kind with whipped cream, sprinkles, and extra chocolate syrup. Just how you like it." She held the drink holder out like an olive branch.

Darby hesitantly took one of the cups from the holder. "Thank you."

"Green tea for you, Jade," Taylor said. "I guess you have some already."

Jade smiled extra wide, like she tended to do when she was trying to encourage Darby. "You can never have too much tea. Thank you, Taylor." The tension between the three of them was stifling. Jade hated how much stress they were all clearly feeling. The friendship that had formed between them was something she had come to cherish. The three of them had spent weeks having fun adventures, trying new things, and getting to know each other. It was too soon for that to fall apart.

"Sit," Jade told Taylor. "It's a little chilly, but we can put more wood on the fire."

"I'm okay." Taylor hesitated before sitting in the chair she tended to occupy when they were hanging out next to the lake. She dug into the bag and handed Darby a pastry and

Jade a cup of sliced fruit. Then she fidgeted for several moments before she glanced at Jade. "I um... I owe you both an apology. Darby," she said, "I'm sorry I was a jerk about you selling the cabin to Jade. I didn't mean to be. I was just..."

"Looking out for Jade," Darby said. "I get it."

"I know it came across that way, but that wasn't what I intended. You got screwed when you bought that place, too. I'm mad for both of you."

"You think I'm passing my problems off to someone else," Darby said. "I guess I am. That's what I do." She shrugged. "I've never been good at sticking things out when the going gets tough."

"Darby, I *want* to buy the cabin," Jade said. "I know it's a mess. I'm okay with that. Worst-case scenario, I knock it down and start from scratch. I'm going to have an inspection, like Taylor suggested, and then I'll decide what to do. But no matter what I'm told, I'm still buying the cabin."

"I didn't mean to make you feel bad, Darby," Taylor said. "I don't really know how to talk to people." She shrugged as her cheeks turned red. "I spent too much time around construction crews, I guess. I've never really had female friends, and sometimes I... Sometimes I'm too hard. I know that. I didn't mean to sound so harsh. I'm sorry."

"It's okay," Darby said.

Taylor shook her head. "No, it's not. I'm going to try harder to not be so...*me*. Forgive me?"

The smile returned to Darby's face. "Yeah. Of course. We're friends, right?"

"Yeah. We're friends."

Jade lifted her tea in a toast. "Yes, we are."

"I'm sorry for talking to you that way too, Jade," Taylor

said. "I know you're smart enough to make this decision. Just because it's not what I would do doesn't mean I should talk to you like you don't know better. I just..." She rolled her eyes back and blinked in an obvious attempt to not cry. "I just really need you guys to give me another chance. I promise I'll do better."

"No," Darby cooed as she stood. She rushed around the fire pit to Taylor's side and hugged her. She pulled Taylor's head to her chest and gave her a squeeze. "No crying. I spent half an hour on my makeup."

Taylor sniffled before muttering, "Get your boobs out of my face, Darby."

"Oh," Darby said, leaning back to give Jade a wink, "nobody's ever said that to me before."

Jade laughed, happy to see that they were back to bantering already. "We all have issues we're working through. Let's agree to be a little bit more tolerant of each other."

"Agreed," Darby said.

"Agreed," Taylor chimed in.

Jade took a deep breath. "Good, and now that we're all back to being friends, you guys have got to help me fix this thing with Liam. As much as I'd love to simply avoid him forever, that isn't possible if I'm going to be in Chammont Point. I have to face this, and I... Ugh. I don't know what to do."

Taylor looked from Jade to Darby and back again. "What thing? What happened?"

Darby's smile widened, and she rubbed her palms together. "Oh, you're going to love this."

FOURTEEN

JADE PARKED OUTSIDE LAKEFRONT RENTALS, and a rock settled in her gut. Though Taylor and Darby had made plenty of jokes at Jade's expense after she gave them a detailed recount of her failed attempt at seducing a seducer, they also helped her formulate a proper apology. The hard part was going to be delivering it. They had offered to go with her and wait in the car in case she needed on-the-spot support. But this was a mess Jade had made on her own, and she had to fix it on her own.

However, as she stared at the store knowing Liam was inside, she wished she'd accepted the offer.

"Woman up," she muttered to herself as she exited her car. She dug deep for mettle to walk to the door, but once there, she felt her courage wither. Her heart began to pound, and her stomach turned upside down. Her knees grew weak, and the lump in her chest grew, making her breath come in shallow bursts.

Fear. She knew this well. Closing her eyes, she reminded herself what Taylor had said several times: The worst thing that could happen was he could tell her he didn't accept her apology and she had to find a new place to rent a paddleboard for the rest of the summer. Though she felt bad and hoped she could fix this, she and Liam didn't have some long history that was going to be erased if he didn't forgive her.

She barely knew him. Who cared what he thought of her?

The reality was, Jade cared. She'd lashed out and felt terrible, and she wanted him to know she wasn't the type of person who acted the way she had the night before.

Though she didn't want to, Jade opened the door and walked into Liam's store. She saw him at the back, restocking a shelf, and looked back at the door. She could still make her escape unnoticed.

"Hey, Jade," Parker called from behind the counter. She smiled and waved with the same greeting she used for everyone.

Liam stopped moving but didn't turn around.

"Hey, Parker," Jade said and gave her a smile in return, though Jade suspected hers came out more like a grimace.

Parker glanced between Jade and Liam, clearly picking up that something wasn't quite right. The last Parker had heard, Jade was furious at Liam and had wished the man's soul to an eternity of torment. Theoretically, unless Liam ran his mouth, Parker had no idea that the tides had turned and Jade was now in the wrong. Jade didn't figure Liam to be the type to run his mouth.

Moving to the back of the store, Jade stopped at Liam's side. "Hi."

"Hey," he said without looking at her.

"We need to... Can we talk about last night?"

He added another bottle of sunscreen to the shelf. "Do you mean the part when you threw yourself at me or the part when you threw me out for refusing your offer?"

Ouch. His pointed words hit the mark and made her already shaky ego crumble. "I mean when you very nicely turned me down instead of taking advantage of me. I was in a bad place last night, and you saw that. You could have used that against me, but you didn't. Thank you."

He didn't answer. He continued shelving the bottles until she grabbed one from his hand and waited for him to look at her.

"Liam, don't act like an ass," she said. "That's my job."

He rested his hand on the shelving unit and shook his head. "Do you know how ridiculous it was for you to be mad that I didn't take advantage of you?"

"Yes, I do. I was confused," she said softly. "I don't like being confused. Uncertainty isn't something I'm used to. I should be by now, but I'm not. You were pointing out things that I didn't want to see, and I didn't respond well. Throwing myself at you, stupid as it sounds now, made me feel like I was taking control of something. I see now that was...wrong. To put it mildly."

Liam grabbed a few more bottles of lotion from the box on the floor and shoved them carelessly onto the shelf. He roughly snagged the box and carried it out of the shop with her following behind. After crushing the cardboard, he shoved it into a recycling bin and spun to face her. "You said some pretty shitty things, not just last night but while we were out on the lake. You don't know me at all, Jade."

233

"Maybe not, but I do know you're playing games," she accused.

He shook his head at her. "I'm not playing games."

"Bullshit," she said pointedly. "You smile and wink and say the most inappropriate things, but then you—"

"Treat you with respect when you need it most? Goddamn, I'm an asshole," he snapped.

She stood taller. He was mad? He'd been throwing mixed signals at her for weeks and *he* was mad? "Yes," she stated. "You kind of are."

"Because I wouldn't sleep with you?"

"Because you've been trying to sleep with me for weeks and when I say yes, you say no. You *are* a fake."

"Is this your idea of an apology, lady?"

"I'm apologizing for my behavior, but that doesn't mean you get a free pass on yours. The last thing I need in my life is another man pretending to care about me to spare my fucking feelings."

"Whoa," Parker said, skidding to a stop. She hovered by the door, wide-eyed. "I think it's time for my break."

"No," Liam ordered. "You stay." He pointed at Jade. "You come with me."

He led her to the stacks of canoes and grabbed one. "Get the oars," he ordered. When she didn't obey, he blew out his breath. "*Please*. I'd like to have this conversation in private, and I'm not giving you the chance to paddle away from me when you get called out for your bullshit too."

She grabbed the oars and followed him across the street to the lake. They climbed in, and Liam rowed. After several minutes, he stopped and looked around at the vast water and trees in the distance.

"I'm not the kind of guy who takes advantage of women, Jade. I would have hoped you'd know that. I know I..." His words faded, and he blew out a long breath before starting again. "I tease and I flirt, but I'd never take advantage of you. I'm sorry you thought otherwise."

Heat touched her cheeks. "I don't think that about you."

"Apparently you do."

"No. I'm... My marriage is ending without warning, and yesterday... Finding out Nick signed the divorce papers was not something I was prepared to deal with. I was thrown for a loop. I knew it was coming. I had just buried my head and ignored it. Like you said I was doing. Finding out he'd taken that step hurt. I was feeling discarded and wanted someone to make me feel worthy for a while. You were there, and when you used common sense—"

"When I respected you," he clarified.

"When you showed me the respect that I deserve," she agreed, "I overreacted. I'm sorry. I'm very, very sorry, not only for the mean things I said but for the way I treated you when you turned me down."

"Apology accepted. Thank you. And for the record, you are worthy. You're incredibly worthy. I'm sorry he hurt you like he did, but that doesn't make you disposable. You're not. If that's what you think—"

"You don't know what I was like before I got sick," she said quietly. "I was self-centered and narrowly focused. I wasn't..." She swallowed hard before voicing a truth she hadn't wanted to face. "I understand why he cheated on me."

Liam was quiet for an unbearably long time. "Whatever you've been through, whoever you were before, those things made you who you are now. And you're worthy. You need to hear that."

Jade shook her head as the familiar prick of tears bit her eyes. "Please don't give me a pep talk."

"You need one."

"No. I don't know what I need, but a pep talk from a shaggy-haired wannabe surfer isn't it." She grinned, hoping he'd realize she was teasing him.

He smiled too, but his smile wasn't sincere. "Remember that really bad ice storm we had six years ago? The entire state was covered."

"Yeah." She wondered where he was going with that.

"My fiancée was killed in a car accident in that storm. A truck came around a curve and hit her head on. He couldn't stop."

Jade's heart dropped to her stomach. "Oh, Liam. I'm sorry."

"It's been six years, and I… I still push people away by acting like an ass because… I don't want to love someone that much again, Jade. I don't want to feel that kind of pain again. That doesn't mean I take advantage of women when they're hurting."

"I'm sorry," she said. "I shouldn't have made you feel like that. I wasn't trying to…" She stopped before telling the lie. "I *was* trying to get you into bed, but I'm glad you didn't take me up on it. I would've hated myself this morning. And you. I really would have hated you."

"The crazy thing is, you're the first person who I think I might like to let in. But you're not ready, and I'm not that kind of guy."

"I know you're not."

"You didn't last night."

She inhaled as much air as her lungs could hold. "My ego was bruised last night. I shouldn't be starting over at this point in my life, but here I am. With nothing and no one except this self-pity that seems to be taking over my life. I really want this part to be over," she said. "I don't want to go through this."

Liam gripped her hand. "You have to, but you aren't alone. You have Darby and Taylor. You have me and this beautiful lake and this quiet town. Your kids. And you have a second chance. You're going to be okay."

Shaking her head, Jade focused on the horizon so she didn't have to see the sympathy in his eyes. "You can tell me all day long that I'm not disposable, but my husband had a replacement lined up for over a year. We aren't even divorced yet, and he's trying to push her onto our kids. I was disposable. And the worst part is that I can't blame him. I guess the reason I keep telling myself to pick up and move on is because that's what he did. I was busy with my career, and he picked up and moved on. As much as it hurts, how can I blame him for that?"

"That's easy, Jade." Liam rested his elbows on his knees. "It's actually really easy. He had other choices. He had the opportunity to make your relationship better. He chose not to. You absolutely get to blame him for that."

"Oh, trust me, I have. I want to hate him, but I can't. I can't even hate her. She stood by him while he stood by me when I was sick. They're both very righteous when you think about it."

He scoffed and shook his head. "No, they're not. You're giving them way too much credit."

"I look back and think about all the time I wasted chasing promotions and accounts but never stopping to enjoy any of the benefits of my hard work. In some twisted way, cancer is the best thing that could have happened. It opened my eyes. I guess you're right. I should thank it. I just wish..." She blinked her tears back. "I don't know what I wish anymore. I'm off-balance. I don't know how to right the ship."

"I know a little about starting over," he said. "You do it one day at a time. I think you're doing great. I know I lashed out last night," he said when she opened her mouth, "but you're doing great. I'm not sure about buying that cabin, but for the most part, I think you're on your way."

Jade chuckled. "I like that cabin. I'm going to fix it up and make it my own."

"No more deer antlers?"

She laughed and pictured the terrible light hanging over the table. "No more antlers *or* turquoise cabinets."

He winced dramatically. "Oh, now you're going too far. You're getting out of hand."

"I'm a wild woman," Jade said with a shrug. "Get used to it."

"Chammont Point is a good place to restart. It's quiet and the people are nice."

She studied the sorrow in his eyes. "Is that how you landed here? Starting over?'

He nodded. "I needed to be someplace that didn't haunt me."

"I know that feeling."

"You've made friends here," Liam said.

"I've made amazing friends here." She put her hand on

his. "I want to be able to include you in that. Just so you know."

"It won't be easy," he warned her. "But you'll make it. I know you will."

For the first time, Jade really believed that. She was about to share that with him when his phone rang.

"That's Parker," he said, pulling the phone from his pocket.

"Hey, you lecture me about using waterproof cases. Why aren't you using one?"

He simply smiled as he put the phone to his ear. "What's up, Park?"

Jade watched curiously as he lifted his brows.

"Okay," he drawled out. "Hang tight. We're on our way."

As soon as he ended the call, he tossed his phone at Jade and grabbed the oars. "Her water just broke."

Jade gasped. "Oh my gosh. She's having a baby."

"She's having a baby," Liam said. While Jade felt a sense of panic wash over her, Liam calmly grabbed the paddles as if he hadn't a care in the world. "Hopefully, she's not having a baby in my shop."

Widening her eyes, Jade looked at the shore in the distance. "My God, Liam! Row faster!"

Jade and Liam rushed into the store to find Parker sitting behind the counter looking terrified as she held her stomach and panted.

"How far apart are the contractions?" Jade asked.

"Uh. I, uh..."

"It's okay." Jade pressed her palms to Parker's face and held her gaze. "You're okay. Everything is *okay*."

"The more times you say that the less I believe you," Parker whimpered.

"Okay." Jade bit her lip so she didn't laugh at herself. "Let's get you to the hospital."

Liam helped Parker stand. "How many rentals are on the water?"

Parker panted. "Seven."

Liam cursed under his breath as he scanned the store.

"You stay," Jade told him. "I'll keep you posted."

"Thanks. I just can't..."

"I know," Jade reassured him. "Help me get her to the car."

Once they had her tucked inside, Liam closed the passenger door and sighed at Jade. "She's like my kid sister. Maybe I should close the store? I could put up a sign or..."

"Are you her birthing partner?" Jade asked.

He winced. "No."

"Then you can't do anything to help her anyway. I'll stay with her."

"Thanks. I'll be over as soon as the last raft comes in."

Parker knocked on the window. "I'm having a baby here, guys! Can you wrap this up?"

Jade chuckled. "I'll call you," she said one more time as she walked around to the driver's side. As soon as she was buckled up, she glanced at Parker. "Breathe."

Parker squeezed the handle above her head and ground her teeth. "Is it supposed to hurt this much?"

"Yes, I'm afraid it is." She glanced at the young woman next to her. "Have you called the dad?"

As tears rolled down her cheeks, Parker blew out a long breath and shook her head. "He left as soon as I told him. He doesn't want anything to do with us."

"What about your family? Your parents or..."

Parker shook her head again.

Jade grabbed her hand and used a soothing maternal tone as she said, "I'm here. We got this. Breathe through the pain, honey. Just breathe."

"I'll breathe," Parker grunted, "but you gotta drive unless you want to deliver this baby."

"I'm driving," Jade said and put her car into gear.

After pulling up at the emergency room entrance ten minutes later, Jade ran to grab one of the wheelchairs parked inside the sliding doors. She helped Parker sit and rolled her inside to notify the receptionist that she was in labor.

"Wait," Parker called when a nurse came around the desk to take her away. "You're coming with me, aren't you?"

The fear in her eyes broke Jade's heart. She could easily see herself sitting there, terrified at the reality of becoming a mother at such a young age. However, Jade had been lucky enough to have not faced motherhood alone.

"I have to park the car," Jade explained. "I'll see you in Maternity." Before Parker could protest, the nurse turned the wheelchair and pushed Parker down the hall. Jade trotted back to her car, pulled her phone from her pocket, and dialed Liam. As soon as he answered, she put him on speaker so she could park. "What's the deal with Parker's parents?"

"They don't approve of her life choices."

"Should we call them?" she asked.

"Absolutely not," he said.

Jade's heart dropped to her stomach. "She's in labor.

Wouldn't they want to be here for the birth of their grandchild?"

"She's not on solid ground with them," Liam explained. "I don't know all the details, but I know it's a touchy subject. Don't get involved with this, Jade. It's not your fight."

She scoffed. "I didn't say I was going to get involved."

"Good. Because I don't think doing so would end well. Look, I promised I'd help her as much as I could while she adjusts. She's going to have her hands full for the foreseeable future. We're not going to make it worse by stirring the familial shit pot. Got it?"

"Got it." Jade parked and turned off the ignition. "So she's on her own?"

"She's got a few friends who come around now and then, but she got in with the wrong guy and... Well, he did what bad guys do. This isn't our problem. I'm here to help her, but I'm not getting involved unless she asks. Neither are you. How's she doing?"

"Scared," Jade said as she headed back to the hospital. "I told her I'd stay with her."

"Thanks. I'm sure that will make today easier for her. But don't stick your nose where it doesn't belong."

Jade scowled at his lecture. "Yeah, I got it, Liam. I said I got it."

"Call me when she has that kiddo."

"I will." Jade walked back into the hospital and followed the signs for the maternity ward, texting Darby as she went. While Jade wouldn't get involved with Parker's family issues, she wasn't going to ignore that this child—and for all intents and purposes, Parker still was a child—needed a support system.

Jade remembered all too well the struggles of being a new mom at such a young age. She had been seventeen when she'd had Xander. Even though her parents weren't thrilled, they hadn't shunned her. She'd also had Nick. They'd gotten married and faced the new struggles together.

He hadn't abandoned her. At least not when it counted.

Parker didn't have that, and Jade wasn't about to let her go through this alone. As she walked into the maternity ward, she sent a final order to Darby to go all out on presents for Parker and the baby with a promise that Jade would pay her back.

Inside Parker's room, Jade took the seat beside her. "I let Liam know you're doing okay. He's excited. I promised to call as soon as the baby's born."

Parker sniffled. "Will you stay with me?"

"Of course. I'm not going anywhere."

"Thanks."

Jade took Parker's hand and did her best to distract her with questions about the baby. Did she know the baby's gender? A little girl. Did she have a name picked out? Marie Louise, after her grandmother.

Jade asked anything she could think to talk about that didn't involve family and the baby's MIA father.

"What's the deal with you guys?" Parker asked when there was a lull in the conversation.

"What do you mean?" Jade asked.

"Between you and Liam. Are you dating or what?"

Jade chuckled. "No. God no. I'm not even divorced yet."

"So?" Parker asked.

Jade shook her head and said, "I don't want to date anyone right now. I don't even know who I am right now."

"Liam's not a bad guy," Parker said. "I know he acts like a fool most of the time, but he's not."

"I know," Jade said. "We talked about that. I get why he acts like he does, but that doesn't mean I want to date him. Or anyone else."

Parker shifted on the bed. "I just want you to know, he's really nice. He cares about people in his own jacked-up way."

Jade smiled, but her reassurances were lost when Parker hunched forward and started whimpering as another contraction hit her. Before too long, Jade was wiping sweat off Parker's head and telling her to push. And several hours after that, Parker collapsed back on the bed as her newborn daughter let out a loud, shaky cry. Jade had never been present for any birth other than her children's, and the sense of wonder that washed over her made her cry.

"Oh my God, she's perfect," Jade whispered. Jade stroked Parker's hair back and fought the urge to give her a big motherly kiss on the forehead. But she did lean down and hug her as much as she could. "Good job, Mommy."

Parker looked up at Jade with a hurricane of emotions in her eyes. "What do I do now?"

Jade brushed her hair back and smiled. "Now you rest, honey. Because it's going to be a while before you get a good night's sleep again."

"No, I mean... I don't know what to do."

The fear on Parker's face nearly brought Jade to her knees. Once again, she understood all too well what the girl was feeling. Her life had changed in one heartbeat too. Her life had been upended in the blink of an eye too. And she'd been left feeling the exact same way. Brushing Parker's dark hair from her face, Jade offered her a soft smile. "You don't have to, sweetie. Nobody ever really does. You have a beautiful baby and friends who adore you. You're going to be okay. I'm going to help. So is Liam. You're going to be okay."

"Here we go, Mom," a nurse said as she brought over a bundle wrapped in a blanket.

Parker opened her arms, and Jade watched as all her worries melted away. The moment she held little Marie, Parker forgot all her troubles. As she should. Leaning close, Jade put her hand on the baby, and they both cooed at her and told her how perfect she was.

"This is what matters now," Jade told Parker. "You take care of her and let us help take care of you, okay?"

"Okay," Parker said with a thick voice as she hugged the baby closer. "I can do that."

"All right, Grandma," a nurse said, "we need to get Mom cleaned up."

Several seconds passed before Jade realized the nurse was talking to her. "Oh, um..."

"Godmother," Parker said. "Jade is my, um, godmother...*ish*."

Jade laughed lightly as she recalled the role Darby had assigned her. If only she had a magic wand to help make her life and Parker's better with a *swish*. If only.

Jade put her hand back to Parker's head. "I'm going to go call Liam and let him know she's here."

As soon as she stepped outside the room, Jade sank into a chair and let the overwhelming emotions hit her. She barely knew Parker, but they were bonded forever now. Baby Marie had felt like family the moment Jade had seen her tiny body in the doctor's hands.

If she'd had any doubt about restarting her life in

Chammont Point, it was gone now. She wanted to be here. She *needed* to be here. Helping Parker find her footing as a mother wasn't simply a task like so many things in Jade's life had been. This suddenly felt like a mission.

This was her purpose now, whether she'd intended it to be or not. Being there to help Parker bring her daughter into the world made Jade realize that everyone's lives were changing all the time. They were learning and growing all the time. Parker was going to have to learn to be a mother, and Jade was going to learn how to be...*herself*.

Jade's mindset shifted, her outlook changed, and it made her consider just how lucky she actually was. Yes, the last year had kicked her in the shins over and over, but she was here. She was still standing, and even without the marriage she had counted on, she was finding a way to carry on.

As angry as she was, as much as she hated what he'd done, Nick hadn't abandoned her. He hadn't left her to fend for herself when she was a terrified seventeen-year-old girl staring down motherhood, and he hadn't abandoned her when cancer was getting the best of her. He'd stood by her both times when he could have walked away.

She didn't know that she'd ever forgive him for being an adulterous liar, but Taylor had been right when she'd said he deserved some credit for not leaving her to fight for her life on her own. If he had, she didn't know who she would have leaned on. Her parents had barely kept themselves together when she was sick. Nick had been the strong one. He'd been the one who helped her fight the battles that had won the war.

She resented him and what he'd done. But she owed him.

Liam had told her she had to look at the hard times and

thank them for the lessons she learned from them and the changes they'd brought to her life. He'd been right. Her cancer had made her take a long, hard look at herself. Nick's decision to leave her made her make changes she needed to make. And like it or not, his decision to stand by her when she'd been sick was something she should be thankful for.

She wiped her cheeks, looked at her phone, and heaved a dramatic sigh before finding his name in her list of contacts. Part of her wanted to throw the phone before she made yet another mistake she'd regret, but the other part of her—the part that was determined to grow—insisted she reach out to him.

She wasn't about to call him, but she did type out a message and reread it three times.

I don't know how to forgive you, but I understand. Thank you for not leaving me alone to fight my cancer.

Swallowing hard, she hit Send.

"Jade?" Liam asked, sounding fearful.

She looked up. "I was about to call you."

He squatted next to her and searched her eyes. For the first time, she didn't see him as some broken thing trying to avoid his problems by playing mind games. She saw the sincerity, the fear, and the sadness in his light eyes. She saw a man who had lost everything and was still struggling to begin again.

"What's wrong?" he pressed on a whisper, as if he didn't want to know.

She shook her head and wiped her cheeks. "Nothing. Everything went fine. She's perfect. She's beautiful."

He stared at her for a few seconds before sighing. "I saw you crying, and I thought... Never mind what I thought."

Her phone dinged, letting her know she had a new message, and she glanced at it long enough to read: *You're welcome.* Her tears welled up again. "Sorry," Jade said, drying her cheeks again, "it was very emotional."

"Apparently." He snagged a few tissues from the box sitting on the table beside the chairs and handed them to Jade.

She looked down the hallway when a flash of metallic caught her eye. Darby rushed toward them, wearing the most outlandish pink and blue 1950s house dress and stilettos. Her hands were overflowing with balloons, flowers, and stuffed animals. Behind her, Taylor was taking long strides to keep up as she carried a cake in her hands.

"We're here," Darby announced, as if anyone could miss them. "Are we too late? Did we miss it?"

"Miss the baby?" Jade asked.

"Whatever happens when babies come out of..." She winced. "You know."

Jade laughed as she wiped her nose. "She had the baby. A little girl named Marie."

The door to Parker's room opened and a nurse came out, pushing the baby in a wheeled carriage. When she noticed all eyes on her, she smiled. "She just needs a checkup. I'll bring her right back."

"Can we go back in?" Jade asked.

"Yes, just be mindful that Parker needs her rest."

That was all the nurse had to say for the group to pile into the room. Jade watched, gauging Parker's response. She was feeling incredibly protective, and if she saw the slightest hint of unease, she'd usher everyone right back out.

However, Parker smiled brightly, and Jade was glad she'd told Darby to go all out.

"Nice work," Liam said as Darby handed Parker a teddy bear.

"I'm going to be here," Jade said. "To help take care of her."

He nodded. "Good. I think she'll need all the help she can get."

"I...um...I texted Nick."

Liam's face sagged.

"To thank him for standing by me when he could have left. Someone told me I should find things to be thankful for."

Liam's smile returned. "That's the first step to letting go."

"So I've heard."

"How do you feel?"

She drew a breath as she analyzed herself. "Better. I feel better."

"Good. Come on. Let's celebrate with some cake. Don't say it," he warned when she opened her mouth. "You can have one bite, Jade."

"Okay. One bite."

FIFTEEN

AFTER A QUICK VISIT to Parker and the baby, Jade pulled into the lot outside the park where Liam had planned a spelunking trip for her, Darby, and Taylor. She was so excited she could barely contain herself. She'd been wanting to do this for so long, and here they were, about to explore the deepest, darkest caves Liam could find.

They gathered around the back of the car. Jade dug into the trunk and handed out the supplies she'd packed for them.

"What's this for?" Darby asked, holding up a head lamp.

"So you can see," Taylor explained, flipping on the light.

Darby's eyes did that blank stare thing before blinking. "Wait. It's going to be dark?"

"We're going into a cave," Liam informed her.

Again, she blinked and tilted her head. "I thought we were spelunking."

"Yes," Jade said, and then she chuckled. "Wait. Do you know what spelunking is?"

Darby looked from Jade to Taylor to Liam. "Um..."

"It's cave exploring," Liam explained.

Darby furrowed her brow and gawked at him. "In the dark?"

"How much sunlight do you think there is in caves?" Taylor asked.

Darby scrunched up her face. "I don't know. I don't hang out in caves."

"Well, there's not much," Taylor said. "Once we get away from the entrance, it's going to be dark."

"How dark?" Darby asked as she widened her eyes.

Liam placed the lamp on his head. "*Dark*. You'll need that to see."

Putting her hands up, Darby cringed. "Wait. Are there going to be bears?"

"Maybe," Taylor said as a grin tugged at her lips.

"No." Jade gave Taylor a silent warning with her mom stare. "I mean, we're not going that far into the caves, but you should have a light. Come on, Darby. We've been talking about this for weeks."

She pouted. "I thought we were talking about something else."

Jade shared curious glances with Taylor and Liam before asking, "What did you think spelunking was?"

Pulling her head lamp on, Taylor said, "I don't think we want to know."

"Well," Darby said, casting a glance at Liam, "it makes a lot more sense why you're here if we're not doing what I thought."

"Don't ask," Jade warned. "Just...don't ask anything else."

Knowing Darby, she thought there would be drinking and strippers involved—those seemed to be her go-tos for entertainment. Jade didn't think Liam needed to be clued into that.

Darby looked down at her bright pink camo pants, somewhat sensible shoes, and long-sleeved shirt. "Is this why you made me dress like a fashionable version of Taylor?"

Jade helped Darby secure the head lamp over her poofy hair. "Come on," Jade asked. "Give it a few minutes. If you don't like it, at least you tried."

"I don't like it," Darby said as they headed toward the opening of the cave. "I *really* don't like it."

Jade gripped her hands. "I want to do this, Darby. Please try. I'll never make you try again."

"Okay, but if I get eaten by a bear, I'm going to be very upset with you."

"Understood," Jade said.

The four of them made their way to the cave while Liam explained the importance of moving slowly and staying together once they got deeper into the cave. Jade glanced back and smiled at the way Darby grabbed Taylor's hand.

"Do not leave me," Darby instructed her.

Taylor chuckled. "Not unless there's a bear. Then you're on your own."

"Taylor," Darby whined.

Liam grabbed Jade's hand as they neared the opening of the cave and pulled her closer. "She's never going to forgive you for this. You know that, don't you?"

"She might have fun."

"There's no men, no alcohol, and not a single bit of glitter in this cave. She's not going to have fun."

Jade chuckled as she glanced back. Darby seemed to have forgotten how discontent she was and wriggled her brows at

Jade. Only then did Jade realize she and Liam were still holding hands. She pulled her hand away and rolled her eyes.

"Come on, ladies," Liam said. "We need to stick together."

They were only a few yards inside the mouth of the cave when Darby whispered, "It smells like a locker room in here."

"I'm not going to ask how you know what a locker room smells like," Liam said.

"Probably for the best," Taylor said. "Can you stop squeezing my hand so hard, Darby?"

"No."

Jade rested her hand on Liam's back as the light of day started to disappear behind them. She didn't want to admit that as soon as they were engulfed in darkness and the damp, musty locker room smell, the fun of spelunking faded. Quickly.

She was more than ready to turn back and mark this particular activity off her list, but she didn't want to be the one to call an end to the so-called adventure. However, she did have to agree with Darby—this wasn't much fun.

"Shh," Liam whispered as he came to a stop. "Listen."

Darby gasped, but Taylor hushed her.

A moment later, a squeaking far too similar to the sound of rats scurrying down an alley began to get louder. Liam looked up, and his light illuminated a gathering of bats directly above them.

Darby whimpered, Jade swallowed hard, and Taylor muttered, "Oh. My. God."

"That's worse than bears," Darby squealed, sounding as if

she were about to start crying. "That's much worse than bears."

"I agree," Taylor said.

"They won't bother you," Liam said.

The words had barely left his mouth when two bats started fluttering about, followed by several more. The swishing of their wings sounded louder than it should. Darby screamed. Taylor squealed.

Jade spun on her heels and shooed Taylor and Darby back toward the cave opening. "Go! Go! Hurry!"

Liam's laugh echoed around the cave as Jade, Darby, and Taylor ran toward the sliver of light in the distance. Jade hadn't realized how deep into the cave they'd gone until she was rushing for the exit. When they finally made it outside, Darby yanked her head lamp off and gasped dramatically.

Taylor rested her hands on her knees and shook her head at Jade. "You are never allowed to plan an outing again."

"We're going to a bar. Right now," Darby insisted. "And I'm drinking straight from a bottle until I get over this." She sniffled as she pointed at Jade. "And you are the designated driver."

A full-body shiver ran through Jade as she looked at the cave. "Yeah. Okay, that's fair."

They were headed for the car when Taylor looked back. "Liam hasn't come out yet. Should we go back for him?"

Jade looked at the cave opening for a few seconds and shook her head. "Nope. The bats can have him."

By the time Jade was able to move into the remodeled cabin, the trees around Chammont Lake had lost their leaves and the chill of winter filled the air. Christmas was just around the corner, and she was thrilled she could experience the holiday in her new home. Though the structure hadn't been completely torn down, Taylor had hired a crew to strip it to the studs. She'd overseen the project as the cabin was expanded to include a home office so Jade could have a dedicated workspace since she'd be spending most of her time working from the lake. Her trips into Fairfax would be limited to meetings and emergencies, and she was fine with that.

With the help of her friends, Jade had selected a natural maple flooring and, much to Darby's despair, light colors that helped the space feel larger than it was. The loft had also been expanded to the length of the new addition, giving Xander and Owen a bigger room to share when they visited. Rather than the precarious ladder they'd had to climb previously, Taylor had installed a set of stairs that doubled as storage.

A wall of windows faced the cove, giving Jade a perfect view of the water. Even though it wasn't of the bigger expanse of Chammont Lake, she'd come to love seeing the calm water in her little corner of the world.

The work Taylor and her team had done was perfect, and Jade couldn't wait to show it off. Though the cabin was still tiny, and her social circle even smaller, she and Darby had planned a housewarming party. While Xander and Owen built a fire outside for people to socialize rather than cramming everyone inside at once, Darby fussed over the food she'd made. Bite-sized sandwiches, cookies, and stuffed cucumber bites which she'd said were specifically for Jade, had been expertly displayed on the table next to a punch bowl with a fizzy beverage. Darby had concocted the drink with cranberry juice, seltzer water, and a "secret ingredient" that she insisted was legal for all ages.

Slowly spinning, taking in the cabin as she had the first day she'd stepped inside, Jade couldn't stop herself from smiling. She'd worked closely with Darby and Taylor to design every aspect—the colors, the window placement, the built-in shelves that lined the wall to the ceiling, and the picture frames for the photos she'd placed there. One of her favorites was an image Parker had taken of Jade, Darby, and Taylor on the beach with umbrella drinks. The trio was smiling brightly while toasting for the picture. Jade couldn't remember a time when she'd been happier than the days they'd spent relaxing by the lake.

Chammont Point was her home—the place where she was able to get back on her feet and start again. And nothing reflected that more than this tiny cabin. This was her place in the world, and she couldn't think of any other place where she'd ever felt so at peace. She didn't have the need to rush here, or to get ahead, or to strive for some goal. This was a place where she could simply enjoy her life. And she intended to.

Her morning routine of paddleboarding out onto the lake had changed with the weather. The cooler temperatures didn't permit being out on the water, but she would find another way to stay active. She finally felt healthy and strong. She wasn't going to let winter steal that from her.

Liam had promised to help her stay active. She was looking forward to the activities he'd suggested, including snowshoeing, cross-country skiing, and ice-skating at the outdoor rink. She wasn't sure how she felt about the last one, but she was willing to give it a try. They had settled into a friendship that gave her the confidence to try new things. He enjoyed pushing her beyond her comfort zone, and she felt safe enough with him to allow it.

As the summer had started winding down, he'd convinced her to try waterskiing. Though she hadn't done so since, she had the pictures to prove that she'd attempted—and failed—at the sport. Jade had been determined to live her second chance to the fullest, and she could honestly say that she'd been doing that.

"Well," Taylor said, "what do you think now that you're all moved in?"

"I think this is perfect," Jade said. "Absolutely perfect. You did an amazing job."

Taylor smiled. "Thanks. And thanks for the push to keep trying with my business. I appreciate it."

"Any new clients yet?"

"No, but people are talking about the pictures I...*you*... posted on social media. It was awesome of you to get that set up."

"You're welcome. Now you have to keep it up," Jade informed her. "Every project you do, be sure to post pictures before, during, and after."

"Will do. If I get any more projects."

"Are you serious about trying again?" Jade asked after a moment.

"Yeah."

Jade lit with excitement. "Let me help. Marketing is kind of my thing. I'll get you some new clients in no time."

Taylor's frown twisted into a bright smile. "Really?"

"Yeah. I, um... I want to start doing some freelance work. I think I'd like to start my own business here in Chammont Point, but I can't just jump in until I know if it'll pan out. I want my work life to slow down, too. I don't think that will happen if I don't give up my executive role in Fairfax. I'd prefer to have a few local clients to pay the bills."

Taylor smiled again. "I agree. That would be great for some of the businesses around here. Too many depend solely on tourist season. It's tough in the winter months. I bet you could drum up enough business for them to make ends meet."

"I hope so. But don't worry. O'Shea Construction will be my priority. We're going to make sure everyone in Chammont Point knows what amazing work you do."

"Okay," Darby sang, joining them with three glasses of her special punch. "We have to toast before people start arriving." She passed drinks to Taylor and Jade and then lifted hers. "I knew from the moment I watched you plummet off the deck there was something special about you."

Jade laughed with surprise.

"The way you fluttered your little arms and kicked your scrawny legs," Darby continued, "was like watching..."

"A baby bird's failed attempt at flying," Jade said. "Yes, I remember."

"As soon as you agreed not to sue me, I knew we'd become the best of friends. And then we met Taylor, and two became three. I wouldn't change a thing. Welcome home, Jade."

"Welcome home," Taylor said and toasted them.

"Thank you." Jade took a sip of the drink, tentatively letting it wash over her taste buds. "Oh my gosh, Darby. This is amazing."

Darby bowed slightly. "I really was a good bartender."

"And the table looks amazing," Taylor told her. "I tried the snacks. You did a great job."

"Hey," Darby said as if she'd just had an epiphany, "since the property manager thing didn't work out, maybe I should be a professional hostess. Trust me, I know how to party." She gasped and widened her eyes. "Taylor, you could totally build me more counter space so I have enough room to bake and decorate. And Jade, you could help me market. It would be amazing." She waved her hand and stared into the distance. "Darby Zamora, Mistress of Ceremonies. What do you think?"

Taylor opened her mouth and looked at Jade. "Sounds...interesting."

"Yeah," Jade said. "Yeah. I can see that. But, um, maybe work on the name because Mistress of Ceremonies..."

"Too BDSM?" Darby asked.

"A little," Taylor offered, holding up her fingers with only a few millimeters of space between them.

Jade scrunched her nose. "A lot, actually. I'd worry about the clientele you'd attract."

Darby squealed. "Oh, this is going to be great. I need to write this down before I lose it."

As soon as Darby darted off toward Jade's home office, Taylor chuckled. "She's going to go with the Mistress thing."

"She absolutely is," Jade agreed. Her eyes lit when she noticed Parker walking in with Marie in a carrier. "Oh, excuse me. Baby snuggle time."

"Have at it," Taylor muttered. She had been incredibly supportive of Parker but steered clear of too much baby time. That clearly wasn't her thing.

"Holy crap, Jade," Parker said. "This place is great."

"Thank you. Have a look around."

"You just want to take my baby."

"Yes, I do." Jade lifted Marie from the carrier. After kissing the little one's bald head, Jade hugged her close. "I haven't seen her all day."

"That happened faster than I anticipated," Liam announced, walking in behind Parker. "I thought you'd at least let her get her shoes off before swiping Marie."

Jade grinned. "My house, my rules. The cost of admission is cuddles."

"In that case," Liam said and swooped in with his arms open.

Jade pressed her hand to his chest and held him off. "Not from you. Go get something to eat. Darby worked hard on the appetizers."

"Are you guys dating yet?" Parker asked as soon as Liam walked away.

Jade rolled her eyes. "No. And we aren't going to start dating." She grinned when her boys walked in and made a beeline toward the table. She was about to warn them against eating all the food when she realized they weren't even interested in the sandwiches and punch. They were talking a mile a minute to Liam.

When she looked back at Parker, she simply got a cocky smirk. "We're *not* interested in dating."

"He's different now," Parker said. "Whatever happened between you guys that day, he's different. He doesn't..." She shrugged. "He doesn't act like himself now. I thought you should know. Not that it matters since you aren't interested in dating." She smiled and walked off.

Jade patted Marie's back, kissed her head, and then whispered, "Your mom is a smart aleck."

The baby cooed, bringing the smile back to Jade's face. Looking around the small room, her heart filled. Almost everyone who mattered to her had gathered to welcome her to her new home. She'd invited her parents over the coming weeks, before winter really set in, but this small group were the ones who would be the foundation of her new life.

Watching them interact—her boys and Liam talking about fishing and Taylor and Darby listening politely as Parker talked about Marie's checkup—Jade thought she couldn't have possibly found a better place to restart.

COMING SOON

The Selling Point

Book #2 of Chammont Point Series

ALSO BY MARCI BOLDEN

Chammont Point Series:

The Restarting Point

The Selling Point

The Breaking Point

A Life Without Water Series:

A Life Without Water

A Life Without Flowers

A Life Without Regrets

Stonehill Series:

The Road Leads Back

Friends Without Benefits

The Forgotten Path

Jessica's Wish

This Old Cafe

Forever Yours

The Women of Hearts Series:

Hidden Hearts

Burning Hearts

Stolen Hearts

Secret Hearts

Other Titles:

California Can Wait

Seducing Kate

The Rebound

ABOUT THE AUTHOR

As a teen, Marci Bolden skipped over young adult books and jumped right into reading romance novels. She never left.

Marci lives in the Midwest with her husband, kiddos, and numerous rescue pets. If she had an ounce of willpower, Marci would embrace healthy living, but until cupcakes and wine are no longer available at the local market, she will appease her guilt by reading self-help books and promising to join a gym "soon."

Visit her here:
www.marcibolden.com

 facebook.com/MarciBoldenAuthor
twitter.com/BoldenMarci
instagram.com/marciboldenauthor

9 781950 348572